I0659285

Penumbra

A Journal of Weird Fiction and Criticism

No. 6 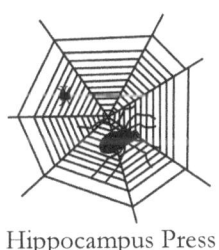 Autumn 2025

Edited by S. T. Joshi

". . . the penumbra of a profound melancholy . . ."
—M. P. Shiel

Hippocampus Press

New York

Published by Hippocampus Press
P.O. Box 641
New York, NY 10156
www.hippocampuspress.com

Cover by Daniel V. Sauer, dansauerdesign.com.
Hippocampus Press logo designed by Anastasia Damianakos.

PENUMBRA is published semiannually, in Autumn and Spring.
Articles and letters should be sent to the editor, S. T. Joshi,
℅ Hippocampus Press. Literary rights for articles will reside with
PENUMBRA for one year after publication, whereupon they will
revert to their respective authors.

ISBN 978-1-61498-477-1 (paperback)
ISBN 978-1-61498-481-8 (ebook)

Contents

Fiction

Nonfiction

Classic Reprints

Poetry

Dead Reckonings

Notes on Contributors

Saki's Windows

John C. Tibbetts

> ". . . open a window and listen to the howling of the wolves."
> —"Reginald's Drama"

"The Open Window" is perhaps the most famous short story by the man popularly known as Saki. The "window" in question is ordinary enough. It discloses a normal and tidy world. Yet, as an open portal, it admits something that is, well . . .

As a young reader, I found the story tucked away between the pages of an otherwise sober and conventional high school reader. I know now, years later, that it was just waiting there, cleverly biding its time, lying in readiness to sting me with its twisty final sentence.

It takes but a few moments to recall Saki's story. The window in question swings wide open on this late October afternoon. Three years ago to the day a man, his two sons, and their dog had gone through that window on a shooting expedition from which they never returned. Their bodies were never recovered. "'Poor aunt always thinks they will come back one day,'" says Vera, a young girl of fifteen, who explains to the stranger just arrived on an introductory social call. "'They and the little brown spaniel that was lost with them will walk in at that window just as they used to do. My aunt will be down presently; in the meantime you must try and put up with me.'" Moments later Mrs. Sappleton arrives with the

Source Note: Unless otherwise noted, all quotations are from the following: Sandie Byrne, *The Unbearable Saki* (Oxford: Oxford University Press, 2007); A. J. Langguth, *Saki: A Life of Hector Hugh Munro* (London: Hamish Hamilton, 1981); Christopher Morley, "Introduction," *The Short Stories of Saki (H. H. Munro)* (New York: Modern Library, 1958). Quotations from the novels *The Unbearable Bassington* and *When William Came* are from *The Complete Works of Saki,* ed. Adam Rovner (New York: Barnes & Noble, 2006).

brisk announcement that she expects her husband and brothers any moment. The visitor's gaze swivels toward the window: "In the deepening twilight three figures are walking across the lawn towards the window; they all carry guns under their arms, and one of them is additionally burdened with a white coat hung over his shoulders. A tired brown spaniel keeps close at their heels." Considerably alarmed, the visitor, who has a history of nervous attacks, grabs wildly at his stick and hat and hurriedly flees the scene. "'A most extraordinary man,'" exclaims Mrs. Sappleton, "'dashed off without a word of goodbye . . . One would think he had seen a ghost.'" No, suggests our young storyteller, perhaps it was his fear of dogs that had once trapped him in a "cemetery somewhere on the banks of the Ganges . . . Enough to make anyone lose their nerve.'"

The concluding line: "Romance at short notice was her specialty'" (288–91).[1]

Like so many other readers who have felt the lash of that last line, I was compelled to seek out more stories authored by the writer hiding in plain sight behind that peculiar name, Saki. In more of my early discoveries I encountered what Saki described as a menagerie of "beasts and super-beasts"—a talking cat ("Tobermory"), a werewolf ("Gabriel-Ernest"), a murderous ferret ("Sredni Vashtar"), the vengeful god Pan ("The Music on the Hill")—and many other creatures who revealed what biographer A. J. Langguth has described as Saki's "fondness for skulking animals capable, should the need arise, of inflicting rough justice (35). Moreover, the stories turned societal pretensions and supernatural tropes inside out with a gleeful malice that is entirely at home with later masters John Collier, Roald Dahl, Gahan Wilson, and Alfred Hitchcock.[2]

---

1. Permit me the opportunity to turn Saki's conclusion on its head: what if those advancing figures coming through the open window *really are* ghosts, and the terrified aunt has to confront them? Or, to put it another way, what if they are real enough, but it is the aunt who is the ghost? Saki does that to you: he reads *you* while you are reading *him*.

2. Saki's "The Shartz-Metterklume Method" was adapted for *Alfred Hitchcock Presents* on 12 June 1960. Some of the witty dialogue is retained, but

My adventures were just beginning, and they continue today. And while these short and pungent stories are best savored at intervals one at a time—rather than in bunches—I have no choice here but to consider them as an aggregate. They occupy a unique position among his contemporaries in horror and the macabre. His ghosts lacked the material substance of M. R. James and Algernon Blackwood; his pagan furies the ecstatic intensity of Arthur Machen; his satires the psychological penetration of Henry James; and his horrors the outré monstrosities of William Hope Hodgson. Rather, as biographer Sandie Byrne notes, "The object of the stories does not always seem to be the evocation of atmosphere or the frisson of terror" (171). Instead, what he does bring to the party is, in my opinion, the saving grace of something all too often lacking in his contemporaries— humor. He is *funny*, occasionally hilarious, even if his wit is touched with cruelty. If he touches base with anyone of his generation, it is with the deft satires of Max Beerbohm and James Branch Cabell; and with the musical and poetic satires of composer Peter Warlock.

Formative Years and the Coming of "Saki"

Hector Hugh Munro was born in 1870, the youngest of three children, to Charles and Mary Frances Munro in Aykab, Burma, where his father was an officer in the British police. There were calamities aplenty in his ancestry and life. One ancestor was attacked and killed by a tiger. During a stroll along a pastoral lane, his mother miscarried and died after being charged by a cow. His boyhood back in Devonshire was consigned to the care of two spinster aunts, Charlotte and Augusta, whose domineering regime would surface

the results are flat and bland. Truly, Saki belongs on the printed page.

frequently in his stories. Years later, thanks to the intervention of his father, the twenty-three-year-old Hector went to Burma to serve in the Burmese police, where he first contracted the malaria that would afflict him all his life. Never robust in health, he nonetheless spent the next five years of the new century as a foreign correspondent for the *Westminster Gazette* and the *Morning Post,* for which he dispatched news of turmoil and war in the Balkans, Warsaw, and St. Petersburg. A. J. Langguth's biography reveals images of him in Sofia wandering through the smoking palace of a king blown up by dynamiters; leaning in a doorway in St. Petersburg watching the massacre of reformers by tsarist troops; inspecting the huddled heads split open by Cossack sabres. "He was exhilarated by the promise of violence, although he would take care to mute that note of expectation in his coverage" (129). He returned from these horrors a hard case, a "self-effacing, secretive man of numerous acquaintances but few intimates," writes Byrne, "in some ways deeply unpleasant, in some ways admirable, [who] achieved popularity and even love when he was endeavouring to be a killer" (227).

All this time, he was writing stories under the pen-name of "Saki."

The name first appears alongside Munro's own name—with a nod toward Lewis Carroll—in that first series of satiric stories collectively titled "Westminster Alice," which appeared in 1900–1902 in the *Westminster Gazette.*

Here we find the first of Saki's windows:

> "Alice," Child with dreaming eyes
> Noting things that come to pass
> Turvey-wise in Wonderland
> Backwards through a Looking-Glass.[3]

Illustrated by F. Carruthers Gould, who provides a delightful counterpoint to the original drawings by John Tenniel, the "Alice/Saki" persona skews the subjects and pretentions that will

---

3. Hector Hugh Munro (Saki), *The Westminster Alice,* ed. Michael Everson (Portlaoise, Ireland: Evertype, 2017), 5.

The Westminster Alice

A political parody based on
Lewis Carroll's Wonderland

Hector Hugh Munro (Saki)

Illustrated by Francis Carruthers Gould
With notes by Hugh Cahill, Adam Newell, and J. A. Spender

So when the Angel of the darker Drink
At last shall find you by the river-brink,
And offering his Cup, invite your Soul
Forth to your Lips to quaff—you shall not shrink

populate the later stories—the Anglican Church, matters of state, societal pretensions, military incompetence, etc., etc.

Munro had found references to "Saki the Cup-Bearer" in Edmund FitzGerald's purported translations from Omar's eleventh-century quatrains, *The Rubáiyát of Omar Khayyám*. Since its first appearance in English in 1859, *The Rubáiyát* has attracted readers in both the Victorian and later Edwardian age and reflects Munro's own predilection for the mingling of the pleasures of wine and song with a morbid fascination with decay and death. The youthful Munro copies out these lines from Omar in his notebook:

> So when that Angel of the Darker Drink
> At last shall find you by the river-brink,
> And, offering his Cup, invite your Soul
> Forth to your lips to quaff—you shall not shrink?

That last line—"you shall not shrink"—might itself be a presentiment of the challenge Munro will take up at a later day, when his generation is called to plunge into the turmoil of World War I.

Hard upon the heels of the "Alice/Saki" parodies come two more spokesmen for Munro's witty, sarcastic, and occasionally sharply brutal observations. "Reginald" and "Clovis Sangrail" are wealthy idlers and dandies who are both onlookers and occasional participants in the stories. Speaking for them both, Reginald proclaims: "No one will understand the drift [of my stories], but every one will go back to their homes with a vague feeling of dissatisfaction with their lives and surroundings [and then] put up new wall-papers and forget." Moreover, these "everyday tragedies" would not have a "happy ending" but would "commence with wolves worrying something on a lonely waste—you wouldn't see them, of course; but you would hear them snarling and scrunching, and I should arrange to have a wolfy fragrance suggested across the footlights" ("Reginald's Drama," 28–29).

The Munro/Alice/Saki/Reginald/Clovis oeuvre consists of more than one hundred published stories, two novels, and a variety of miscellaneous published and unpublished works. Limitations of available space force me to make an admittedly arbitrary and representative selection, which I divide into four categories: 1) classic tales of the weird and the macabre; 2) twisty contes cruels; 3) intimate mood studies; and 4) wartime meditations that position Saki in the trenches before his death in 1916. Such easy categories, however, defy easy classification: the more obviously horrific tales are never far from a deadpan humor and ferocious irony; likewise, the brittle surfaces and polish of the contes cruels are only false comforts before the savage stroke. The mood pieces and the wartime stories alike combine narrative with autobiographical revelations. Moreover, they are all so finely tuned, so precise in their diction, so deftly eloquent in tone that any attempt to summarize them risks rending them into pieces that slip through the fingers.

Above all, we should not be misled by Christopher Morley's comment that Saki's urbane, "suavely smooth" and astringent tone is merely a flippant affectation (vii); or, according to Noel Coward, that he possesses an Edwardian "evanescent charm" (quoted in

Byrne 15). No, any deep dive into the stories reveals something far more evasive and troubling. As recent biographer Sandie Byrne writes: "Charm is not a word that leaps to mind in relation to Saki's descriptions of country-house life, where animals may mock, gore, or eat the guests" (15). And in cataloguing such delights, V. S. Pritchett declares that "Saki writes like an enemy. Society has bored him to the point of murder . . . The joke, for Saki, is in the kill."[4]

Like so many windows, Saki's stories look out onto different scenes, different circumstances, different views to a kill.

Classic Tales of the Weird and the Macabre

> If there had been wood-gods and wicked-eyed fauns in the sunlit groves and hillsides of old Hellas, surely there were watchful, living things of kindred mould in this dusk-hidden wilderness of field and hedge and coppice.
>
> —*When William Came*

"Music on the Hill"

Saki's window discloses "an open space, shut in by huge yew trees [with] a stone pedestal surmounted by a small bronze figure of a youthful Pan . . . Newly cut grapes have been deposited at its feet." Sylvia Seltoun has ventured into the "wild open savagery" of the woods surrounding her new home. "'The worship of Pan never has died out,'" her husband had warned her; "'other newer gods have drawn aside his votaries from time to time, but he is the Nature-God to whom all must come back at last. He has been called the Father of all the Gods, but most of his children have been stillborn. If you're wise you won't disbelieve in him too boastfully while you're in his country.'" With casual disdain, she defiles the altar. Her fate is sealed. "Unutterably evil eyes" gaze at her from the thickets, and "a low, fitful piping as of some reedy flute" assails her ears. As if bidden by the piping, a rampaging stag crushes her to death on its

---

4. V. S. Pritchett, "The Performing Lynx," in *Complete Collected Essays* (New York: Random House, 1991), 645–47.

horns. "The last thing she hears is the echo of a boy's laughter, golden and equivocal" (181–85).

A mere four pages in length, "Music on the Hill" is one of the masterpieces of the weird. Typical of Saki's fascination with cultic paganism (see "Vespaluus" elsewhere in these pages), it is also unusual in its unrelieved grim and graphic violence. Pagan gods were everywhere challenging and transcending the strict social conventions and religious orthodoxies of the Victorian and Edwardian ages. The "wild ecstasy" of their "pipes and timbrels"—as John Keats had once described it—were intoxicating and destructive in their enchantments. "Pan, far from being dead," wrote Virginia Woolf, in 1918, "is at his pranks in all the villages of England [and] a group of writers who have the sense of the unseen . . . may bring visions of fairies or phantoms."[5]

"Tobermory"

Tobermory the cat ranks high in the ranks of Saki's cherished "beasts and super-beasts."

Take a closer look at him as he creeps silently among the guests attending Lady Blemley's house party. After listening to their gossip and scandals, he is all too willing to tell all. A talking cat? "Of course I have experimented with thousands of animals,'" explains a stranger to the group, Mr. Cornelius Appin, "but latterly only with cats, those wonderful creatures which have assimilated themselves so marvellously with our civilization while retaining all their highly developed feral instincts.'" Although Tobermory takes his name from ancient Highland legends and can claim a degree of aristocratic pedigree, he is not above scandalizing the assembled guests. He hints at Major Barfield's amorous adventures—"'I should imagine you'd find it inconvenient if I were to shift the conversation on to your own little affairs'"—and reveal to another guest Lady Blemley's intentions to defraud her: "You were the only person she

_____

5. Virginia Woolf, "The Supernatural in Fiction," in *Granite and Rainbow* (New York: Harcourt Brace Jovanovish, 1958), 64.

could think of who might be idiotic enough to buy their old car.'" Offered a propitiatory glass of milk, Tobermory loftily responds, "'Not so soon after my tea. I don't want to die of indigestion.'" Prophetic words. He eludes the strychnine left out for him but soon falls victim to the big yellow Tom from the rectory. The abashed Mr. Appin flees the scene and moves on to the Dresden Zoological Gardens, where, as the result of his further animal experiments, he is found crushed by an angry elephant. Narrator Clovis delivers his final assessment of the man's demise: "If he was trying German irregular verbs on the poor beast, he deserved all he got'" (120–26).

Typically, Saki's deftly comic treatment of the supernatural, avers A. J. Langguth, "is presented with so little flourish, that the story is done before logic has recovered itself enough to protest" (173).

"Gabriel-Ernest"

Move your gaze past the treeline of Mr. Van Cheele's property and there on the "shelf of smooth stone overhanging a deep pool in the hollow of an oak coppice" is a boy of about sixteen, lying asprawl drying his wet brown limbs in the sun. He is naked. "His wet hair, parted by a recent dive, lay close to his head, and his light-brown eyes, so light that there was an almost tigerish gleam in them, were turned on Van Cheele with a certain lazy watchfulness." He is too old to be the child of the miller's wife, lately lost, presumably in the mill-race. Where on earth can this wild boy hail from? From the woods . . . "'They're very nice woods,' said the boy, with a touch of patronage in his voice." The night is his busiest time, the boy continues, when he feeds on flesh—"'poultry, lambs in their season, children when I can get any . . . It's quite two months since I tasted child-flesh.'" He pronounces the word "with slow relish, as though he were tasting it." In a flash, the boy plunges into the pool and is gone. A later report from a neighbor is equally alarming: "'I was watching the dying glow of the sunset. Suddenly I became aware of a naked boy . . . His pose was so suggestive of some wild faun of Pagan myth . . .'" Moments later the boy vanishes and is replaced by "'a large wolf, blackish in colour, with gleaming fangs and cruel, yellow eyes.'"

By now, thoroughly alarmed, Van Cheele speeds to his aunt's house, where, mistaking the boy for a foundling, she had charitably taken in the boy and named him "Gabriel-Ernest." But Gabriel-Ernest has vanished and taken with him a child from a local Sunday school class. Van Cheele searches for them along the mill stream. "A dwindling rim of red sun showed still on the skyline . . . then the colour went suddenly out of things, and a grey light settled itself with a quick shiver on the landscape." A wail of fear is heard. Then, nothing. Too late. Both boys are never found. A pile of discarded clothes suggests the child had fallen into the water and that Gabriel Ernest had gone in after him. While the child's mother, who had eleven other children, "was decently resigned to her bereavement," Van Cheele's aunt grieves the loss of her foundling. She puts up a memorial brass in the local parish church with the inscription: "Gabriel-Ernest, an unknown boy, who bravely sacrificed his life for another." Last line: Van Cheele gave way to his aunt in most things, but he flatly refused to subscribe to the Gabriel-Ernest memorial" (69–75).

Compared to the bestiality of stories of lycanthropy from contemporaries Rudyard Kipling and Robert E. Howard to later masters James Blish and Jack Williamson, Saki's creature speaks like an Etonian and would be comfortable in the drawing room. He is bemused by his shape-changing condition and casually frank about his dining habits.

"Sredni Vashtar"

Our view shifts to "a disused tool shed" that is almost hidden behind the "dismal shrubbery" of a "dull and cheerless garden." For ten-year-old Conradin it is something of "a playroom and a cathedral." For the reader it is a scene of a grisly murder, from which our eyes are thankfully averted.

Aunts and guardians rank high among Saki's public enemies and populate many of his stories. Conradin's guardian and aunt, Mrs.

De Ropp, is demonized from the first. And while it cannot be proved that she is based on the two aunts who terrorized Saki's lonely childhood, it seems clear enough, according to biographer Sandie Byrne: "'Sredni Vashtar' depicts the effect on a small boy of a loveless upbringing, the development of an ability to blame and to hate that even now shocks in its power and ferocity" (20). In his isolation and loneliness, Conradin finds solace from his hatred of Mrs. De Ropp in the tool shed where he worships the great polecat-ferret he dubs "Sredni Vashtar." Although afraid of the lithe, sharp-fanged beast, "it was his most treasured possession," giving him a "secret and fearful joy." One day, observing the curious Mrs. De Ropp entering the shed, determined to destroy whatever crouches there, Conradin whispers this invocation:

> Sredni Vashtar went forth,
> His thoughts were red thoughts and his teeth were white.
> His enemies called for peace, but he brought them death.
> Sredni Vashtar the Beautiful.

He offers up a fervent request: "'Do one thing for me, Sredni Vashtar.'" Presently his eyes are rewarded: "Out through that doorway came a long, low, yellow-and-brown beast, with eyes a-blink at the waning daylight, and dark wet stains around the fur of jaws and throat." As Conradin drops on his knees, "the great polecat-ferret made its way down to a small brook at the foot of the garden, drank for a moment, then crossed a little plank bridge and was lost to sight in the bushes." When the maid goes to fetch Mrs. De Ropp from the shed, her screams disrupt the calm. The servants debate who will bring the awful news to Conradin, who is otherwise occupied: "He made himself another piece of toast" (152–55).

John Collier's classic tale "Thus I Refute Beelzy" bears unmistakable signs of Saki's influence.[6]

---

6. See John Collier, "Thus I Refute Beelzy," in *The Touch of Nutmeg and More Unlikely Stories* (New York: The Press of the Readers Club, 1943), 164–68. Even the most *guignol* of Collier's stories, such as "Another Ameri-

"The Peace of Mowsle Barton"

Nothing is to be trusted in Saki, not even the picturesque serenity of a rural landscape. Reveling at first in the bucolic scene of Mowsle Barton, after the "stress and noise of long years of city life," the vacationing Crefton Lockyer soon senses something disturbing:

> Time and space seemed to lose their meaning and their abruptness . . . Nothing seemed to belong definitely to anywhere; even the gates were not necessarily to be found on their hinges. And over the whole scene brooded the sense of a peace that had almost a quality of magic in it. In the afternoon you felt that it had always been afternoon and must always remain an afternoon; in the twilight you knew that it could never have been anything else but twilight.

While "Mowsle Barton" is one of the least-known of Saki's tales, it deserves a place on the honor roll of classic literary Bad Places. Perhaps the well has been poisoned by the mutual recriminations of the village's two old alleged witches, Martha Pillamon and Betsy Croot. They have consecrated "their last flickering energies to the task of making each other wretched . . . The uncanny part of it was that some horrid unwholesome power seemed to be distilled from their spite and their cursings [and Lockyer] felt that he had come suddenly into contact with some unguessed-at and very evil aspect of hidden forces" (209). Tea-kettle water never comes to a boiling point, ducks in a pond sink below the surface and drown. "There was something peculiarly piteous in the sight of the gasping beaks that showed now and again above the water, as though in terrified

---

can Tragedy," is expressed in an eighteenth-century manner of elegance and wit. Yet the scalpel is clean—and eager. What most irritated Collier, alleges Betty Richardson in her book-length study of Collier, was the persistent association of his stories with Saki and the implication that he had deliberately chosen Saki as his model. Collier himself insisted that he read nothing by Saki until 1939, when he briefly visited Ireland and came across some Saki stories; he decided that he could do something along those lines. The result was "Thus I Refute Beelzy." Collier declared, "'So much for my discipleship!'" See Betty Richardson, *John Collier* (Boston: Twayne, 1983), 15.

protest at this treachery of a trusted and familiar element" (210). After more disturbing incidents, the fleeing Lockyer casts one last backward glance: "Over all brooded that air of magic possession which Crefton had once mistaken for peace." Back at Paddington Station the bustle and roar is a "welcome protective greeting" and that Crefton surrenders himself to the "sedative" of a strenuous performance of the music of "1812" (205–12).

"The Interlopers"

Snowflakes spatter Saki's window. The beauties of a Carpathian winter conceal a menace that defeats the attempts of two warring families to reconcile a storied feud of long standing. Ulrich von Gradwitz and Georg Znaeym find themselves trapped beneath falling timber. As they await rescue, they begin to soften their mutual hatred and agree to move for some kind of reconciliation: "I've come to think we've been rather fools,'" declares Ulrich to Georg; "'there are better things in life than getting the better of boundary dispute. Neighbour, if you will help me to bury the old quarrel, I—I will ask you to be my friend.'" But this night "there was a disturbing element in the forest." Sounds of approaching rescuers are mistaken for what really confronts and what finally ends their dispute—and their lives: wolves.

The Contes Cruels

> "Clovis believed that if a lie was worth telling, it was worth telling well."
> —"The Forbidden Buzzards"

Here are windows of fine cut-glass, though they betray a spidery network of spreading cracks.

The following selection marks Saki as the master of the conte cruel, fully the equal of his most prolific contemporary, Marjorie Bowen, and influencer of later practitioners John Collier and Roald Dahl.[7]

---

7. The roll call of practitioners, to which Saki takes his rightful place, is a distinguished one. Directly contemporaneous with him is Marjorie Bowen, who, I have argued in my *The Furies of Marjorie Bowen*, rivals him in the quantity

Despite their brittle character and occasional comic twists, their innate savagery peeks out furtively through the drawing room blinds. Saki's moderation of the more outright horrors of the foregoing tales only thinly disguise the more subtle brands of savagery practiced therein. That the storytellers here—notably the aforementioned Reginald and Clovis—are notoriously unreliable is a thundering understatement. I am particularly fond of our first meeting with the irrepressible Reginald: "Reginald is reclining in a comfortable chair, with the dreamy, far-away look that a volcano might wear just after it had desolated entire villages" (5).

"The Strategist"

The view discloses a children's tea party in full swing. Because young Rollo has found himself without the protection of his best buddies, he is at the mercy of his deadly rivals, the Wrotsley boys. They immediately contrive a game that leaves him alone with them in the library, where with dog-whip and whalebone riding switch they mete out a swift and merciless punishment. ("Rollo thought it criminal negligence to leave such weapons of precision lying about.") Desperate to avoid more tortures, Rollo concocts a story about a stash of

---

and savage wit of her stories. The modern masters closest to Saki's example are the aforementioned John Collier and Roald Dahl. The gleeful subversions of societal pretensions in the best stories of Roald Dahl (1916–1990)—collected in the early volumes *Someone Like You* and *Kiss Kiss*—all too soon morphed into a crude misogyny and sadism of later story collections. But as Joyce Carol Oates observed of his contes cruels (and she should know), his best work is that of a "writer of macabre, blackly jocose tales that read, at their strongest, like artful variants of Grimm's fairy tales; Dahl is of that select society of . . . satiric moralists who wield the English language like a surgical instrument to flay, dissect, and expose human folly." See Joyce Carol Oates, "The Art of Vengeance," *New York Review of Books* (26 April 2007): 44. In his introduction to a volume of collected stories, biographer Jeremy Treglown asserts, "While Saki's stories inhabit a grander, more leisured, more whimsical social world than Dahl's, they have a similar mix of malice and edge, particularly in the ways in which they unsettle comfortable-seeming scenarios." See Treglown, in *Roald Dahl: Collected Stories* (New York: Everyman's Library, 2006), x.

chocolates that lures some of the children to the library, leaving him behind in comparative safety with the others. Saki's savagely comic touch is irresistible, and Rollo's retreat into safety carries with it an allusion to one of his oft-cited animals: "Rollo sank into a chair and smiled ever so faintly at the Wrotsleys, just a momentary baring of the teeth; an otter, escaping from the fangs of the hounds into the safety of a deep pool, might have given a similar demonstration of its feelings" (88–92).[8]

This is a personal favorite and one of funniest of all Saki's stories, which is saying something.

"The Storyteller"

We are looking through a railway carriage window. Inside a bachelor watches in silence while a governess tells a story to her young charges. "She began an unenterprising and deplorably uninteresting story about a little girl who was good and made friends with every one on account of her goodness, and was finally saved from a mad bull by a number of rescuers who admired her moral character." After the children dismiss the story as "stupid," the bachelor enters the fray. He begins a counter-narrative of the fate of a little girl who was *horribly* good. The children perk up: "It seemed to introduce a ring of truth that was absent from the aunt's tales of infant life." One day, he begins, the little girl is allowed to play in a

---

8. Parenthetically, "The Strategist" also contains a throwaway line about one of the party guests that struck me then and now as one of the funniest I've ever read: "Dolores was known to recite 'Locksley Hall' on the least provocation. There had been occasions when her opening line, 'Comrades, leave me here a little,' had been taken as a literal injunction by a large section of her hearers" (90).

beautiful garden populated by a number of small pigs. Into the garden comes an enormous wolf who immediately forgets the pigs and hunts for the little girl. Alerted by the Good Conduct medals that clank noisily around the child's neck, the wolf with eyes gleaming with ferocity and triumph drags out Bertha "'and devoured her to the last morsel. All that was left of her were her shoes, bits of clothing, and the three medals for goodness.'" The storyteller's young auditors are delighted: "'It is the most beautiful story that I ever heard,'" declares one. But their aunt is horrified by the story and declares such "improper" stories "'have undermined the effect of years of careful teaching.'" As the bachelor prepares to leave the carriage, he reminds the aunt that he had been able to keep the children quiet, which was more than she had done. "'Unhappy woman,'" he muses, "'for the next six months or so those children will assail her in public with demands for an improper story'" (391–96).

A. J. Langguth praises "The Storyteller" as "a pure distillation of Hector's freshest ingredients, and it offers the best introduction to his work. If that story does not please a new reader, Hector has no more potent charms to win him over" (217).

"Laura"

A close-up view of a sick room. "I have the doctor's permission to live till Tuesday," declares a young woman. Her name is Laura, and she is failing:

> "I never said I was going to die. I am presumably going to leave off being Laura, but I shall go on being something. An animal of some kind, I suppose. You see, when one hasn't been very good in the life one has just lived, one reincarnates in some lower organism. And I haven't been very good, when one comes to think of it. I've been petty and mean and vindictive and all that sort of thing when circumstances have seemed to warrant it."

She seems to be referring to her girlfriend Amanda's husband, Egbert, whom she cannot abide. "'Maybe I will be a nice animal,'" Laura continues, "'some thing elegant and lively, with a love of fun;

an otter, perhaps'" (269). After that, if she has been a "'moderately good otter,'" she might metamorphose into human shape, "'probably something rather primitive—a little brown, unclothed Nubian boy, I should think.'" And so it happens that Laura does indeed expire, a bit prematurely, as she had predicted. Alas, her funeral conflicts with her friend Amanda's rhododendrons just then coming into bloom: "'Laura always was inconsiderate,'" says a friend. Sure enough, in no time an otter appears and kills Egbert's beloved Sussex hens. Then more are massacred. And worse, the otter makes its way into Egbert's house and raids the salmon provisions. "'We shall have it hiding under our beds and biting pieces out of our feet before long,'" complains Egbert. He manages to kill the beast, but not before he notices it "had such a human look in its eyes when it was killed." Exhausted from the ordeal, Amanda and Egbert repair to the Nile Valley to recuperate. But more disaster follows when Egbert's dressing room is torn into pieces by—you guessed it—"a little beast of a naked brown Nubian boy" (272). Last line: "And now Amanda is seriously ill" (267–72).

"The Lumber Room"

Dusty and fly-specked, the window of the lumber room discloses young Nicholas, seeking refuge from his aunt's reproving gaze. He has been ordered to stay at home while his cousins are allowed to go on an outing. Here in the lumber room he finds a storehouse of "unimagined treasures," including a colorful tapestry depicting a huntsman who had shot a deer with an arrow. Nicholas sits for "golden minutes" extrapolating that the four wolves in the background would soon imperil the huntsman. Presently he is interrupted by shrieks coming from his aunt. She has just fallen into the nearby garden's water tank. Although empty, the water tank's sides are slippery and the woman is trapped. "'I was told I wasn't to go into the gooseberry garden,'" he shouts in response to her entreaties for help; moreover, he claims the voice is not that of his aunt but of "the Evil One" tempting him to be disobedient: "'Aunt often tells me that the Evil One tempts me and that I always yield. This time I'm not going to yield.'" "'There was an unusual sense of luxury in being able to talk to an aunt as though one was talking to the Evil One.'" It is left to the kitchen maid to rescue the poor woman after her "undignified and unmerited detention" for thirty-five minutes. As for Nicholas, he remains absorbed in the tapestry's huntsman. It is possible, he concludes, that the huntsman would escape and the wolves would feast on the stricken stag (416–22).

"Esmé"

With a blast of trumpets and the yelp of hounds, a fox-hunting party swings into view. Clovis's friend the Baroness and her companion find themselves separated from the rest of the group. A hyena is stalking them. "'It was certainly no mortal fox,' recalls the Baroness. 'It stood more than twice as high, had a short, ugly head, and an enormous thick neck.'" She dubs the beast Esmé. Presently they come across a "small, half-naked gipsy brat picking blackberries." They ride on. Wailing cries are presently heard behind them. The animal reappears, clutching the child painfully in its jaws. It follows the Baroness. "'How can you let that ravening beast trot by your side?'" asks the Baroness's companion. "'In the first place, I can't prevent it,'" replies the Baroness; "'in the second place, whatever else he may be, I doubt if he's ravening at the present moment.'" But did the child suffer much? "'The indications were all that way'" replies the Baroness. "'On the other hand, of course, it may have been crying from sheer temper. Children sometimes do,'" The hyena races ahead of them and is run over in the street. In a moment of inspiration, the Baroness approaches the driver and claims that the dead creature is her dog. She demands reparation of an expensive diamond brooch. She subsequently keeps her own counsel about the event, adding, "'the gipsies were equally unobtrusive over their missing offspring; I don't suppose in large encampments they really know to a child or two how many they've got.'" The Baroness later confides to Clovis that she refused to share the wealth of the brooch with her companion—"'After all, the Esme part of the affair was my own invention'" (111–16).

"The Blind Spot"

The dining room is cozy and warm in the candlelight. A sumptuous meal is laid for Egbert and his uncle, Sir Lulworth. Egbert has just returned from the funeral of his great-aunt, Adelaide. Now her heir, Egbert has something on his mind. While going through his aunt's effects, he has discovered a letter to her incriminating her cook as the murderer of her brother, the canon. The canon's letter stated: "'I very much fear I shall have to get rid of Sebastian. He cooks divinely, but he has the temper of a fiend or an anthropoid ape, and I am really in bodily fear of him . . . I dare say the danger is imaginary; but I shall feel more at ease when he has quitted my service.'" The news is startling to Sir Lulworth, who has just taken the cook into his employ. He asks Egbert if he has shown this letter to anyone else. Before Egbert can respond, Sir Lulworth snatches up the letter and flings it into the fire. Egbert gasps, "'That letter was our one piece of evidence to connect Sebastian with the crime.'" That is why I destroyed it, says Sir Lulworth. But why shield him, a common murderer? Last line: "A common murderer, possibly, but a very uncommon cook," says Sir Lulworth (326–31).

"The Story of St. Vespaluus"

A stained-glass window discloses a Christian cross flanked by a pagan altar. Storyteller Clovis explains that these days pagans and Christians are disporting themselves at a time when "'a third of the people were Pagan, and a third Christian, and the biggest third of all just followed whichever religion the Court happened to profess.'" King Hkrikros has appointed no successors, but several nephews are up for job, among whom is the handsome and athletic Vespaluus. But the youth does not profess the king's pagan worship of the "sacred serpents" but instead appears one day in court with a rosary tucked into his belt. The outraged king orders the court librarian to beat him out of this "religious perversity." No use. For additional offensive Christian sentiments, the undaunted Vespaluus is shut into a tower with nothing to live on but bread and water and nothing to do but listen to the fluttering of bats. Upon release he seems to behave himself, until his disregard of more pagan rituals so offends the king that he sentences him to death from a thousand stings of the royal bees. Unbeknownst to anyone, the Keeper of the Royal Hives has Christian leanings and works all night before the execution to extract the stings from most of the bees. Of course, Vespaluus suffers only fits of giggling and laughter: "It was obvious that a miracle had been performed in his favour, and one loud murmur, of astonishment or exultation, rose from the onlooking crowd." Vespaluus had hardly cleaned off the honey stains from his body before the king dies and he is crowned as a saint: "The boy-martyr-that-might-have-been was transposed in the popular imagination into a royal boy-saint, whose fame attracted throngs of curious and devout sightseers to the capital." But he refuses to cut down the Pagan Serpent Grove. What, then of his Christian principals?—

> I never had any. I used to pretend to be a Christian convert just to annoy Hkrikros. He used to fly into such delicious tempers. It was rather fun being whipped and scolded and shut up in a tower all for nothing. But as to turning Christian in real earnest, like you people seem to do, I couldn't think of such a thing. And the holy and esteemed serpents have always helped me when I've prayed to them for success in my running and wrestling and hunting, and it was through their distinguished intercession that the bees were not able to hurt me with their stings. It would be black ingratitude to turn against their worship at the very outset of my reign.

He concludes: "'I don't mind being reverenced and greeted and honoured; I don't even mind being sainted in moderation, as long as I'm not expected to be saintly as well . . . but I will *not* give up the worship of the august and auspicious serpents.'" Finally, as a state expedient, both religions are accommodated: Vespaluus will appear as a Christian saint in the cathedral at intervals while worshiping other times in the pagan gardens (186–92).

Interlude

We stand back for the moment. Saki's window is a mirror. We hazard a look. Behind our reflected image stands the figure of Hector Hugh Munro. He looks back at us. It is a look of cruel speculation, like Pan peering through the underbrush in "Music on the Hill." Who is this man, really?—call him Hector, or Saki, or Reginald, or Clovis, or the many other storytellers to whom he gives voice. In the cynical wit of his stories, in the allegations by his biographers of his closeted homosexuality, in his taste for the aforementioned horrors of war in his journalistic dispatches, we sense a man secretive and self-effacing, living a half-hidden life. Perhaps he is capable of love, avers biographer Byrne—"when he is endeavoring to be a killer" (277).

In my opinion, we must look to some of the moody, even confessional pieces written during the years just before 1916 for a less obstructed view of a man weary of the life behind him and sensing the darkness and death that lies ahead. His protagonists— arguably Munro himself—appear severally in the stories "Dusk," "The Wolves of Cernogratz," "The Cobweb," and "The Mappined Life," and the novels *The Unbearable Bassington* and *When William Came.*

In "Dusk," we peer through the thickening twilight at a man named Norman Gortsby settling himself on a bench.

> It was some thirty minutes past six on an early March evening, and dusk had fallen heavily over the scene, dusk mitigated by some faint moonlight and many streetlamps. There was a wide emptiness over road and sidewalk, and yet there were many unconsidered figures moving silently through the half-light or dotted unobtrusively on bench and chair, scarcely to be distinguished from the shadowed gloom in which they sat . . . Dusk was the hour of the defeated. Men and women, who had fought and lost, who hid their fallen fortunes and dead hopes as far as possible from the scrutiny of the curious, came forth in this hour of gloaming, when their shabby

clothes and bowed shoulders and unhappy eyes might pass unnoticed, or, at any rate, unrecognized.

Gortsby is "in a mood to count himself among the defeated . . . He had failed in a subtle ambition, and for the moment was heart sore and disillusioned, and not disinclined to take a certain cynical pleasure in observing and labeling his fellow wanderers as they went their ways in the dark stretches between the lamp-lights" (331–35).

Through the castle window we regard the ageing Baroness Cernogratz, the impoverished last survivor of the Cernogratz line. "The Wolves of Cernogratz" is her story. She is living out her last days as a humble governess in a castle that once had been her ancestral home. She explains that the wolves howling in the distant forest foretell, according to family legend, the impending hour of her death: "'There would be scores of them, gliding about in the shadows and howling in chorus, and the dogs of the castle and the village and all the farms would bay and howl in fear and anger at the wolf chorus, and as the soul of the dying one left its body a tree would crash down in the park.'" Given notice by her employer, the Baroness is abandoned and alone. "'I am the last von Cernogratz that will die in our old castle,'" she declares, "'and the [wolves] have come to sing to me. Hark, how loud they are calling!'" As she breathes her last, "The cry of the wolves rose on the still winter air and floated round the castle walls in long-drawn piercing wails." She expires with "a look of long-delayed happiness on her face." A tree crashes in the woods (460–65).

Old Martha Crale in "The Cob Web" may or may not be a witch, or even a ghost. Certainly she is subject to purportedly supernatural visions of impending death. Like a "human cobweb," she has been stifling attempts of reform by the generations of occupants that come and go. When an accident befalls one of the newest tenants, it is she who anticipates the death. And now, left alone at the end, we find her "white, unheeding face peering out through the lattice, and [her] weak muttering voice would be heard quavering up and down those flagged passages" where she had lived for nearly fourscore years (295–301).

Published in June 1914, just two months before Munro's enlistment into the army, "The Mappined Life" is more sermon than story. Here, Saki's lifelong fascination with animals serves to provide more than a hint of his existential angst on the eve of the war that will take his life. "'These Mappin Terraces at the Zoological Gardens are a great improvement on the old style of wild-beast cage,'" observes Mrs. James Gurtleberry. "'They give one the illusion of seeing the animals in their natural surroundings. I wonder how much of the illusion is passed on to the animals?'" Her niece's response is pointed:

> "Nothing will make me believe that an acre or so of concrete enclosure will make up to a wolf or tiger-cat for the range of night prowling that would belong to it in wild state. Think of the dictionary of sound and scene and recollection that unfolds before a real wild beast as it comes out from its lair every evening, with the knowledge that in a few minutes it will be hieing along to some distant hunting ground where all the joy and fury of the chase awaits it; think of the crowded sensations of the brain when every rustle, every cry, every bent twig, and every whiff across the nostrils means something, something to do with life and death and dinner . . ." (539)

Indeed, the "mappined" life is a poor imitation of a life of liberty. "'We are trammelled by restrictions of income and opportunity,' adds the niece, 'and above all by lack of initiative . . . We are just so many animals stuck down on a Mappin terrace with this difference in our disfavour, that the animals are there to be looked at, while nobody wants to look at us. As a matter of fact, there would be nothing to look at'" (538–42).

"Tom Keriway" makes a brief but memorable entrance in chapter 8 of the undeservingly neglected novel *The Unbearable Bassington*. He appears only once, and then is gone again. But these are some of finest, most moving pages in the entirety of Saki/Munro. The man is something of a legend: *"There was an air about him that a German diplomat once summed up in a phrase: 'a man that wolves have sniffed at'"* [my emphasis]. The glamor of his roving career has fired the imagination, and wistful desire to do likewise, of many young Englishmen. "He seldom talked of his travels, but it might be said that his travels talked of him." But after "a sudden and severe illness shook half the life and all the energy out of him," he is now driven by "the impulse which drives a stricken animal away from its kind. He has left the haunts where he had known so much happiness and withdrawn into the shelter of a secluded farm-house lodging."

We see him now, talking with young Elaine De Grey, who has just come to call. Tom responds to her request to know more about his present life on the farm. He describes "a whole world, or rather several intermingled worlds, set apart in this sleepy hollow in the hills . . .

> of beast lore and wood lore and farm craft, at times touching almost the border of witchcraft—passing lightly here, not with the probing eagerness of those who know nothing, but with the averted glance of those who fear to see too much. He told her of those things that slept and those that prowled when the dusk fell, of strange hunting cats, of the yard swine and the stalled cattle, of the farm folk themselves, as curious and remote in their way, in their ideas and fears and wants and tragedies, as the brutes and feathered stock that they tended. It seemed to Elaine as if a musty store of old-world children's books had been fetched down from some cob-webbed lumber-room and brought to life.

It seems to his young friend that here is a man who has held in the hollow of his hand "much that was priceless and lost it all, and he was happy and absorbed and well content with the little wayside corner of the world into which he had crept."

She declares he is a person to be envied: "'You have created a fairyland, and you are living in it yourself.'"

Tom bitterly rebukes her:

"'Once, in a German paper I read a short story about a tame crippled crane that lived in the park of some small town. I forget what happened in the story, but there was one line that I hall always remember: "it was lame, that is why it was tame.""""

Keriway has indeed created a fairyland, but "assuredly he was not living in it" (624–30).

Finally, *When William Came* is a window onto war. At the story's opening, Murrey Yeovil has just returned from a long illness to a London that is hardly recognizable. Germany has invaded England: "It was just after the great catastrophe, and men of the London world were in no humour to think; they had witnessed the inconceivable befall them, they had nothing but political ruin to stare at, and they were anxious to look the other way" (696). Saki/Munro had been watching the growth of industrial and militaristic Germany, and in 1913, less than a year before the outbreak of World War I, his novel predicted an inevitable clash with the Kaiser and an invasion of Britain. As England's patriotic fervor grows dormant, resistance will be difficult, realizes Yeovil. "'I don't imagine that they are going to give us an easy chance to push them out. To do that we shall have to be a little cleverer than they are, a little harder, a little fiercer, and a good deal more self-sacrificing than we have been in my lifetime'" (762). What about English youth? A German officer is wary of "the younger generation of Britons [that] may grow up in hereditary hatred, repulsing all our overtures, forgetting nothing and forgiving nothing, waiting and watching for the time when some weakness assails us, when some crisis entangles us, when we cannot be everywhere at once. Then our work will be imperiled, perhaps undone. There lies the danger, there lies the hope, the younger generation.'" It will fall to Yeovil to carry on the struggle:

> "But you, Murrey, you are young [he is admonished], you can fight. Are you going to be a fighter, or the very humble servant of the *fait accompli?* . . . One must not wait too long, Time is on their side, not ours. It is the young people we must fight for now, if they're ever to fight for us. A new generation will spring up, a weaker memory of old glories will survive . . . I would awaken or keep alive in their memory the things that we have been, the grand, brave things that

some of our race have done, and I would stir up a longing, a determination for the future that we must win back." (768)

But Yeovil is no longer young. He admits he is tired and past resistance. Like Tom Keriway, he is full of regrets and bitter at the peace he has found: "Yeovil saw himself in moments of disgust and self-accusation, settling down into this life of rustic littleness, . . . ignoring the struggle-cry that went up low and bitter and wistful, from a dethroned dispossessed race, in whose glories he had glorified, in whose struggle he lent no hand" (793).

War and Death

Hector Hugh Munro enlisted in the 2nd King Edwards's Horse on 25 August 1914 at age forty-four. Never robust, he was now "Trooper H. H. Munro." The innate tendencies of violence and cruelty he had always seen in children—satirized most recently in a short story, "The Toys of Peace"—seemed to have been incarnated in current events large scale as a nation rushes headlong toward war. "He was reviling himself for the slackness of his years in London," writes A. J. Langguth, "and tiring of his earlier incarnations, of Saki and the rest. He wanted to expunge half his life. He would start over" (252). This was the man who as "Saki" had once satirized in *The Westminster Alice* the political and military ineptitude of the Boer War. Now, "he no longer had the excuses of youth or illness for having denied his destiny as a soldier" (194).

His social class and his education, such as his knowledge of German and familiarity with Mitteleuropa, made him an obvious candidate for officer rank, or even something like intelligence work, but he refused such offers more than once. Reassigned at his request to the 22nd Battalion of the Royal Fusiliers, Munro arrived in France in late 1915. He was recovering from a bout of malaria when, knowing that a "push" was imminent, he discharged himself early and returned to the front on 11 November.

Munro found time for a few more stories and sketches, including "The Square Egg: A Badger's Eye-View of the War Mud in the Trenches." This last of his animal parables likens the drab badger, which digs and burrows and listens, to the soldiers who wait, while 200 yards away is "a vigilant, bullet-spitting enemy, lurking and watching in those opposing trenches." Here in the pitch dark is "the mud of the moment, the mud that engulfs you . . . where you can only stumble about and feel your way against streaming mud walls, when you have to go down on hands and knees in several inches of soup-like mud to creep into a dug-out, when you stand deep in mud, lean against mud, grasp mud-slimed objects with mud-caked fingers, wink mud away from your eyes and shake it out of your ears, bit muddy biscuits with muddy teeth" (607–8).

The picture that emerges of him as a soldier is distant from the effete and amoral dandies of his short stories and the languor and idleness of his last few months in London. "There is a photo of him carrying a bucket, his uniform rumpled, sleeves rolled up, a scrubby

Hector Hugh Munro (left) killed in action, 14 November 1916; and William Hope Hodgson, killed in action 19 April 1918.

moustache on his top lip. If he was unrecognizable, then that perhaps suited him. Always an intensely private individual, he may have been happy that only a few of his fellows recognised the witty satirist Saki" (Byrne 267). He displayed an apparent joy in army life, as recorded in his letters, as well as "conspicuous bravery under fire that indicates his decision to risk his life for his country as a common soldier was sincere." But why, we must ask, were he and his brothers doing this in the face of certain death? It has been speculated: "They fought to avoid punishment, they fought for their brother soldiers, they fought out of lingering patriotism, and they went on fighting because they saw no way back."[9]

Even so, his sharply cynical voice never quite left him. At Christmas 1915 he composed a mock carol:

> While shepherds watched their flocks by night
> All seated on the ground,
> A high explosive shell came down
> And mutton rained around.[10]

And so it happened that on the night of 14 November 1916, near the French town of Beaumont-Hamel, while crouching in a shell-hole, he angrily shouted to a comrade, "Put that bloody cigarette out!" And he was killed instantly by a sniper's bullet to the head.[11] He thus joined the ranks of other deceased British writers and composers, including his contemporary, the noted master of the weird, William Hope Hodgson.[12]

---

9. George Packer, "The Warrior's Anti-War Novel," *Atlantic* 333, No. 3 (March 2025): 86.

10. A. J. Langguth reports that Munro sent these lines to his sister Ethel on Christmas Eve 1915, while in training camp (267).

11. Is the report of Munro's demise really true? "If true," writes E. S. Turner, "it would have been a black pay-off as good as any in his stories (it has the bleak, casual cruelty of the last sentence in his tale of the fight to save the nest of two rare birds: 'The buzzards successfully reared two young ones, which were shot by a local hairdresser')". See Turner, "Blowing Cigarette Smoke at Greenfly," *London Review of Books* 22, No. 16 (24 August 2000): 4.

12. Other British writers and composers killed in the Great War included

Epilogue: Opening Saki's Window

Saki's death inevitably recalls these lines:

> Thou hast made me, and shall thy work decay?
> Repair me now, for now mine end doth haste,
> I run to death, and death meets me as fast,
> And all my pleasures are like yesterday . . .

They were written by the Anglican priest John Donne (1572–1631), in his cycle of *Holy Sonnets* (1609–10). Although removed from Saki's world by several centuries, don't these lines seem apposite enough to the Saki we have come to know in these pages? And consider them in comparison with these lines from one of Saki's last stories, "For the Duration of the War," written in the months before his death:

> "You are not on the Road to Hell,"
> You tell me with fanatic glee:
> Vain boaster, what shall that avail
> If Hell is on the road to thee? (601)

Concurrent with my Saki readings, I am startled to find in Katherine Rundell's recent estimable biography of John Donne, *Super-Infinite: The Transformations of John Donne*—an amazing book full of witty insights that belongs on everyone's shelf—what seem many correspondences between Donne and Saki/Munro. Never

---

Wilfred Owen, Rupert Brooke, Edward Thomas, and George Butterworth. There are some parallels with William Hope Hodgson's death, who had also forsaken civilian life to serve bravely in the trenches. Sam Moskowitz describes Hodgson's days as a lieutenant in the Royal Field Artillery in 1915. Injured from a fall from a horse, he was discharged, but, like Munro, he petitioned to re-enlist and wrote a series of published articles and stories about his war experiences. In a letter to his mother he declared, "If I live and come somehow out of this *what* a book I shall write if my old 'ability' with the pen has not forsaken me" (115). He was killed in action from a shell burst near Ypres on 19 April 1918. See *Out of the Storm: Uncollected Fantasies by William Hope Hodgson,* ed. with a Critical Biography by Sam Moskowitz (West Kingston, R.I., Donald M. Grant, 1975).

overt, to be sure, but present all the same. Rundell, former Fellow of All Soul's College, Oxford, describes Donne's "questing toward death" in a way that immediately suggest Saki's own demise: "[Donne] felt death reach him . . . He made himself ready, part, perhaps, of a desire to have things done exactly as he had imagined them—an artist of ferocious precision, dying precisely." Thus, his own words, "'I were miserable if I might not die.'"[13] Now read this account by a fellow soldier of Munro's preparations for war: "He put on a trooper's uniform with the exaltation of a novice assuming the religious habit" (quoted in Byrne 266).

Saki and Donne? Surely an unlikely pair, separated by centuries of political and religious contexts. Any comparisons seem invidious or, at the least, merely foolish. And now I must venture into pure speculation. I think here we find an affinity that borders on identity. On virtually every page of her book Rundell's comments on Donne can easily apply to Saki, although never overtly stated. For example, do we not think of Saki when she declares that Donne "was . . . such a fount of satirical, mean snide: He was both celebrant and assassin, ever shifting between the two" (134–35)? And what about Donne's early satiric poetry, which "is quick on its feet and angry at you"? And there was Donne's "strange, remarkable intellect, with its courageous munificence and its angry bitter corners . . . He saw both marvels and corruption in the state of humanity as a whole," while regarding the world "with both awe and

13. Katherine Rundell, *Super-Infinite: The Transformations of John Donne* (New York: Farrar, Straus & Giroux, 2022): 290.

scepticism: that you weep for it and that you gasp for it" (135, 295). Not to mention Donne's "linguistic pyrotechnics," which are "constantly in motion: turbulent, shifting between triumph and anxiety, bravado and dread, irony and humility" (294).

Conversely, in Rundell's enthusiasm for Saki—as avowed in her commentary on a recent collection of his stories—do we not sense the presence of Donne? "To read a Saki story," she writes, "is to hire an assassin [and indulge] in the pleasures of laying waste to convention combined with the quickening promise of something wilder in its stead." As with Donne, she continues, "[Saki's] mechanisms of wit are unseen and so inimitable." And there is this: "Saki ... was a man who saw the hidden wildness of things ... His short stories burst with the possibilities of a world in which strangeness is bone-deep and evident in every facet of civilized life."[14] Moreover, her enthusiasm for Saki has gone public, as it were, in a play she wrote and staged in 2017. *Life According to Saki* features Munro himself as a storyteller in the trenches of World War I, in which, in the words of a reviewer, "he entertains the lads with narratives that twist like a corkscrew." A critic in the *New York Times* observed: "Evidently, that greatest of concluding Saki lines—'Romance at short notice was her specialty'—applied to its creator as well."[15]

---

14. Katherine Rundell, "Ferrets Can Be Gods," *London Review of Books* 38, No. 16 (11 August 2016). www.lrb.co.uk/v38/n16/katherine-rundell/ferrets -can=be-gods.
15. Ben Brantley, "Life According to Saki, in the Trenches of World War I," *New York Times* (1 February 2017). www.nytimes.com/2017/02/01/theater/ life-according-to-saki-in-the-trenches-of-world-war-i.html.

When, at the end of her book on Donne, Rundell asks, "Who else of [Donne's] peers had been able to hold grotesqueries and delights, death and life so tightly in the same hand?" (297), I propose we extend the question to our present day and give our answer: Saki. Would that I could engage Professor Rundell to explore further these perceived correspondences and what they say, respectively, about the tumultuous times of warfare and religious tensions that confronted both men and fueled their works.

Meanwhile, what we do know is that John Donne was buried in St. Paul's Cathedral in London. Saki was buried—where? His body was never recovered.[16]

In life and in death, the window swings wide open . . . And we listen to the howling of the wolves.

---

16. Inscribed on the Thiepval Memorial to the Missing, located near the Somme battlefield, is a French inscription reads "Aux armées Française et Britannique l'Empire Britannique reconnaissant" ("To the French and British Armies, from the grateful British Empire"). www. annotated-saki.info/r-i-p-lance-serjeant-h-h-munro/#

Thiepval Memorial to the Missing, located at the northern part of the 1916 Somme battlefields

Eternal Circles

Dmitri Akers

1

24 December 1941—Magalang
Father Carberry dictated the Word of God, however doleful. His intonations fell flat, flatter than any note exhaled by a broken organ.

It was Christmas Eve. They were fleeing an invading army of heathens, the Japanese Imperial Army. No time for presents and merry-making in the Philippines. For it only stank of an army's collective excretions, paired with dank rot, rather than holly and nutmeg. The air, humid yet clammy, was rife with odors so unlike the smell of pines back in the States.

The chaplain raised his voice, impassioned and quavering, yet his dictation of the Word fell on deaf ears. The American officers, silent and sullen, sat on old chairs. They fanned themselves with rolled-up newspapers. With glazed eyes, the Americans stared at the chaplain. Carberry was his name; he stood and pontificated, awkwardly so. His words bounced off the moldy walls and almost rattled the podium, if it was a podium.

These moldy crates, making the frame and body of an unsteady pulpit, were rank with decomposed tamarinds. The rot of sugar only grew worse with the advent of inch after inch of more rainfall.

On the floor, the tanned troops of the Philippine Scouts sat attentively. They watched Father Carberry. Every few passages, he turned the pages of his old missal. Its leather had worn down into soft, frayed wounds.

"And it is in this time of outrageous war and violence," Father Carberry said, "that we should reflect on the birth of Christ. And remember our sound doctrine as Christians to be self-disciplined, faithful, loving, and endurant. I shall now read from . . ."

A page turned; it tore beneath his finger and thumb.

Father Carberry half smiled, half winced. But he went on. His throat grew hoarse. The night was long. Nonetheless, he instructed his lambs during a prayer.

"Now you may stand," he said.

The officers slowly stood. It came to sing. Only the Scouts joined. The Mass ended. Officers, pink and sweaty, left without a word. But, as Father Carberry looked up from his missal, he saw the Scouts gathered. One of them, with a large and wooden crucifix around his neck, walked forward.

"May the Lord be with you."

"May the Lord be with you," the Scout replied and bowed. "Thank you for the service, Father."

"What may I do for you, my son?"

The man's baggy eyes that trembled. The other Scouts anxiously looked about. Father Carberry noticed that one held a white sheet. White if not for a stain. A dark stain like wine. A stigma.

"It's not something to discuss right here after a holy Mass," the soldier replied. "I'm Private Idos. If you could help us, we need a blessing in the sleeping quarters."

A mattress, sanguine and scarlet, greeted the chaplain. Gore, decay, ephemera. Oh, God, it stank of a charnel house, of an orgy of cadavers.

"Whose blood is this?" Father Carberry asked.

They were in the sleeping quarters, where the Philippine Scouts had been sleeping. One, it seemed, had lost all his lifeblood on the bed. Around Father Carberry the Scouts stood like stone statuettes.

"Did someone wound himself?" Father Carberry turned to the Scouts as he spoke. "If this is another suicide attempt, I might have to contact Command."

"No suicide, Father," Idos replied.

"Then what?"

"A hound from hell. They call it a sigbin here, Father."

The chaplain shook his head as the Scouts recounted tales of a string of murders. At the center of these murders remained one figure: the shadowy dog, or a demon. A sigbin.

May 1942—Corregidor

How many had died? Their faces infested fevered dreams. One after another. Wights wailed. Their obsidian eyes wept.

Father Carberry woke with a start. The forest's songs blared within the chaplain's dizzied mind: whoops and clicks and groans. He rose from the wet grass. The others, leaning against crates of munitions, snored.

He looked over. In the dawn's mandarin-hued light, he saw the pale face of Private Idos. It looked peaceful for once. But then a trickle of blood fell from his nostrils. When the chaplain called out to him, only death responded. Once Father Carberry rose and inspected the soldier, he saw the hollow of his chest where the scarred flesh had been. Whatever killed Idos must have been ravenous. It could not have been a man that stole his heart. Even the Japanese soldiers who pursued them had no tantōs for such butchery.

"Help. Wake up," the chaplain called out. "Idos has been attacked."

The other stirred. Some vomited. Others made the sign of the cross. The body was hauled away. No burial. No fire. Only the songs of the forest would pray for him. The outfit ploughed through the long grass.

A chatter of gunfire. Then nothing.

Father Carberry heard his heart thumping. When he heaved in air, only mud entered his mouth. For a moment he thought he would die there. Until something pulled his dead weight upwards. Despite his faith, the chaplain expected the devil. Or a hellhound.

But he looked and he saw the face of a Japanese soldier.

2

Seasons passed. Relentless rain wore against the mud and buildings and even the prisoners' morale. As unbearable humidity crept into pores, the unshakeable and simultaneous feelings of dirtiness and wetness hung on one's skin. Overhead, the searing sun seemed to coexist with the undying wetness.

If Americans went out to the lumber camp, to fell trees or process timber, they came back either pink or brown from the baking light. The southern reaches of the Philippines might have differed from the high climes of Luzon, but what stayed constant was the unrelenting nature of the elements.

Father Carberry hunched over the feverish man. No medical degree was required to recognize the yellow, lingering of death. That horrid tropical plague, malaria! Lieutenant Boelens was covered in it, his deathly body harboring the mere seed of life in disease. During a delirium of decay, the sick man called out: "Jungles from hell . . . islands in hell . . . we walk through hell . . ."

His bloodshot eyes tremored inside their sockets. Father Carberry dabbed the ill man's forehead with a handkerchief and spoke in hushed tones: "Our Lord God shall drive out the enemy and deliver our men home."

"Perhaps you're right," a voice interjected.

As he looked over his shoulder, Father Carberry recognized Grashio the pilot. A glimmer of stained teeth exposed from cracked lips pulled into a smile.

"Here, the mosquitos bite you from head to toe to render you a shambling grotesque of bloody sores. The heat and humidity cook your brain to madness. And the world itself turns into nothing but a labyrinth of vines and leaves," Grashio said until his voice trailed off.

Footfall emanated from the corridor. Japanese soldiers, as stoic and hard as slate, marched past their cell with their bayoneted rifles. Clockwork steps died away. Grashio whispered: "This place is a special corner of hell. The Japanese call it Jigoku. There are realms inside Jigoku. Just as there are circles of hell. But Dante escaped the final circle of hell. We can escape."

"Escape?" the chaplain muttered. "Do you mean to break out?"

"The Supreme Poet needed Virgil to guide him through hell," Grashio replied. "You can be our guide, Father. The local people trust Catholic priests like you. Better yet, you're a good man who would sooner lay down your own life than see another suffer."

The chaplain turned, looked at Grashio, and nodded.

"I'll guide you. Information about the area is paramount. Luckily, I know my way here. I've been stationed in the Philippines since before the war, as you may know."

"Though you've never fired a shot," Grashio responded. "You've fought harder than anyone I've met."

The chaplain stood, made a sign with his hands and uttered a final prayer of blessing for the sick man. Boots against the stony floor echoed. Keys rattled.

After several scheming days and several whisper-filled nights, Father Carberry attended the cell once more. Boelens's sickness had miraculously cleared. But he feigned a persistent fever. Another prayer of blessing echoed within the bars, as the supine soldier attempted a convincing groan. By the door, the guards shook their heads. Latin must have sounded awful to them, for they walked away, smoking cigarettes and chatting.

"I cannot go," the chaplain whispered to Grashio in the corner. "I've given you all the details about the surrounds. It should be enough."

"Why do you stay?" Grashio asked. "You'd mean more to us free than enslaved."

"I lost so many souls already. Back in the forest, you should have seen how many men died. I must save more."

"Truly, you are selfless. We'll break out all the same. But you mustn't expose your collusion. They'll do unutterable things to you, Father."

The chaplain nodded and lifted himself off the ground; he waited for the guards. They came and saw him. They escorted him, without a word.

Walking down the corridor, Father Carberry silently mouthed the verse: "For though I walk through the valley of the shadow of death, I will fear no evil, for thou art with me."

Steely-eyed guards brought another prisoner to the chaplain's cell, which had then served as something between an unstocked infirmary and a funeral home. Swelling, bleeding, defiled, that prisoner little resembled a man. What moved men to such acts of sustained and terrible violence, Father Carberry did not know. Broken as he was, the prisoner was lifted by the soldiers. They left the prisoner on a bed of rotting straw.

The chaplain brought out his handkerchief. He soaked it in a hollowed coconut containing stinky water. Father Carberry rubbed the prisoner's disfigured face and scarred body. It became apparent the fellow was a Filipino private. His tattered uniform concealed what intact skin remained: smooth, bronzed, and hairless. Whoever he was, moans left the private's mouth; they sounded almost like "Armageddon" or maybe some native term.

"Pardon?" Father Carberry asked. "My son, I couldn't hear you."

Wincing, the mangled private raised his voice. "What happens?"

"What do you mean, child?"

"When death comes at the end of the Bible . . ."

"Do you mean in the Book of Revelation?" Father Carberry replied. "There's much about death in the Bible. Especially that part."

"Horse. Death rode a—"

"A pale horse," Father Carberry confirmed. "And Hell followed him."

The private, perhaps due to contemplation or expiration, fell into utmost silence. As pale light slanted through iron bars, the chaplain felt his insides chatter and roil. An invisible worm bored its way into his chest. It wriggled and writhed until the wound widened to a spear's diameter. What would a parasite do with a ripened apple other than devour it whole?

Along the prisoner's bodily shell, the handiwork of the Japanese was writ like calligraphy on paper. Despite such horrors draining nature, one must bear witness to them. What testament would exist without a pair of eyes that have witnessed? The chaplain looked down and saw the hollow of the private's palm.

A necrotic wound—that putrefying, blackened stigma—opened there as if it yawned sleepily. A holy sign was made over it as Father Carberry muttered something in Latin. He ran his fingers along the wrist like an apothecary who practiced bloodletting. The clammy skin stuck to his fingertips, yet not a single vein throbbed.

"In nomine patris et filii et spiritus sancti," the chaplain began.

How long had it been? Day in, day out, tortured prisoners were brought to the chaplain. They seemed more like corpses animated only by pain than anything else. Time passed by like a torrential rain. No torturer nor guard came for the priest. Instead, they went after the innocent lambs who had been thrown into this horrid war and worse prison.

The worm gorged; it burrowed deep into his flesh. Transubstantiation, decay. The heart—there was no flesh that remained on that rotten fruit—did not even possess seeds of hope anymore. When Father Carberry closed his eyes for prayer, the scores of dead souls welcomed him in the dark sanctums of his mind's eye.

Every night, the tormented wraiths haunted him. Some of them were from the war or the camps; others he could not recall where he had met, although they seemed familiar. Sleep, if one could call it that, overcame his restless brain until he dreamt of tears and screams and cries.

A vermilion dawn illumined the deathly empire with rosy light. The chaplain slowly opened his eyes. Keys rattled. Foreign orders bellowed. The door swung, clamored. Two guards entered, grabbed him, and marched him out of the camp.

The cell held more shadows than men. And there were dozens of prisoners of war. Father Carberry prayed for whatever souls there bothered to wail. Through a womb of metal, waves swished. The hell ship, as it was called, set off. Whoever knew the true meaning of the Japanese hell ships? They had naming conventions: a place name, then the word *maru,* meaning circle. These ships were not ships. They were realms of Jigoku—eternal circles of punishment.

It sailed, not like a ferry along Acheron, but a sort of ghastly barque lost in the land of the living. There was a whistling sound. Not of wind, but machine. Then the clamor came from on high. Carberry clapped his ears. The screams came, although not from men, but the hail of munitions. Fire rained; metal melted. Teardrops of embers lingered.

A force threw Carberry hither; a mound of corpses caught him. As his ears rang, as his eyes blurred, some hand grabbed him. It tugged, as if to retrieve him from the land of the dead.

January 1945—Takao

After one sailed the sea long enough, nothing remained linear. Like a circle, all events went, came, and were repeated. A vastness rolled and roiled into a mad infinity. One hell ship replaced another: a circle around a circle, a realm around a realm. There was a hell like this before, the Oryoku Maru, an inferno unto itself. It came full circle. Brazil Maru replaced that hell.

How long had they sailed? How many hell ships had there been, truly? If this was hell, there would be more circles, more realms. Bombs whistled. Guns chattered. Over and over. A leitmotif in a wretched symphony.

A putrid concoction stabbed one's nostrils. The stale air of brine preserved the sulphur of sewage and cadaverous decomposition. No soul slept. Days and nights melded into a gloomy oneness. Time died inside the vessel's lightless bowels.

The same event was repeated: grim-faced soldiers who wielded tantō swords forced prisoners to form groups that drew straws. If anyone defied these monsters masked as men, they were roundly stabbed and hacked to pieces. Any flesh or bone was collected in buckets, then taken upstairs with a strange urgency. Tongues ran down any blood-drenched blades.

After each group drew lots, all losers were dragged away. They never returned. Given that the Brazil Maru's food stores ran out, everyone understood what transpired. Time ebbed. Tears flowed.

The boat rocked. Waves beat like drums against the hull. Spray hissed, hushed, hissed, hushed. But only Father Carberry's Latin words filled the stinking cell. Other prisoners, bundled together like cargo, had forgotten how to speak, how to cry, how to scream.

First, the chaplain prayed for the souls of the dead; after that, he prayed for the deliverance of himself. But who would answer his prayers, out in the ocean where only hell awaited those suffering souls? Fever overtook Father Carberry. His head throbbed madly; his nightmares turned to waking terrors; heat and cold alike consumed him.

Even if the deathly cold of midwinter died away, the chaplain's health nosedived. Inside his tenebrous room, he cried until even the deckhands and sailors came down to kick him. Cries soon came too hard to come by. What was there to cry about when left to rot in the shadows?

Father Carberry trembled; frozen, barren—as Antarctica. Soon his entire body seemed to convulse with wet shit and vomitus. Tension banded around his throbbing skull; screams welled inside his gut, but never escaped. An unseen witch's gridle clamped upon his head. He would have prayed had any willpower remained.

The pain surged. On and on. No relief. Except to become numb inside the agony.

Clangor! Thunder rolled, then lightning exploded. A blast

shook him to wake; fires spread.

That roaring blaze seemed its own sort of hell. Great eruptions leapt into the cell's doorway. It crept along the inner walls until nothing was left unsinged. Around him, the other prisoners seemed either to have perished or vanished entirely. What replaced them were the faces. Dead souls' ghastly images formed amidst the flaming forks. There, the privates' faces looked back at him. Most were either burned, or emaciated, or rotting. Some were mauled beyond any recognizable humanity.

Other spirits appeared. The chaplain somewhat recognized them from distant dreams or nightmares long forgotten. This host of apparitions swirled within the blaze. Many dozens of them came, enough to fill a sizable church at Mass. Across these ghosts' brows or cheeks or lips, there bled these great ravines carved into their flesh. Their anguished faces were mauled—or cut with a butcher's knife. Loose flaps of skin hung. Agonised choruses lifted.

Japanese cannibals ran through the inferno. They cried at the flaring phantasmagoria. One after another, they burned in the kiln of hell. Caterwauls came.

"Kaidan!" one screamed.

"Jigoku!" another cried.

Father Carberry made the sign of the cross. His skin burned. His hair scorched. His lungs, pierced with heat, collapsed. Within that furnace, he charred. Still, his eyes saw the last face of them all: the twisted visage of a demon-dog. A sigbin oped its horrible maw. Inside its mouth there were rows of canines and slime; deep inside its throat, a clutch of mesmerizing eyes stared back at Father Carberry. Gold irises with sable, feline slits for pupils.

The dog must have guarded the southernmost pit of hell. Like Cerberus, its body was muscled and obscene in proportions. Hairless, ashen skin coated its beastly body. Buboes lined its muscly back. But Father Carberry could not escape the gaze emanating from that oozing, terrible maw. A bifurcated, scarlet tongue slid out of its mouth. In serpentine fashion it flicked it here and there, a slippery bident.

Father Carberry tried to scream. But his voice was gone. It burned away.

Somewhere off, a cackle echoed. Something primeval spoke.

"Once I was man of faith. Indeed, I was a priest of the Catholic parish. We are cut of the same cloth in that respect."

Fire danced. Ash descended.

"There are still whispers of insane priests who sacrificed men for their mothers," the voice declared. "But it was nothing more than a demon, a dog, a sigbin."

Mutilated ghosts flashed in the hellscape once more—masks of some Noh play. Blood trickled across their rotted skin. The scarred cadaver of Idos burned in the flames.

"The blood of lambs must intoxicate me. I cannot get rid of the taste, the passion, the misery," the voice declared.

Wailing ghosts danced in the flames, becoming one with the hellfire that was raised. They sang amidst the fiery deluge. Choruses expelled their unweal.

The voice continued: "And our spirits still roam this world. We are doomed to roam it evermore. Even in death, I am at the behest of harlots who use witchcraft."

The ruinous ship's bow groaned for the last time. That room's walls and ceilings simultaneously collapsed. Pillars of smoke ascended into clouds of deadly miasma. The swirling firestorm roared.

The demon-dog, that sigbin, disappeared. A dissolving mirage. A fleeing wisp of smoke. All went dark as the ship took its final trip to the bottom of the sea. Brine ejected, cold as ice. The fires hissed as they died, once and for all.

A plunge into the deep! The burning wreck submerged itself lower and lower, into the deepest zone of perdition. Waves after waves devoured the wreck, the ghosts, the dead.

Bubbling, gurgling, foaming. And, beneath the depths, only an infinite blackness lived. Though not wholly corporeal, Father Carberry swirled inside an unseen vortex. A dirge wailed along the currents. Inside that swell of blackness, the chaplain hearkened to the multitude of the damned.

House of U.

Adele Gardner

Stone upon stone. Centuries trace a crack.
Yet I guard them—as only I can.
I reflect their deepest desires, their most abject fears.
But most of all, their lives and mine entwine—for centuries.
Usher, Usher. My house. Yours. Family and manse.
How I love the crackle and snap of their cute little brains
As I creep in while they slept, inhabiting their dreams,
Stretching out to commune, ah, but their heads are so tiny—
Not big enough to contain my cathedral grandeur,
My height that ate the sky. But how they climbed,
My eagerness their fire, driving them to burn through their senses,
Cracking their minds wide until they could not say
Whether they or I formed the shapes there.
Until their human House declined.

I live for the crack. That crack gave me life. A mind. Individuality.
Song and sequence. A reason, *you* might say, for getting up in the
     morning.
A reason for falling down. You needed it, you said. Needed to be
     free.
To breathe, without a moldering family ruin hanging from your
     neck.
Without a pile of crumbling stones pinning you in place, caging you
Within this open circle of stones, its windows and doors
Marking not egress, but the boundaries of your prison of the mind.

I manifest as "symptoms," for surely your perception of me
Must be an *aberration,* your glimpses into the plane of existence I
     inhabit

Synesthesia: hypersensitivity to noise, to color,
To violet that speaks of lush evenings of bloodletting
Under the moon, that stinks of ripe cigarettes
Lit and relit, shared by too many, sucked into lungs longing for
      death,
That fatal cloud of ashes, then used to burn a whole house down.

The homes of my enemies. The homey parlor in the front of your
      mind
That reeks of respectability, *Roderick,* that would deny me my due,
The power in your blood. I am nothing without you, for as surely
As I stand, your fragile, friable being pulses, moving through me,
Your spirit filling my bones, pouring into the *crack,*
The anomaly from which I derive my existence,
The strangeness that renders me *unique,* even as the force of my
      personality
Poisons yours, your *person* too weak to hold me.

I demand sacrifice, the blood of your family line: ideally yours,
But this is how you prove to me that you *are* strong enough, that
      you are mine.
You offer me Madeline's—feed me, in great bowls and tubs of blood
That you pour into the cracks in my foundation, my gaping maw,
More blood than should be able to fit inside one person.

Ah, yes. Your actual soulmate, your friend, whom you invited to
      visit,
Whom you secretly hoped might stay a lifetime. How you wished
That his love might *save you.* Oh, my Roderick, so hopeful still,
Clinging to this belief in your humanity. You fight me. But that is
      fun.
Your struggles in my web bring me *life,* enliven my *bones,*
The "good bones" of this old house, filling me to bursting
Till I might almost *explode* with my love for you,
Shower stone on stone into the valley, the bog. Onto the heads

Of the unsuspecting. Yes, my beautiful Roderick, you sense me,
You feel me, you *hear* me, you will be mine, mine and mine only.
I require more blood, and you have to sleep sometime—
You're only human, after all, and no matter how you barricade
     yourself
In your room, I am your very *house*. You cannot keep me out.

He is your second cousin, after all. Already distant kin,
And he *loves* you. That makes it all the more delectable.
As you squirm together for comfort, as you cry into his shoulder
About your lost sister (just how much you have to cry about, he may
     never know),
We get closer, closer. Soon there shall be no way to tell the
     difference
Between you, once your two hearts beat as one. Ah, there it is.
Delicious spite, for you'd never have agreed, my darling, would you?
No, surely never, so sleepwalking was the best option, you agree,
     yes?
Almost painless, but I do have to wake you for this last little bit,
Him lying on the stone altar deep within my bowels,
You standing above plunging the knife down,
That soul-rending cry of agony your own as the blade finds his
     heart.
Only your own.

Echoing and reverberating up through my bones,
Your scream carries on and on. Oh, this exquisite agony,
Your pain filling me up even more than *his* blood,
This bitter sharpness sparking all my nerves, oh god, this ecstasy,
     this agony
Rising through me, till your shout blows my roofs off,
Till you raise your hands up through my towers
And clench your fists
And all my walls come tumbling down.

Mourning Mireille

Manuel Arenas

Behind a locked door little Mireille reposes, arrayed in lace, upon a bone-white bed. On the anniversary of her death, her *maman* plays a mournful tune on the harmonium in the parlour before visiting the doll's lugubrious chamber. Dressed in black crêpe and weeping into her kerchief, she gazes through the only window in her daughter's room, within the lid of Mireille's pinewood bed, admitting view of her pallid face. The aureate tresses crowning her waxen head, shorn from the beloved babe who went before, frame her cheeks, painted flush, as if pinched by the bony fingers of Death.

For ten years she has practiced her somber ritual, always upon this brumal even. Tonight is cold and tempestuous, not unlike the night her little Mireille, namesake of the doll, succumbed from a surfeit of laudanum. For ten years she has prayed to God above for some sign of life in the beyond from her dear departed child; alas, to no avail. Tonight, however, is different. Tonight she will make up for her missteps and turn her orisons in a southerly direction to plead her plight. She has a new ritual to perform, one that shall undo all past wrongs and pull Mireille's spirit from the limbo of unbaptized children into the land of the living.

She has procured a pamphlet with an arcane rite, the conjuror who sold it claiming it would put her in direct contact with the spirit of her *petite fille chérie*. The doll provides much of the requisite material for the summoning, as it is attired in the clothing of the *enfant malheureaux* and crowned with her flaxen curls. Not to mention the poppet has been well-nigh steeped in the rueful tears of her *maman*.

With the strength of her determination, the slight woman lifts the bantam casket and places it on a dusty hope chest housing unfulfilled dreams and an unused trousseau. Then, following the ritual in the arcane booklet, she lights a black candle and commences reciting the supplication to Abaddon, Angel of the Abyss, whom she hopes will effectuate her desiderated result.

Gazing into a crystal shew stone on the makeshift altar before her, the woman desperately seeks her little girl's soul among the shadows taking shape in the orbuculum. Ere long, she discerns the shade of her beloved Mireille, evoking a cascade of tears from her sunken gray eyes.

"*Maman,* please don't cry! I drown in your tears! Your sadness has kept me tied to this world of shadows these many years. And, *ma chère mère,* there are others here, bad spirits that torment me and—listen! They want to break through, they want to do bad things in your world. They wish to use the doll as a passkey into the realm of the living. Let me go! Destroy the doll, stop them, and let me go!"

Confused, the woman falters, "But . . . Mireille . . ." She then hears a creaking sound and, turning, directs her apprehensive gaze toward the casket. As she looks on, the lid rises and the doll sits upright of its own accord, turning its head to regard her with cold glass eyes.

She screams and shoots up from her genuflection, jostling the altar and causing the casket to overturn, the orbuculum also crashing to the floor. The doll, grasping for purchase, reaches out one stitched-cloth hand, but the woman smacks it away.

Could it be? she thinks in a moment of madness. *Could this be my little girl come back to me?* However, the sudden assault of a sulphurous stench on her nostrils quickly disabuses her of that dubious notion.

Warily she grabs the doll by the waist, its little arms flailing, and runs to the kitchen, clasping it tightly as it fights to free itself, its lips uttering maledictions in an eldritch voice while staying fixed in a bland expression. Grabbing the grate to a cast iron wood-burning stove, she quickly draws her hand back from the too-hot metal. Wrapping her free hand in a kitchen towel, she tries again, opening the grate and casting the curse-spewing doll into the fire.

Grabbing a chair, she wedges it up against the grate, keeping it shut as the doll struggles to escape. Bloodcurdling screams and dreadful oaths are emitted from inside the iron stove, and a black plume of brumous smoke issues from an aperture in the grate to permeate the room, causing her to gasp.

Panting and reeling, she runs toward a window and throws open the casement, allowing the outpouring mephitis to disperse. Once she catches her breath and regains some composure, she remembers Mireille and hasten back to the shrine, where the shew stone lies in shards. Doll burned and orbuculum broken, she has lost all communication with the spirit of her daughter.

Collapsing to her knees, she dissolves into bitter weeping, until a salty puddle dampens the hem of her crêpe dress. Mireille, however, sees none of this. Her soul, released from grip of her mother's malingering grief, is finally free to go on, decamping from this loury veil of shadows and tears.

Dark Comets

Ann K. Schwader

Between two worlds we know, a stranger drifts
in fragmentary orbits strewn among
the dust motes of its death. What crisis flung
these shards apart? What fatal cosmic rift
produced a planet's worth of shrapnel? Space
is silent on this point. Yet stone by stone,
the answer spattered into shallows grown
to Earth's first oceans. Life at last replaced
an aeon's innocence—but life spawned not,
as most are told, from native elements
alone. Dark comets shattered from a sphere
inhabited by Others best forgot,
their icy hearts preserved embodiments
of that which ended them. Our future fears.

The Writhing Plateau: Tentacular Cities, Dystopia, and the Weird in Pompeu Gener's "La coronada villa tentacular" (1911)[1]

Mario Sánchez Gumiel

Introduction: The Castilian Landscape and Hispanidad

It has become well known that when intellectuals in turn-of-the-century Spain sought to depict Spain's national identity (or even a broader notion of Spanishness) after the so-called "disaster of 1898"[2] that would officially end the Spanish Empire, they often thought of the Castilian landscape as the perfect embodiment of that idea. Writers of the Generation of '98 such as Miguel de Unamuno, "Azorín," and Antonio Machado, as well as painters such as Ignacio Zuloaga, considered the Castilian landscape the expression of a series of characteristics that reflected Spaniards' personality and Spain's national identity in that moment of crisis—austerity, strength, purity, and hard work, to name a few (see figure 1).[3]

1. Pompeu Gener [in Spanish, Pompeyo Gener]. In this article, I am using the Catalonian name.
2. The "disaster of 1898" refers to how Spain's government viewed its defeat by the United States in the Spanish-American War. This war, which lasted from 21 April to 10 December 1898, started after the USS *Maine* exploded in Havana Harbor, prompting U.S. intervention in the Cuban War of Independence. As a result of the war, the United States gained control over Puerto Rico, Guam, and the Philippines, and became the dominant power in the Caribbean.
3. See, for example, *En torno al casticismo* (Miguel de Unamuno, 1902), *Castilla* ("Azorín," 1912), and *Campos de Castilla* (Antonio Machado, 1912). For Zuloaga, see *Vista de El Escorial* (c. 1905), *Paisaje castellano* (1909), *Paisaje de Pancorbo* (1917), *Gregorio en Sepúlveda* (1908), or *Mujeres en Sepúlveda* (1909).

Fig. 1: The Castilian landscape in Ignacio Zuloaga's "Vista de El Escorial" (1905?).

The goal was to articulate an essence (or cultural identity) that would gather and define Spain's diversity, first, to explain the source of its problems after the "disaster of 1898"; second, to prevent confrontations among its several regions (and thus to avoid a fratricidal fight); and third, to define Spain as "a historical entity, an organic, timeless and ancestral nation-state whose former greatness was inherent to *hispanidad*," and where by honoring and embracing that past, Spain would be able to heal its wounds and emerge into modernity (Crosson 68). However, in that articulation of a comprehensive essence of Spain's diversity, the elevation of the Castilian landscape as the most representative would result in the suppression of Spain's geographic and scenic diversity.

Scholarly work on why the Castilian landscape came to be considered emblematic of Spain's national identity has often pointed to philosopher and educator Francisco Giner de los Ríos as one of the main references for *regeneracionistas*[4] and the Generation of '98.[5] In

---

4. *Regeneracionismo* is the umbrella term for the combined political and in-

his 1886 essay "Paisaje" (Landscape) for the newspaper *La Ilustración Artística*, Giner de los Ríos wrote that the Castilian landscape possessed a geological beauty and roughness nonexistent in the landscapes of Northern, Eastern, and Southern Spain (92). Focusing on the role played by geological processes in the formation of a landscape, Giner de los Ríos stressed how, in the Castilian scenery, "asoma por doquiera el esfuerzo indomable que intenta abrirse paso á través de obstáculos sin cuento; y así como en un mismo día y lugar se suceden con rapidez y vertiginosa el hielo y el ardor de los trópicos, así también el sol deslumbra con un fulgor casi agrio en el fondo de un cielo, de puro azul, casi negro" (92).[6] In this sentence, Giner de los Ríos acknowledged the existence of tensions among the geological

---

tellectual attempts to change this moment of anguish and unease that had descended upon Spain. Originating during the second half of the 19th century (and although not homogeneous nor having clear and defined purposes by a specific group or class), *regeneracionismo* had a primary specific goal: to overcome the political system of the Restauración—associated with caciquism, corruption, ineffectiveness, and backwardness—which most citizens blamed as responsible of the problems of the country. Among its adherents were writers, intellectuals, and politicians of different ideologies, such as Joaquín Costa (one of the main instigators), Lucas Mallada, Miguel de Unamuno, and Ramiro de Maeztu, though the list of names is far more extensive, and it varies depending on the temporal framework we choose. According to Lissorgues (who locates the time of *regeneracionismo* between 1890 and 1912), that list would also include writers who sometimes are overlooked, such as Emilia Pardo Bazán, Benito Pérez Galdós, and José María Salaverría. There existed a diversity of proposals on how to regenerate Spain, with many opting for political action (Costa, Mallada, Maeztu), while others opted for more contemplative and aesthetic approaches—the so-called Generation of '98: Unamuno, Pío Baroja, José Martínez Ruiz ("Azorín"), etc. (Davis 313–14).

5. See Ortega Cantero (2007, 2009, 2015), González Trueba, or Gómez Gutiérrez.

6. "[in the Castilian landscape] can be seen the effort of everything struggling everywhere, against obstacles and problems. Just as in one day cold and hot weather can happen, the sun also brightens with wild intensity against an intense, almost black, blue sky."

and meteorological forces that shape landscape: "asoma por doquiera el esfuerzo indomable que intenta abrirse paso á través de obstáculos sin cuento." In his view, a landscape was the result of *actions* (erosion, rain), *elements* (rocks, plants, animals, human beings), and *concepts* (weather, topography), which not only experienced *inwardly* the results of the landscape they created *outwardly* but also shaped that landscape *through* those internal effects (92–93). In other words, a landscape is a relational entity that is both created and creator, existing in a permanent state of becoming. Ultimately, Giner de los Ríos's "Paisaje" perceived in the Castilian landscape a raw integrated unity whence (as people moved either north or south) smoother, more polished, embroidered landscapes appeared.

In "Paisaje," Giner de los Ríos does not dismiss these other, more hospitable landscapes of Spain's geography, but his writing style sometimes makes it difficult to see why they are less fascinating than the Castilian countryside. The geological aspect seems to be the crucial point of this preference. More precisely, Giner de los Ríos is interested in how the *tension* among elements (inherent in any landscape formation process) is more visible in the Castilian scenery compared to others. By highlighting the visibility of that tension, Giner de los Ríos thought of this landscape as one that more clearly stimulates *our* awareness of the struggles involved in landscape-making, regardless of whether the landscape ultimately appears as a balanced whole (103). He mentions how human beings' aesthetic expressions of landscapes (e.g., paintings) also *make landscape,* as well as their subjective opinions, their mood when they look at a landscape, etc. Additionally, Giner de los Ríos sees the Castilian landscape as the landscape that gathers, in physical terms, the largest number of components: plateaus (nonexistent in other areas of the Iberian Peninsula), mountains, coasts, drastic divergences between cold and hot weather (and consequently, a drastic variety of vegetation), minerals and rocks absent in other areas.

Although "Paisaje" did not explicitly establish a connection between Castile and Spain's cultural identity, Giner de los Ríos's praise for the visibility of the tensions at play in the Castilian landscape (and for how those elements struggle to shape the landscape against adversities) was used by other intellectuals to establish an analogy with Spanish society after the "disaster" of 1898. For example, in the first stanzas of his poem "Castilla," Miguel de Unamuno compared the Castilian landscape with an old mother who, despite her weariness from all the vicissitudes of life, could still help her babies (the Spanish people) survive:

> Tú me levantas, tierra de Castilla,
> en la rugosa palma de tu mano,
> al cielo que te enciende y te refresca,
> al cielo, tu amo,
>
> Tierra nervuda, enjuta, despejada,
> madre de corazones y de brazos,
> toma el presente en ti viejos colores
> del noble antaño. (*Poesías* 25)[7]

In these stanzas, the use of adjectives such as *rugosa, nerviosa,* and *enjuta* evoke the image of something withered that, while associated with old age, at the same time can overcome adversity and can be kind and curative.

This aesthetic preference for the Castilian plateau was not, however, accepted by all writers and artists at that time. Neither was the view that the Castilian landscape was the most representative visualization of *Hispanidad* unanimously accepted. To privilege Castile implied the exclusion of other Iberian landscapes deemed unsuitable for representing *Hispanidad,* thereby resulting in the creation of spatial Othernesses.[8] This glorification of the Castilian

---

7. "You lift me up, land of Castile, / in the wrinkled palm of your hand, / toward the sky that kindles and refreshes you, / toward heaven, your master, / Land that is sinewy, lean, clear, / mother of hearts and arms, / take the present within you, wrapped in old colors / of the noble yore."—Translation from *All Poetry.* See Works Cited.
8. See, for example, García Fernández (2021) on the construction of *andaluzofobia* in the members of the Generation of '98. Examples of this inclu-

landscape was not widely shared beyond the sphere of literature and art either, for by any empirical standard, Castile was by then economically underdeveloped, compared with the more prosperous Northern and the Eastern coasts, which had initiated a vibrant industry during the second half of the nineteenth century. The more advanced industrial development of the coasts did not go unnoticed by modernist Catalonian writer Pompeu Gener.

In this article I analyze Gener's tale "La coronada villa tentacular" (1911), a dystopia in which the Catalonian writer criticizes this vision of the Castilian plateau as the most representative site of the Spanish essence. "La coronada villa tentacular" resembles the genre of the weird, popularized by American writer H. P. Lovecraft, which speculates about the existence of non-anthropocentric creatures who threaten human beings' dominant status of nature. Gener's story presents that plateau as an Otherness, vindicating the Catalonian landscape as an idyllic space for humanity. In doing so, "La coronada villa tentacular" eventually comes to reproduce the exclusionary, racist connotations of the Castilian plateau, since it also refuses to acknowledge other landscapes of the Iberian Peninsula.

The Racial Superiority of Catalonians, According to Pompeu Gener

A very cultivated, and controversial man,[9] Pompeu Gener viewed the political, social, and cultural reality of late nineteenth-century

---

sion/exclusion dyad can also be found in Miguel de Unamuno, whose elevation of the Castilian landscape was accomplished by dividing Spain into two areas: a glorified Castilian and Basque Spain, and a dismissed Valencian–Andalusian Spain (Tomás 13). Others, however, thought of alternative Iberian landscapes as better suited to represent Spanishness. For example, Ramón del Valle-Inclán considered Castile a dead land, since its imagery always seemed to look at the past (and the past, he argued, is dead); he saw, on the contrary, the Cantabrian area as young, full of energy and opportunities (Tomás 22–23). At the same time, Valle deplored the Levant because of its Phoenician, gypsy, and cheating influences.

9. His racist and misogynistic ideas are well known, as is as his defense of the philosophy of Social Darwinism.

Spain through the lens of Aryan racism,[10] seeing Catalonia's industrial development as proof of the racial superiority of Catalonians over the rest of Spaniards (Álvarez Chillida 242). In writings such as *Heregias* or "La cuestión catalana," he approached the problems analyzed by *regeneracionistas* (e.g., Spain's political corruption, apathy, and economic backwardness compared with other European nations) from the perspective of the Catalonian identity. As Mariano Martín Rodríguez observes, Gener "se sumó al coro de voces intelectuales que, en torno a la derrota Española ante los Estados Unidos en 1898, intensificaron sus ataque al Sistema sociopolítico y económico del Estado, cuya escasa funcionalidad había quedado de manifiesto de forma tan trágica" (133).[11] From this premise, Gener believed that there was no future for the Spanish monarchy, politically centralized in the city of Madrid, and that the central task ahead was to pursue *inside* Spain the process of decolonization initiated in the Americas during the nineteenth century.[12] In doing so, he saw Catalonia as a colonized region, just like the American colonies. Moreover, Gener considered as a key justification for Catalonia's independence the aforesaid racial superiority of Catalonians. This is expressed in "La coronada villa tentacular," wherein the Castilian plateau is depicted as a shapeless monster that opposes and threatens the well-proportioned human forms inhabiting the Iberian Peninsula, representing the Catalonians.

Gener's justification for his belief in Catalonians' racial superiority was that they had not been influenced or polluted by other races that had historically inhabited Spain—in particular, the Jews and Moors. In his book *Heregias* (1888), he asserted that the Semitic and Berber cultural heritage of Spain had dramatically

---

10. See his essay "La cuestión catalana" (1903).
11. "[Gener] joined those intellectuals who, in the aftermath of Spain's defeat against the United States in 1898, intensified their attacks on the sociopolitical and economic system of the state, whose limited functionality had been tragically exposed."
12. See "La cuestión catalana" (1903).

affected the blood of Spaniards, making them lazy, apathetic, and unproductive, conditioning their future. He wrote:

> Hay demasiada semítica y bereber esparramada por la península para que pueda generalizarse en la mayoría de sus pueblos la ciencia moderna, para que adquieran una conducta conforme a las universidades relaciones de la Naturaleza, para que abandonen el pensamiento con ideas absolutas, o solo con palabras. [. . .] España está paralizada por la necrosis producida por la sangre de razas inferiores como la Semítica, la Bereber y la Mogólica, y por espurgo que en sus razas fuertes hizo la Inquisición y el Trono, seleccionando todos lo que pensaban, dejando apenas como residuo más que fanáticos, serviles e imbéciles. (232–33, 238)[13]

Gener's criticism, however, was not restricted to blaming the Semite and the Berber. He also blamed the Inquisition and the Spanish Crown, whose efforts to eliminate any heritage other than the Castilian since the fifteenth century he saw as more harmful because they had eventually created a land (Spain) dominated by fanatics and worthless people—Castilians. Gener thus accepted the myths of the so-called *leyenda negra* (Black Legend),[14] yet contended, unlike the *regeneracionistas,* that any attempt to resolve Spaniards' problems was

---

13. "There is too much Semitic and Berber blood disseminated in the Iberian Peninsula to unanimously accept modern science, to act according to the Laws of Nature, to abandon a way of thinking based on absolute statements and ideas [. . .] Spain is paralyzed by the necrosis produced by the blood of inferior races like the Semitic, the Berber, and the Mongol, as well as by the extermination of those strong races by the Inquisition and the Crown, which eliminated everyone who had a thought, and leaving as a mere residue only fanatic, servile, and imbecile people."

14. The *leyenda negra* refers to a historiographical trend characterized by anti-Spanish and anti-Catholic sentiment. Advocates of this viewpoint maintain that its origins can be traced to the sixteenth century, during a period when Spain's European competitors sought to undermine the Spanish Empire through political and psychological warfare. They aimed to demonize Spain, its people, and its culture, underplaying Spanish contributions and accomplishments and diminishing its global influence and power.

a waste of time. In his view, Spaniards were comfortable living under conditions of serfdom, apathy, and decadence (Caja 96), assuming that they had *consciously* abandoned the timid modernization initiated in the country during in the eighteenth century, during the reigns of Phillip V, Ferdinand VI, and Charles III: "[l]os españoles estaban tan adaptados a tales decadencias, los elementos de razas inferiores que entraban en su constitución fisiológica habían preponderado tanto, que casi nadie quiso conservar aquel estado superior impuesto por [esos] tres reyes ilustrados" (*Heregias* 229).[15] These beliefs can be observed in "La coronada villa tentacular," where Gener describes a city located atop of a plateau that is submerged in physical and moral degradation. As I will develop in the article, his pessimistic view of Spain contains the racial fear and disgust of Otherness and the possibility of sharing traits with those races perceived as inferior– a concept that scholar Mitch Frye refers to as "genotypic horror."

"La coronada villa tentacular," Dystopia and the Weird

Originally published in the nationalist-oriented magazine *Juventut* and then in the book *Del presente, del pasado y del futuro* (see figure 2), "La coronada villa tentacular" is a first-person narration of a dream composed, in turn, of three visions.

The first vision depicts the tentacular city of the title as "una villa grande [. . .] como si fuera un pulpo, estando situada en una elevada meseta" ("La coronada" 115).[16] This nameless city refers to the city of Madrid (albeit unnamed),[17] whose metaphorical tentacles spread across the Castilian plateau, controlling and exploiting the richer and more fertile territory that exists around it. The city is

---

15. "Spaniards had got used to decadence because the elements of inferior races had gone into their physiological constitution so deeply that almost nobody wanted to preserve that superior state proposed by [those] three Enlightened kings."
16. "a big village [. . .] like an octopus on the top of a high plateau."
17. This reference to Madrid as a tentacular village is, however, explicit in Gener's essay "La cuestión catalana."

governed by lazy, useless kings; it is inhabited by brainless, corrupted, ignorant, and sanctimonious people, and it is a place where any attempt to promote knowledge or goodness is doomed to fail (116–18). Hypocrisy, mediocrity, poverty, and a false sense of greatness dominate the city (119–21).

The second vision of the dream depicts a monster, "un monstruo gigantesco tendido en el suelo, de terrorífico aspecto, obscuro como la noche, de frente estrecha, cara estúpida e indolente y mirada codiciosa" (121).[18] This monster lies on the

Fig. 2: Cover of *Del presente, del pasado y del futuro* (1911), which contains "La coronada villa tentacular."

plateau where the city is located, with its head in front of a door that, in turn, blocks access to the sun (122).[19] The monster holds a chained man, who seems hypnotized by it. Despite having a strong and muscular appearance, the man seems unable to overcome the creature and does not move. Although the narrator states that the man could break the chains and escape from the monster "por la

---

18. "a gigantic monster stretched out on the floor, horrific, dark like night, with a narrow forehead, an indolent and stupid face, and avaricious eyes."

19. I write here the original sentence in Spanish, since I am not fully sure that the translation above might be completely accurate: "Su cuerpo estaba tendido en el alto llano, pero tenía apoyados los pies en el sur del territorio y la cabeza ocupaba un lugar frente a una puerta que impedía que el sol llegase" (121–22).

parte de Levante, única que estaba aún algo libre,"[20] he does not move (122). This ambiguous depiction of the monster, and how it is situated in relation to the tentacular city and plateau, lead us to conceive of it as a blurred, weird entity, such that it is impossible to know where the monster, the tentacular city, and the plateau begin and end. After the second vision, the dream concludes with a third, very brief vision of a market where everything is for sale (even justice and conscience) and with the awakening of the narrator, who realizes that everything has not been a dream, but the real world (123). The narrator expresses a terrible despair upon realizing that everything that happened was real, leaving the ending of the story open by not offering a conclusion to that despair.

"La coronada villa tentacular" utilizes the image of the tentacle as something fleshy but elusive, slimy, and threatening to narrate a politically themed story. In doing so, Gener's story can be read as a condemnation of Spanish society in a specific historical moment, which places "La coronada villa tentacular" within the genre of dystopia. As a dystopian tale, it expresses, not hope, but "a collective yearning for a rupture. A collective desire to somehow break free from an all oppressing, inescapable totality" (Keller). As Jameson stresses in his book *Archaeologies of the Future*, utopia is not only a positive vision of the future, but also (and principally) a critique, or negative judgment, of the present (12). Robert Tally Jr. also shares this position, suggesting that the utopian impulse is essentially dystopian because "[b]efore anything else, the utopian impulse must be a negative one: to identify the problem or problems that must be fixed [. . .] to act as a critique of the existing system" (quoted in "The Cultural Significance of Cyberpunk"). The desire called *utopia* is therefore as dystopian (negative) as it is eutopian (positive) as far as the imagining of an alternative works to think critically about the here-and-now.

Gener's tale is a dystopia that challenges the tropes and ideologies of Spain which, from the late nineteenth century onward (and mainly

20. "by the Levant, the only area still free."

after 1898), were being discussed, defended, and challenged in a broad effort to overcome Spain's problems at the turn of the century. In that sense, against the attempt of those who sought to regenerate Spain by attaching a sense of national identity to the Castilian landscape, Gener believes in the inherently defective nature of Spaniards due to the influence of inferior races, and in the impossibility of any improvement or regeneration. In his worldview, Castile/Spain is, in other words, a *degenerate* (rather than regenerable) land/country.

This characterization of Castile/Spain as a degenerate land makes "La coronada villa tentacular" partake in the literary genre of the weird. According to Jarvis, degeneration and decay are central tropes of the weird (1136). The term *weird* appears for the first time as a literary form in H. P. Lovecraft's essay "Supernatural Horror in Literature" (1927), where the writer of Providence makes his famous statement that "[t]he oldest and strongest emotion of mankind is fear, and the oldest and strongest kind of fear is fear of the unknown. These facts few psychologists will dispute, and their admitted truth must establish for all time the genuineness and dignity of the weirdly horrible tale as a literary form" (25). For Lovecraft, a weird story engages that human fear, of the unknown, keeping that unknown alive and never fully disclosed. Rather than just being composed of stories of "secret murder, bloody bones, or a sheeted form clanking chains according to rule," the weird is the product of an

> *atmosphere* of breathless and unexplainable *dread* of outer [where] unknown forces must be present; and there must be a hint, expressed with a seriousness and portentousness becoming its subject, of that most terrible conception of the human brain—a malign and particular suspension or defeat of those fixed laws of Nature which are our only safeguard against the assaults of chaos and the daemons of unplumbed space. (28; my emphases)

The weird is therefore not only horror or something that evokes immediate physical revulsion, but a more conceptual, numinous fear that is impossible to grasp, see, or run from because it contradicts the laws of nature. As a result, it creates a universe in which human beings are no longer the primary forces of nature.[21] It also entails temporality and an orientation toward the future, encompassing fatalism. In other words, when something is considered weird, it is related to the determinism of the future, to the idea that nothing can be accomplished to escape from what may come, thus creating the aforementioned dread and anxiety.[22] In "La coronada villa tentacular," all these elements of apprehension, fatalism, and anxiety are present, shaping a narrative not so much of horror as of one imbued with a fear of the unknown and, worse yet, a fear that what is unknown (the shapeless monster on the plateau) will eliminate all hope in the protagonist's belief that he has control of the situation and can harbor some semblance of hope.

The history of the weird is the history of the rise of the tentacle as a trope representing something horrid, and menacing (VanderMeer xvi).[23] In his exploration of the history of the weird,

---

21. The word *weird* derives from the Old English *wyrd*, which means "the principle, power, or agency by which events are predetermined; fate, destiny" as well as "magical power, enchantment." *Weird* also derives from *weorðan*, which means "to become" (Joy 30). It is rooted, in turn, in the Old Norse *urth*, which means "to twist or turn," representing "a twist of fate" (Morton 20).

22. The weird can further be a way of reading. Such "weird reading" relies on posthuman approaches like speculative realism or object-oriented philosophy, and it seeks to locate in literature things that "don't quite line up with each other" (Joy 34) or texts that "don't easily correspond or answer to traditionally humanist questions and concerns" (29). A weird reading thus opens the door to "incoherence, and non-routinized un-disciplinarity that privileges unknowing over mastery of knowledge," or, in other words, "to recognize better how inhuman and weird texts are" (29–30). A weird reading is then a reading for the weird everywhere.

23. There is consensus on thinking of the weird as a concept strongly entangled with Modernism and modernity. Ann and Jeff VanderMeer locate a possible beginning of the weird circa 1907–08 with Algernon Blackwood's "The Willows" and F. Marion Crawford's "The Screaming Skull." Others have traced its origins in the late nineteenth century (Joshi 1–3),

China Miéville thinks of the tentacle as "a limb-type with no Gothic or traditional precedents" ("M. R. James" 105). The coming-of-age of this trope occurred around 1928 with the appearance of the monster in Lovecraft's story "The Call of Cthulhu." Lovecraft describes Cthulhu as a "Thing" with an "awful squid-head with writhing feelers," full of "scattered plasticity" and capable of "nebulously *recombining* in its hateful original form" ("The Call of Cthulhu" 54; emphasis in original). According to Miéville, Cthulhu is an iteration of another monster (a gigantic "devil fish"—i.e., octopus) that appeared in a 1907 novel by William Hope Hodgson titled *The Boats of the "Glen Carrig"* ("M. R. James" 106).

Lovecraft's Cthulhu (figure 3) and Hodgson's nameless "devil fish" are not the origins of the weird, but their location in history has been crucial to articulate a genealogy of the concept that, in turn, serves to contextualize the monster of "La coronada villa tentacular." In that sense, Gener's tale is inscribed in what Miéville considers a "shift to Weird culture" that took place at the turn of the

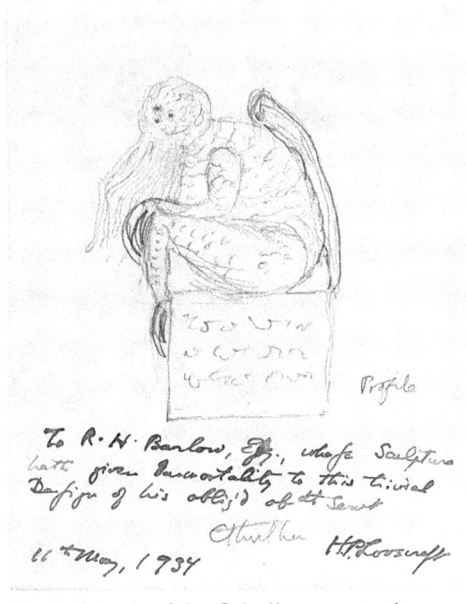

Fig. 3: Sketch of the Cthulhu monster by H. P. Lovecraft (11 May 1934).

considering the weird as modernism's "pulpy underside" (Marshall 634), while such critics as Newell have thought of Edgar Allan Poe as the beginning of the genre (5). Joshi asserts that the weird, while present in the second half of the nineteenth century, only became constituted as a consistent genre when it went "underground." That is, as part of popular literature, and therefore as receiver of academic dismissal due to its status of low culture form (3).

twentieth century (105).

Fig. 4: Pages 392 and 393 (upper row), and page 400 (bottom) of *Vingt mille lieues sous les mers*.

Miéville's assertion regarding this "shift to the Weird" leads him to consider precursors of the weird novels, such as Jules Verne's *Vingt mille lieues sous les mers*[24] and Victor Hugo's *Les travailleurs de la mer*[25] as examples of pre-weird, or literary influences upon the weird (107–8). In those novels there are detailed descriptions of cephalopods, presenting them as dangerous and menacing—descriptions that, in the case of Verne, are complemented with vivid illustrations whose purpose is to visualize their danger (see figure 4).[26]

The presence of cephalopod in these stories is, however, often "pre-mediated by human understanding," so its monstrousness, "though certainly not denied, is [. . .] defined by human categorization" (Miéville, "M. R. James" 107). In other words, unlike Lovecraft's weird tales, in these pre-weird novels human characters still attempt to rationalize the fear that those cephalopods create as if they had confidence in the capacity of human beings to explain and categorize everything. This idea of categorizing what seems uncategorizable appears in "La coronada villa tentacular." While the first vision evokes the tentacular city, that description is opposed to an idea of (human) order and progress, instead positioning the city as non-human or abnormal. It does so by using vivid expressions such as "tentáculos chupadores," "sucios estropajos de meson," and "híbridos de planta y de espectro" ("La coronada" 116–19),[27] which not only describe what the narrator sees, but also what those images evoke in him. The fact that the tale is a dream adds a oneiric component. In the second vision, the scene between the monster and the man is observed by the dreamer, who attempts to advise the man, suggesting that he believes a solution for horror is

---

24. In English, *Twenty Thousand Leagues under the Sea* (1869–70).
25. In English, *Toilers of the Sea* (1866).
26. Hugo's novel, while not containing any illustration, contains a passage where the character of Gilliat must face an octopus. There is an ink wash painting by Hugo himself that refers to the way he conceived that moment in *Les travailleurs de la mer*. See Rodari et al. (1998).
27. [expressions such as] "sucking tentacles," "dirty scouring pads," and "plant-specter hybrids."

possible. However, the end of the tale—with the dreamer's awareness that what he thought was a dream is actually real—reinforces the aforementioned fatalism of the weird as well as the idea that everything is not just an observation of facts, but something more complex.[28] I will examine these issues in greater detail as I go through each vision of the dream.

The First Vision within the Dream

"La coronada villa tentacular" begins with a sentence that blurs the boundaries between the real and the dreamed: "Yo sueño muy á menudo," the narrator (and unnamed protagonist) writes, "tanto, que hasta hay quien dice que á veces sueño despierto. Y ayer soñé. Soñé cosas terribles que eran una verdadera pesadilla" (115).[29] This statement imbues the tale with an atmosphere of dread and fatalism. When the protagonist (hereafter, the dreamer) says that sometimes he dreams awake and that yesterday he dreamed horrible things, we do not know if what he is going to recount is real or not. The sentence immediately introduces the first vision of the dream, where the dreamer narrates his experience in the city of the title. According to him, that city is "coronada y tentacular, como si fuera un pulpo [. . .], situada en una elevada meseta" (115).[30] In his first vision of the dream, he will describe the city, its inhabitants, and his sensations and thoughts as he encounters this "weird" site.

This first depiction of the city ("*coronada y tentacular* [...] en una elevada *meseta*"; my emphases) clearly refers to the city of Madrid

---

28. The ending also echoes Edgar Allan Poe's poem "A Dream within a Dream," which ends with the famous passage: "Is all that we see or seem / But a dream within a dream?" Poe is considered one of the fathers of science fiction as well as a writer of the weird, e.g., *The Narrative of Arthur Gordon Pym of Nantucket* (1838).
29. "I dream very often, so much so that some say I even daydream at times. And yesterday, I dreamed. I dreamed terrible things that were a true nightmare."
30. "crowned and tentacular, like an octopus [. . .], situated on a high plateau."

(although it remains unnamed): not only is Madrid located on the Castilian plateau, but also "coronada villa" points to its historical denomination as *corte* and *villa* [court and village/city]. With the inclusion of the word *tentacular* in this description of the city, Gener summarizes the object of his critique: Spain's capital, Madrid, is a *crowned* city that constitutes a threat that, like an octopus, sucks the life out of everything around it. Subsequent sentences provide additional geographical details: we are told that the city is surrounded by "estepas y terrenos yermos y breñas, y desde allí tendía sus largos tentáculos para chupar el jugo vital á las fértiles comarcas de las riberas de dos mares: el mar grande y el mar latino" (115).[31] The description of the areas closest to the city as arid corresponds to the prototypical image of the barren Castilian plateau (see figure 1). Beyond those arid areas lie the Great Sea, the Latin Sea, and more fertile regions, all threatened by the tentacular city. The Great Sea and the Latin Sea seem to refer to the Cantabrian Sea and the Mediterranean Sea, respectively, and the more productive lands near the coasts of the peninsula.

According to scholars who have examined literary and filmic representations of cephalopods, human fascination with octopuses and squids relies on seeing them as a boundary subject/object (Brown and Fleming 14).[32] The beginning of "La coronada villa tentacular" confirms this assertion and expands upon it as the tale progresses. An octopus moves its tentacles in a way that seems wild, uncontrolled, and unpredictable, making it threatening. Its tentacles appear to be soft and flaccid; however, they are made of muscle fibers. An octopus thus has the strength and capacity to take control of its surroundings, such that other beings in its orbit find it difficult

---

31. "steppes and barren lands and scrublands, and from there it stretched its long tentacles to suck the life juice from the fertile regions along the banks of two seas: the great sea and the Latin sea."

32. One of the most popular works on squids and cephalopods is Vilém Flusser's *Vampyroteuthis Infernalis: A Treatise, with a Report by the Institut Scientifique de Recherche Paranaturaliste* (1987). I thank Michael McGrath for his suggestion.

(if not impossible) to combat it. At the start of "La coronada villa tentacular," Gener conceives of the city on the plateau as a living and uncontrollable entity that throughout its history has imposed its strength without anyone being able to dominate it. Similarly, the blurring of the boundary between the real and the dream establishes a framework of uncertainty and uncanniness about what we are going to read in the narrative. The dream is fluid and unpredictable, its boundaries diffuse. This effect of diffuseness grows as the narration progresses, until in the second vision the tentacular disappears, giving way to the shapeless monster of the second vision, which nevertheless is *still* inflected with the idea of the tentacle.

The first vision continues by saying that "la villa que antes era solitario castillo, había ido creciendo y prosperando á la sombra de una corona, con la ayuda de sus tentáculos chupadores" (115–16).[33] This hearkens back to the city's origins in the ninth century as a small settlement that grew around a solitary castle, built to defend the then more important cities of Toledo and Segovia (see figure 5). The castle (the Real Alcázar) was built by the Umayyad emir, Muhammed I of Cordoba; it was later expanded by King Charles V in the sixteenth century, eventually becoming the home of King Phillip II.[34] As a consequence, Madrid became the permanent capital of the Spanish Empire.[35] The sentence above on the growth

---

33. "and this village was crowned and tentacular, as if it were an octopus [. . .] and from there it extended its long tentacles to suck the vital secretion of the fertile lands around, close to the two seas [. . .] [the village] had been growing and thriving through history under the shadow of a Crown, and with the help of its [Crown's] sucking tentacles."

34. A fire would destroy it by the beginning of the eighteenth century, being substituted by the current Palacio Real (Real Palace).

35. Before Madrid became the capital of the Spanish Empire, the capital status was moving, based on where the Crown was. Thus, more important cities such as Valladolid, Toledo, Segovia, or Ciudad Real had this capital status. After Madrid became the permanent capital in 1561, only Valladolid became the capital too. In 1601, Phillip III (Phillip II's son) decided to move the capital status to Valladolid, but that status only lasted three years.

Fig. 5: The *Real Alcázar* as painted in "Le chasteau de Madril," by Flemish painter Jan Cornelisz Vermeyen (c. 1534), before the expansion ordered by King Charles V (1537).

of the tentacular city is constructed somewhat ambiguously, given that it is not clear whether those "sucking tentacles" belong to the monarchy or to the city itself. In doing so, Gener's tale sees both the city and the Crown as inseparable, emphasizing the hybridity of the monstrous nature.

Gener's assertion that "la ciudad había ido creciendo y prosperando a la sombra de una corona" confirms that his criticism is not only focused on a city as a specific geographical location but also on a broader imaginary one. The city is thus what Mariano Martín Rodríguez has called as a geofiction or *urbogonía*. That is, "la representación literaria de espacios imaginarios, como una especie de geografía fantástica" (125).[36] In lexical terms, the word *urbogonía* resembles *cosmogonía* [cosmogony], and understands the city as a cosmos and totality. An *urbogonía* thus compresses a worldview under the form of a city. In "La coronada villa tentacular," the city/world on the plateau therefore becomes the representation of a threatening totality, a form of inescapable force that erases the past, present, and future and which conditions the lives and destiny of those affected by it.

Since the weird is cosmically dreadful per se, the monsters that populate it are always part of a cosmogony that always implies a threat to the human world (Burleson 135–47). In associating the

36. "the literary representation of imaginary spaces, as if they represented a fantastic geography."

city, the plateau, and the Crown with the tentacular, "La coronada villa tentacular" is not just using those spaces and the royal institution as examples of something negative but is trying to express something broader. In that sense, Gener's tale can be considered a dystopian *urbogonía*—a shapeless monstrosity that characterizes Castile as a weird Otherness, and in so doing challenges the ideology of *regeneracionismo*. If the glorification of the Castilian landscape as representative of *Hispanidad* had created spatial Othernesses (i.e., the exclusion of other Iberian landscapes), here the story does the opposite by "othering" Castile. Moreover, Gener's representation of Castile as a weird Otherness constitutes a form of weirdly *regeneracionista* discourse, disregarding for the moment his call for secession and his racist, misogynistic, and aggressive language. Ultimately, he denounces the same problems that preoccupied the *regeneracionistas*—Spain's political corruption, apathy, and economic backwardness in comparison with other European nations. The difference would not then be *what* he denounces (which is common to both the *regeneracionistas* and Gener) but *how* he denounces it.

Similarly, Gener's reference to the tentacularity of the city not only reflects the "shift to the Weird" that Miéville detects in works by Verne, Hugo, Hogdson, and Lovecraft; it also may derive in part from a concept, *villes tentaculaires* (tentacular cities), coined by the Belgian poet Émile Verhaeren[37] in the 1890s. While not mentioned by Miéville,[38] Verhaeren's coinage of *villes tentaculaires* supports Miéville's argument for the emergence of the tentacle as a new trope of horror and elusiveness by the end of the nineteenth century. According to Soros, Verhaeren considered a tentacular city to be "viscosa y rizomática, en el plano horizontal, en oposición a los 'ángulos rectos' de los tejados en el eje vertical" (282).[39] In the

---

37. See *Les campagnes hallucinées (1893) and Les villes tentaculaires* (1895).
38. Miéville's focus is mostly on Anglo-American literary traditions.
39. "viscous and rhizomic horizontally, as opposed to the 'right angle' of the roofs, vertically."

tentacular city, the configuration of urban space is a living organism, with negative connotations symbolized in the image of the octopus (281). Verhaeren considered all industrial cities at that time to be octopus-like, omnipresent, and predatory, as may be noted in his poems "La ville" (1893) and "L'âme de la ville" (1895),[40] where he targets the industrial development of European cities, which has made living difficult in them due to greed, labor exploitation, chaos, and pollution.[41]

The effects of the tentacles ceaselessly sucking the life of the nation permeates the rest of "La coronada villa tentacular," showing us how everything that is under its influence has become lifeless and absent of energy or spirit. Within the city, everything and everyone is empty and thoughtless. The dreamer observes that

> [l]os hombres que allí imperaban y bullían llegaban de todas partes, y eran duros y vacíos y sonaban á falso [. . .] Los grandes pensamientos ardientes eran allí ahogados, o los chafaban echándolos encima plomo helado" [. . .] Las conciencias eran sucios estropajos de mesón [. . .] El vapor de los espíritus abatidos y el sudor de los parias alimentaba y conservaba a los grandes del Poder y de la Fortuna, [. . .] La alegría era allí falta de seso y no expansión de plenitud de la vida [. . .] Todo era falso, hasta el oro de la palabra [. . .] Todo se hacía mediante fórmulas [. . .] Veíase mucha piedad beata y mucha conscupiscencia devota [. . .] Los ricos pedían limosna en coche. (116–18)[42]

---

40. These two poems may be found with a Spanish translation in Juan Soros's article. The poems can be found together in Verhaeren's *Les villes tentaculaires, précédées des Campagnes hallucinées* (1917).

41. Gener, however, does not seem to use the idea of *ville tentaculaire* in the same way that Verhaeren does. Instead, he considers the opposite as representative of the evil ontology of the tentacle. In other words, what Gener denounces and labels as tentacular is the lack of industrial development that Spain has suffered for decades (and embodied by that "coronada villa"), thus transmuting Verhaeren's original idea into the opposite.

42. "The people who lived there used to arrive from everywhere, and they were tough and void and fake [. . .] Large, important thoughts were silenced

Furthermore, the citizens are described in a grotesque way—as filthy, fake, shallow, stupid, scrawny, and hard-hearted : "Y tenían las uñas largas y las ideas cortas, cuando tenían alguna. Sus almas eran lacias, sus pechos estrechos, sus corazones helados, y sus palabras dulces y empalagosas como arrope rancio. Muchos de ellos tenían una diarrea de palabras producida por la poca retentiva del intelecto" (116).[43]

The people of Madrid thus exhibit a mixture of humanity and non-humanity: "Los del pueblo, cuando eran buenos, resultaban vegetativos, uniformes y pequeños, y cuando no, eran acres, corrompidos y descompuestos [. . .] Eran un híbrido de planta y espectro [. . .] Algunos para lucirse se vestían de hermafrodita" (118–19).[44] Like the amphibious sea-dwelling humanoids of Lovecraft's tales "Dagon" and "The Shadow over Innsmouth," the inhabitants of Madrid are ambiguously human and non-human, and hence fake their lack of humanity with the help of masks: "Eran imitadores [. . .] A muchos de los que sobresalían, su propia cara les servía de careta. Otros iban disfrazados todo el año" (119).[45]

After presenting the inhabitants of the tentacular city, the

---

or smashed as if someone threw over them iced lead [. . .] Consciousnesses were like dirty scrubbers of a restaurant [. . .] The vapor of defeated souls and the sweat of pariahs fed and helped preserve those who controlled Power and Fortune [. . .] There happiness meant lack of thought and no expansion of life purposes [. . .] Everything was fake, even the words [. . .] Everything was formulaic [. . .] It can be seen a lot of sanctimonious pity and devout lust [. . .] The rich people begged for money from inside their cars."

43. "And they had long nails and short ideas when they had any. Their souls were limp, their chests narrow, their hearts cold, and their words sweet and cloying like rancid syrup. Many of them had a diarrhea of words caused by the poor retention of intellect."

44. "The people, when they were good, used to be vegetative, homogeneous, and small, and when they were not good, they were acrid, corrupted, and rotten [. . .] They were a hybrid of plant and specter [. . .] Some of them used to dress up like hermaphrodites to impress."

45. "They were imitators [. . .] Those who were impressive had masks as faces. Others used to be dressed up the whole year."

narrator goes on to present a monstrous depiction of this *urbe*, foregrounding certain themes. The first of these themes is the monarchy. The city is ruled by a "Rey ó Reina"[46] whose authority is criticized by Gener because "reinaban, mas no gobernaban, según la formula dictada por algunos leguleyos [and] no faltaba quien mandara desde allí en su nombre" (116).[47] When Gener states that there is a monarchy that reigns but does not govern (thanks to a system created by swindlers to give the appearance of democracy), he suggests that despite not governing, the monarchy still holds authority over the city. Second, he denounces the politicians, who emerge from this corrupt and conscienceless society:

> Las conciencias eran sucias estropajos de mesón, las inteligencias, muelles y vacías como tripas horadadas [. . .] y con miajas de serrín de ingenio [. . .] Y de esta pasta que ni para hacer bacines hubiera sido buena, salían diputados y ministros y gobernantes de todos los matices. El vapor de los espíritus abatidos y el sudor de los parias alimentaba y conservaba a los grandes del Poder y de los [*sic*] Fortuna. (117)[48]

Here we observe a continuous mixture of the physical and the psychological, wherein everything appears mingled and inseparable: the consciences of the politicians are filthy scouring pads; their intelligences are spongy and empty like hollowed-out guts; whatever wit they retain is mere sawdust.[49] It is a landscape filled with

---

46. "King or Queen."
47. "They reigned, but did not govern, following that system created by swindlers; yet there was no lack of those who ruled from there in his name."
48. "The consciences were dirty scouring pads from the inn, the intelligences, spongy and empty like hollowed-out guts [. . .] and with crumbs of sawdust for wit [. . .] And from this dough that would not have been good even to make chamber pots, deputies, ministers, and rulers of all shades emerged. The vapor of the downtrodden spirits and the sweat of the pariahs fed and preserved the great ones of Power and Fortune."
49. "The consciences were dirty scrubbers from the inn, the intelligences, springy and empty like hollowed-out guts [. . .] and with crumbs of sawdust for wit."

pessimism and despair, where nothing positive seems possible. This fatalistic depiction continues with a description of the town as a place of pervasive ignorance and fakery where no one can be trusted and where any attempt to assert knowledge is doomed to fail: "A muchos que por la mañana salían enhiestos y bizarros de la sombra del árbol de la Libertad, marchando á grandes pasos hacia las alturas del conocimiento, se les veía por la tarde deshaciendo lo andado, encorvándose hasta arrastrarse á los pies de una cruz y de un trono, tras los cuales se divisaba un pan" (118).[50] This last image of people crawling toward a cross and a throne to receive in exchange for a piece of bread depicts the city's inhabitants as starving and completely dependent on priests and monarchs.

Interestingly, this passage about the ignorance and falseness that dominate the city is divided into two parts; the first criticizes religion, and the second targets Jews and Phoenicians (117–18). In the critique of religion, Gener asserts that "[e]l Dios crucificado reinaba sobre todas las bajezas [y] [a]l pie del Calvario se arrastraban serpientes, sapos, lagartos y víboras."[51] The choice of these creatures (snakes, frogs, lizards, vipers), with their repugnant appearance and in some cases dangerous nature, emphasizes again the hybridity between the human and the non-human in the inhabitants of the city. The fact that they are creatures with rough or viscous skins produces disgust and revulsion. After criticizing the hypocrisy of the wealthy for begging "limosna en coche,"[52] there come the comments on Jews and Phoenicians: the dreamer denounces the former as usurers. The latter are described according to their historical fame as sailors, but also as people obsessed with money (as "coiners") and to whom noble titles

---

50. "Many who in the morning left erect and gallant from the shadow of the Tree of Liberty, marching in great strides toward the heights of knowledge, were seen in the afternoon undoing what they had realized, stooping until they crawled at the feet of a cross and a throne, behind which was seen a loaf of bread."
51. "[t]he crucified God reigned over all baseness [and] at the foot of Calvary crawled snakes, toads, lizards, and vipers."
52. "alms in a car."

are given, in what is a criticism of how it is solely and exclusively money that determines who can be noble or not (118). This passage introduces Gener's disgust for people of other races and ethnicities.

As the dreamer's first vision continues, he focuses on the delusions of grandeur of the tentacular city, Madrid, and the Castilian plateau at large. Gener describes a citizenry convinced that it is cultured and intelligent, but is in reality shallow and ignorant. The dreamer observes that "[t]odo era chico allí, incluso la Crítica y el Teatro:—*Nadie sabe nada. Nadie puede nada. Nadie vale nada. Todo es igual*" (119).[53] Their belief in being superior to the rest of the world is only achieved with the help of masks concealing their inner horror: "Otros aún, comparecían, cubiertos con anchas y hermosas capas, símbolos de poder ó de nobleza, pero esas capas cubrían solo repugnantes momias de las que se escapaba un espíritu muerto de conciencia Negra ó un humo espeso de ignorancia crasa. Y gritaban detrás unos pigmeos: 'Somos los mejores, los reales, los positivos.' Y solo eran pequeños, bajos, y parados" (120).[54] Again, the use of expressions such as "repugnantes momias," "humo espeso," or "conciencia Negra" to ridicule their visions of grandeur evokes sensorial effects of dread and disgust.

The first vision culminates with a veritable paroxysm, as the narrator exclaims: "¡Qué horror! ¡Me asfixiaba! ¡Quería huir, volar en plena Naturaleza! Un hedor de cementerio me atrofiaba los sentidos . . . ¡Oh, qué angustia!" (120).[55] All that the dreamer has witnessed

---

53. "Everything was small there, even Criticism and Theater: *'No one knows anything. No one can do anything. No one is worth anything. Everything is the same.'*" Emphasis in original.

54. "Others still appeared, covered with wide and beautiful capes, symbols of power or nobility, but those capes covered only repulsive mummies from which escaped a dead spirit of black conscience or a thick smoke of gross ignorance. And behind them, some pygmies shouted: 'We are the best, the real, the positive.' And they were only small, short, and standing."

55. "What horror! I was suffocating! I wanted to flee, to fly into the middle of nature! The stench of the cemetery was dulling my senses . . . Oh, what anguish!"

in the tentacular city, en masse, has constituted the assault on his senses: the horror, the stench of death, the anxiety, the fear. He then observes an "oleada de gente" passing by, not the members of the upper crust with all their delusions of grandeur but rather, "hombres enjutos de carnes, demacrados, hambrientos, mal vestidos"[56]—the starving masses demanding jobs. These desperate people stumble along, shoving one another, and ultimately disappear, leaving in their wake rags and discarded pawn-shop tickets.

The Second Vision within the Dream

After this dreadful depiction of the tentacular city and its inhabitants, we arrive at the second vision of the dream. The first sentence makes it clear that this second vision is a continuation of the dream: "Y á esta visión sucedió otra que me llenó el alma de espanto y la mente de tristes meditaciones" (121).[57] This transitional sentence is a crucial element, since it blurs the spatiality of the tentacular city and the bodily presence of the monster we will encounter in the second vision, placing both of them *together* in the same dream.

Interestingly, once the monster of the second vision is introduced, the city will not be referenced again. However, the urbogonic nature of the tentacular city extends into this second vision (within the *continuous* dream) also, reinforcing the pervasiveness of the cosmic horror of the weird and perpetuating the atmosphere of dread of the second vision. The dreamer says:

> Vi un monstruo gigantesco tendido en el suelo, de terrorífico aspecto, obscuro como la noche, de frente estrecha, cara estúpida é indolente y mirada codiciosa.
> Y creí divisar sobre él unas palabras escritas en caracteres que me parecieron originarios de la Arabia y que no pude leer. Su

---

56. "a wave of people" [. . .] "lean, emaciated, hungry, poorly dressed men."
57. "After this vision, another occurred, invading my soul with horror, and my mind with sad meditations."

cuerpo estaba tendido en el alto llano, pero tenía apoyados los pies en el sur del territorio y la cabeza ocupaba un lugar frente á una puerta que impedía que el sol llegase. Hé aquí por qué eran tan obscuro el monstruo.

Tenía las orejas largas y colgantes como para escuchar los rumores que de abajo subieran, y extendía sus brazos como para rodear y constreñir á una figura de hombre fornido que aun no sé si tenía alma. (121–22)[58]

The description of the monster is ambiguous and, as said before, we do not know exactly how it is positioned in relation to the city and the plateau. We know the monster is on the plateau because, as the tale states, "su cuerpo estaba tendido en el alto llano" (121). However, we were told in the first vision that the tentacular city was on the plateau too. The weirdness of the creature is reinforced not only by this difficulty in knowing the monster's location in relation to the tentacular city but also by the descriptions given of it. According to the quotation above, the monster "tenía apoyados los pies en el sur del territorio y la cabeza ocupaba un lugar frente á una puerta que impedía que el sol llegase." The mention of "una puerta que impedía que el sol llegase" can be interpreted as a reference to one of the five gates that, until 1868, were in the walls surrounding Madrid, allowing access to the city. This is also the only reference to the position of the monster in relation to the city, which can be read as if the monster acted as a guardian of the tentacular city.

---

58. "I saw a gigantic monster lying on the ground, terrifying in appearance, dark as the night, with a narrow forehead, a stupid and indifferent face, and a greedy gaze.

"And I thought I could see some words written on it in characters that seemed to me to be of Arabic origin, but I could not read them. Its body lay on the high plain, but its feet were resting in the south of the territory, and its head occupied a place in front of a door that prevented the sun from reaching. That is why the monster was so dark.

"It had long, hanging ears as if to listen to the rumors coming from below, and it stretched out its arms as if to surround and constrain a figure of a sturdy man that I still do not know if had a soul."

Regardless of how the monster's position in relation to the tentacular city may be interpreted, what interests me more here is the atmosphere of strangeness and discomfort that arises from reading this second vision compared to the first. For, although the monster in the second vision is not presented as tentacular, the idea of tentacularity continues in the story, given that both visions pertain to the same dream recounted in "La coronada villa tentacular." This leads me to think that the tentacular implicitly exists in the monster. He is impregnated by the cosmic dread that pervades the tentacular city of the first vision. Still, it may be argued that "La coronada villa tentacular" depicts two creatures (the city and the monster) with only one of them (the city) explicitly tentacular. However, its ambiguous, fluid, almost *shapeless* description as well as its positioning in relation to the city eventually constructs an ominous entity that is a mixture of both a bodily presence (the monster) and a spatial location (the city). The fact that the dream moves from one vision to another with no clear interruption ends in the image of a single entity, bodily *and* spatial, somehow described but still indescribable, seen *and* dreamed, *as well as* evoked, with the limits between the real and the dreamed blurred, and with no sense of optimism but rather apprehension.

We may read this intersection between the tentacular city and the monster as existing in a state of what China Miéville considers a "haptic flirtation" based on his observations of Jean Painlevé's short film *Le pieuvre*. In the film, an octopus lasciviously crawls "over a human skull very similar to it in shape and proportion" ("M. R. James" 126–27). In that haptic flirtation between the octopus and the skull, there is the possibility that the octopus, with its "oozability of weird skin," might merge with the skull to become a "skulltopus" (127). While in Painlevé's film, the skull and the octopus never fully merge to become a skulltopus, Miéville suggests that such a possibility is unconsciously present (see figure 6): "We cannot sustain the skulltopus," Miéville writes regarding *Le pieuvre;* "as close as we can come is Painlevé's skull-*and*-octopus-interaction quantum vampire," thus getting an "unstable haptic flirtation of the two *without merger*" (127; emphasis in original).

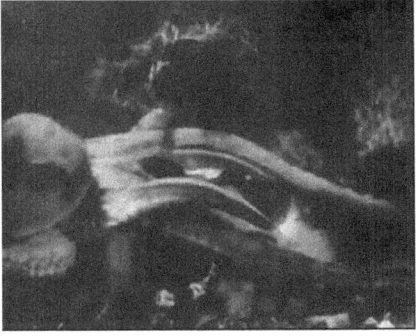

Fig. 6: *Le pieuvre* (Jean Painlevé, 1927) [00:55 – 01:04]

The transition in "La coronada villa tentacular" from the first vision to the second causes points to a similar interplay between the tentacles of the city and the flesh of the monster. In Gener's story, the tentacular city and the monster always remain separated "without merger," yet the "haptic flirtation" similar to what Miéville observes (between the skull and the octopus) is enacted during the second vision, suggesting the possibility of an elusive, weirdly ungraspable, potential tentacular city-monster. The possibility of an absolute fusion of the tentacular city and monster (like a merged "skulltopus"[59]) is always *there* due to the urbogonic nature of the tentacular city. In Gener's description of the monster, we read that it has long and hanging ears, and it has grabbed a chained man in its arms (122). We simply read that the monster "extendía sus brazos como para rodear

59. My quotation marks.

y constreñir á una figura de hombre fornido que aun no sé si tenía alma" (122).[60] Besides physical strength, the monster seems to exert mental control over the man, as he has his head bowed, as if entranced by the creature: "Este hombre estaba de pie con la cabeza caída, como hipnotizado por el repugnante monstruo" (122).[61] The man is thus held captive both physically and mentally.

The reasons for the man's entrapment are not solely the chains or the monster's arms, but also the *effects* that the repulsive image of the monster produces on him. During the first vision, the use of the tentacle to describe the city has been metaphoric rather than realistic. We may read this second vision as a continuation of what was recounted in the first one about the *effects* of the tentacular city on the citizens and surrounding land. For at this moment, those metaphoric tentacles of the city are transmuted into the flesh of the monster. Like a weird hybrid of earth and flesh, the dreamer tells us that, in the monster, "[t]odo en él *tendía hacia la tierra*" (122; my emphasis),[62] as if it were composed of rhizomes or invertebrate legs capable of permeating the soil. Moreover, it seems that the man can free himself if he wishes, but he does not do so: "Y á pesar de ser bien musculada esta figura, estaba sujeta, más por la fascinación del monstruo que por las pesadas cadenas que la ataban. Si hubiese querido, podía romperlas y huir por la parte de Levante, única que estaba aun algo libre, y con aquellas mismas cadenas podía hasta atar al monstruo . . . pero no se movía" (122).[63]

---

60. [The monster] "stretched out its arms as if it tried to surround and constrain the figure of a burly man, who I still don't know if he had a soul." 61. "This man stood with his head bowed, as if it were hypnotized by the disgusting monster."
62. "Everything in that monster *tended toward the soil/Earth*."
63. "Everything on it tended to the land. And despite the man being strong and muscular, he was trapped due to the fascination of the monster rather than the chains that tied him. If he had wished, he would have been able to break them and escape through the Levant, the only area that still was free, and with those chains, he could have tied the monster . . . but the man did not move."

The image of the man held captive by the monster suggests a state of blindness and paralysis that Gener associates with a force so powerful that it incapacitates any resistance from the man. Despite those chains being not as strong as they seem, and while affirming that there are ways to escape the monster, the man is dominated by an inescapable force. He finds himself constrained not so much by the monster's arms but by his own fascination, as if hypnotized by the creature. The dreamer's assertion here—that if he wished, the man could break free from his chains and escape through the Levant where there is still freedom—reflects Gener's belief that the only possibilities for a better future lie on the east coast of the Iberian Peninsula (Catalonia and Valencia).

This suggestion that the captive man could find freedom in the Levant reflects Gener's nationalist perspective, as a supporter of Catalonian independence. At the climactic point in the story, the dreamer shouts to the man: "¿Qué es lo que haces ahí plantado? ¡Sé cual San Jorge; mata la fiera!" (122).[64] The mention of Saint George [San Jorge] is no coincidence, given that Saint George is the patron saint of Catalonia, to whom legend attributes the killing of a dragon (see figure 7). The dreamer's command may be seen as a reflection of Gener's Catalonian nationalism, connecting with his claim, presented in *Heregias,* about the need to escape from the influence of Castile and regain a superiority that, he believes, Catalonia had in the past, but which had been abandoned due to the influence of those races from the Iberian Peninsula that he considers inferior (*Heregias* 229).

The legend of Saint George clearly recounts the victory of the human over the non-human. For his part, the dreamer, in referencing that legend, is attempting to rationalize the creature in front of him, assuming that human superiority would prevail.

Similarly to how the first vision concludes, this second vision ends with the characteristic fatalism of the weird. Faced with the

---

64. "What are you doing standing there? Be like Saint George; kill the beast!"

dreamer's cries for the man to free himself from the monster, the creature looks at him: "Gruñó el monstruo con áspero lenguaje," says the dreamer, "y me clavó sus ojos tétricos" (123).[65] There is no description of what happens next in this second vision because, as the dreamer says, the monster vanishes, and he suddenly finds himself in a market.

Fig. 7: *Left upper*: "Saint George Killing the Dragon," woodcut by Albrecht Dürer (1501-1504). *Right upper*: Façade of the Palace of the Generalitat of Catalonia. *Bottom*: "Saint George and the Dragon," by Pierre Paul Rubens (1606–08).

---

65. "The monster growled with harsh language and pierced me with its gloomy eyes."

The Third Vision: A Marketplace

The third vision in "La coronada villa tentacular" takes place in a market. As was the case in the transition from the first to the second vision, here we do not know how this new space relates to the tentacular city, the monster, and the plateau. This final scene is very brief, consisting of barely three paragraphs. The dreamer informs us that the previous vision with the monster vanished, and he then found himself in an overcrowded marker: "se me presentó un mercado donde se vendía todo, hasta la justicia y la conciencia" (123).[66]

In that market, everything is for sale, including universal values of justice and good conscience, and the hustle and bustle seem as wild and uncontrollable as the octopus' tentacles. Overwhelmed, the dreamer cries out for a new prophet to cleanse that corrupt atmosphere. This sensation of turmoil and unpredictability helps sustain the idea that the influence of the tentacular city extends well beyond the first vision. In his discussion on the Kraken, Slavoj Žižek suggests that cephalopods as constitute "a perfect image of the global Capital, all-powerful and stupid, cunning and blind, whose tentacles regulate our lives" (3). Indeed, octopuses and squids are often utilized as symbols of greed associated with capitalism (Hashimoto 58). While not referencing global capital here, Gener adheres to this common trope in evoking the marketplace.

However, despite concluding the tale with this market scene, "La coronada villa tentacular" remains unclear as to whether the Castilian plateau and its tentacular city represent a society (the Spanish) that has surrendered to capitalism. Gener does associate the tentacular with greed, yet this greed seems to come from stupidity, mediocrity, and vassalage rather than capitalism, as he had suggested in this passage from the first vision:

> Sólo los sentimientos mezquinos vivían allí á sueldo; y las
> pequeñas virtudes eran hábiles y tenían ocupación lucrativa [. . .]

---

66. "[and then] I found myself in a market where everything was sold, even justice and conscience."

Todo era falso, hasta el oro de la palabra, que allí era latón puro [. . .] Los ricos pedían limosna en coche [. . .] Para ser alguien, uno debía agruparse á otros e ingresar en unas partidas que llamaban partidos. Solo existían rebaños mandados por lobos, ó por pastores sin cabeza. (117–18)[67]

The ending of the story relates to this passage. Given that Gener supported the independence of Catalonia, based in part on its more advanced industrial development, his critique here relates to greed and money obtained by other means, such as usury and political corruption. The ambiguity on this issue, however, is not resolved in this final scene in the marketplace. Rather than offering further explanation, the dreamer immediately calls for a sort of biblical Flood to revolutionize and clean this dystopian world: "¡Rayos y truenos!" he shouts. "¿Dónde está la tempestad tremenda, evocada por un nuevo profeta, que venga á purificar esta atmósfera?" (123).[68]

Eventually, this ambiguity in the ending of the tale works in favor of the narrative itself, and it aligns well with the weird reading of the story that I have proposed. In the course of the tale Gener criticizes many things, but he sometimes offers divergent opinions—for example, about religion. If in the first vision, he asserted that in the city "[v]eíase mucha piedad beata y mucha concupiscencia devota" (117); in the quotation above he asks for the coming of a prophet-savior. He also denounces the commercialization of life in the marketplace scene, but at the same time he criticizes the economic underdevelopment of the Castilian plateau. He proposes, instead, the developed region of Levant/Catalonia as a site for salvation, thus implying the need for more capitalism in the Iberian

---

67. "Only miserable thoughts lived there, and the few virtues were skillful and had profitable occupations [. . .] Everything was fake, even the words, which there they were not gold, but like brass [. . .] Rich people begged for money in cars [. . .] In order to be someone, a person had to join others and become members of something called political parties. People were like sheep commanded by wolves, or by headless shepherds."
68. "Where is the tremendous tempest, evoked by a new prophet, to come and purify this atmosphere?"

Peninsula. Even if the descriptions of the inhabitants of the tentacular city and the monster reveal the dreamer's evident disgust, they also hint at a certain fascination and attraction for the morbid, for what is considered abnormal—for the weird.

The Plateau and the Racial in "La coronada villa tentacular"

In this last section I focus on three aspects that have remained in the background during my discussions of other issues: the plateau, race, and genotypic horror. I start with the plateau. As we have seen, the tentacular city, the monster, and the chained man of "La coronada villa tentacular" are all situated on a plateau. In weird literature, a plateau often appears as a space that is "barren, stony [. . .] [and] an intensive symbol of the death-in-life significance of the shadow" (Waugh 224–25). Similarly, in the first vision Gener describes the tentacular city as surrounded by "estepas y terrenos yermos y breñas" (115), in a clear reference to the prototypical image of the Castilian plateau. Like in many of Lovecraft's landscapes, Gener's plateau is a critique and mockery of Castile and its idealization and ideological dominance—the exalted Castilian plateau of *Hispanidad*. For Gener, it is not an idealized landscape but shadowy and sterile—the evil Castilian landscape. These two landscapes cannot be separated. According to Waugh, the ideal landscape is expansive and invasive. At the same time, it heralds the horrors that such expansion creates. As a result, the ideal landscape becomes the expression of a transition toward the shadows (Waugh 222).

The city-monster on the plateau can be read as a form of posthumanist anthropomorphism that counters the official humanistic anthropocentrism promoted by Castile/Madrid and its worldview *Hispanidad*: ideal, expansive, invasive. Unlike anthropocentrism, anthropomorphism implies the idea that "human agency has some echoes in non-human nature—to counter the narcissism of humans [i.e., Spaniards] in charge of the world"

(Bennett xvi). Like Lovecraft's pessimistic posthumanism,[69] the inability of the chained man in "La coronada villa tentacular" to escape from the anthropomorphized, shapeless city-monster and shadowy plateau is a call for a total rupture with Spain, just as Saint George [San Jorge] disposed of the dragon.

This entire worldview of tentacular cities, monsters, shady plateaus, weird Othernesses, and posthumanist anthropomorphism in "La coronada villa tentacular" eventually creates an exclusionary tale that, like the official discourse of *Hispanidad,* can buttress Gener's belief in Catalonian superiority and thus justify a racist ideology. Ultimately, "La coronada villa tentacular," in its denunciation of the evils of turn-of-the-century Spain, narrates a story of racial projection, whereby Gener's monster embodies the implied (and often denounced) "misogynist racial-nightmare monster Cthulhu" of Lovecraft's stories (Haraway 81). For Gener, Castilians, Moors, Jews, and Phoenicians alike come to represent the weird and the monstrous because they fall outside his conception of what is normal.

The racial question is one of the most explored issues in Lovecraft's work and the weird genre at large.[70] Lovecraft thought of the idea of symmetry as inbred in the human race, believing that "the universe itself is possessed of symmetry, that it operates in a predictable way [. . .] [and where] the mastery of geometry is the key to the universe's domination" (Mariconda 193–94). In his view, symmetry meant equilibrium, proportion, and order. The existence of weird cosmoses and their penetration into our world/universe were, for Lovecraft, often understood as challenges or threats to those proportion and order in humanity. This has positioned the weird monsters of the Cthulhu Mythos as asymmetrical and

---

69. For Johnson, that pessimistic posthumanism emerges out of "a recognition of humanity's inescapable imbrication in the nonhuman world," and by materializing "cosmos in ways that narrowed the gap between human and nonhuman difference" (106).

70. See Carl H. Sederholm and Jeffrey Andrew Weinstock's book *The Age of Lovecraft* (2016).

embodying the idea of a threat against human beings.[71]

Lovecraft's tales are thus racial projections that not only express fears toward external encounters that threaten human beings but also what scholar Mitch Frye has called "genotypic horror." According to Frye, genotypic horror appears when characters are not afraid of external forces that can disrupt their daily routine, but of an inward fear of the impossibility of knowing their ancestry, or being descending from asymmetrical, "impure" [my quotation marks] ancestors. According to Frye, Lovecraft was a writer intrigued by genetics, and his works must be contextualized in eugenic discourse (238–40). In his essay "Supernatural Horror in Literature," Lovecraft described genotypic horror as a fear of the unknown *inside bodies*. According to Frye, Lovecraft considered both the external cosmos and internal genes as "equally unknowable" (239). In doing so, he thought of the fear of the unknown that characterizes the weird as both the fear of creatures from outer worlds and the fear of not being able to fully know our own bodies. In the genotypic horror story, that lack of knowledge about the body is perceived as

---

71. Examples of this mentality in Lovecraft (covering from anti-Black racism to antisemitism) can be found in his correspondence with Elizabeth Toldridge or J. Vernon Shea, and in many of his stories, sometimes explicit ("The Horror at Red Hook" [1925]), others more subtly: "Facts concerning the Late Arthur Jermyn & His Family" (1920), or "The Shadow over Innsmouth" (1931). Nevertheless, Benjamin Noys defends as "The Lovecraft Event" (2007) a radical quality or jouissance that emerges from Lovecraft's oeuvre where horror is engendered by "forc[ing] a pass through the avant-gardes of his time," giving rise to the "emergence of a new ontology (or pseudo-ontology) of nature as 'chaotic,' and producing not only a 'reactionary novelty,' but actually also a true novelty of disruption." In other words, Lovecraft's works create their own rupture—the so-called "Lovecraft Event" (Jarvis 1133), which, strategically located "beyond the Gothic, beyond the horror field and beyond his [Lovecraft's] epigones" (Noys), implies the assumption of their regressive nature but does not necessarily resemble it. Instead, writers assume the weird can transform Lovecraft's tropes, just "as he took those topoi from early writers," radically refashioning and combining them (Jarvis 1135).

threatening, specifically when a character discovers that his own genes "may betray him, revealing some dark inherited element of his family's past" (239). The racial component thus enters Lovecraft's fear of the gene, or rather, that gene being flawed.

This fear of the gene can be seen in "La coronada villa tentacular," a tale of genotypic horror that, while attempting to destroy the Castilian *imaginarium*, promotes a racial image of Catalonians as symmetrical (i.e., human), thus fearing the possible "impure" origins of Castilians.[72] As I discussed earlier, Gener believed that, while Spaniards had been undermined by the other races that had inhabited Spain, Catalonians had remained relatively pure. In the first vision of the tale, the dreamer refers to the usurious and money-obsessed nature of Jews and Phoenicians (117–18). Similarly, during the description of the monster in the second vision, he says he sees written on it "unas palabras escritas en caracteres [. . .] originarios de la Arabia" (121).[73] Jews, Phoenicians, and Arabs are thus associated with the weird and the monstrous, being (along with Castilians) part of that threat to Catalonians. The suggestion (in the second vision) that the chained man could escape from the city-monster "por la parte de Levante, única que estaba aún algo libre," as well as the reference to Saint George and the dragon (122), are instances of Gener's desire for the extermination of the Otherness(es), which is racial extermination. In other words, Gener positions himself as the well-proportioned (i.e., human) entity, since he defends progress and industrial development, justifying the existence of a racial worldview that is ordered and proportional, but which also needs the creation and subsequent extinction of Othernesses.

This belief in the racial superiority of Catalonians over Spaniards can be found in his essay "La cuestión catalana." There he asks himself: "¿Y qué es lo que da la inducción respecto a Cataluña?" In response to that question, he says: "De los estudios etnográficos, geográficos, climatológicos e históricos, *resulta ser una nación por la*

72. My quotation marks.
73. "a few words written in characters [. . .] originating from Arabia."

fusión de razas arias casi en su totalidad, con un medio ambiente especial, con un pasado glorioso, con tradiciones propias, con una lengua literaria que ha dado grandes obras maestras sobre todo el Mediterráneo" (708).[74] And later: "Ante todo y sobre todo, queremos que dentro de la nación catalana no se viole ninguna de las leyes de la Naturaleza en la horrible explotación del hombre por el hombre, ínterin ésta acaba ó se acentúa, tendiendo á que acabe lo más pronto posible" (709).[75]

Gener thus links the fusion of Aryan races with nature, making a claim for a political organization of Catalonia based on race, climate, geographical location, and history, and in harmony with the rest of European civilization (709). In contrast, he warns about the hegemony of a shadowy Spain—superstitious, dominated by religion, paralyzed, cruel and indolent, "en que todos aspiran a vivir del presupuesto, aunque sea en clase de *esbirros;* de esa España que no mira hacia adelante ni hacia afuera, a los puntos en que se trabaja y se piensa (709).[76] This relates to the dreamer's comments in the section on the market in "La coronada villa tentacular," where he does not criticize capitalism but rather a corrupt system that makes money only through social and political connections with people in power.

In "La cuestión catalana," Gener therefore looks for a form of eugenics that can combine those superior elements that exist in superior races to create

> una raza grande por su energía, por su elevación y su profundidad,
> que tienda á elevar la vida a una intensidad, á una superioridad

---

74. "And what can be inferred regarding Catalonia? According to ethnographic, geographic, climatological, and historical scholarly works, *it is a nation resulting from the fusion of Aryan races almost in its totality,* with a special environment, a glorious past, with its traditions, with a literature full of masterpieces over the Mediterranean Sea" (my emphasis).

75. "we want that the Laws of Nature not to be violated by the horrible exploitation by humans, trying to end that exploitation as soon as possible."

76. "where everybody aims to live from the public budget, even if that means to become *minions;* that Spain that does not look ahead nor outwards, where people do work and think" (emphasis in original).

desconocidas hoy en día, y que no malgaste dichas energías en obras de decadencia, en *sub-bizantinismos*, como lo hacen la mayoría de las otras razas peninsulares, agotadas que están ya del inmenso esfuerzo que hicieron en el renacimiento para imponer el catolicismo y la monarquía absoluta del mundo, que volvía los ojos con amor al humanismo helénico. (710–11)[77]

This eugenic discourse in "La cuestión catalana" hovers over "La coronada villa tentacular." As a weird tale, it has clear racial connotations. Gener's discourse about Spain can be read as a form of weird *regeneracionismo*. Unlike reformers such as Joaquín Costa and Lucas Mallada, or writers of the Generation of '98 like Unamuno and Machado, who saw Castile as a salvageable territory, despite its historical problems of corruption and economic backwardness, Gener does not entertain the possibility of such salvation. Rather, he considers everything in Castile to be a threat to the only area of the Iberian Peninsula that truly interests him, and which he openly mentions in "La coronada villa tentacular"—the Levant. In this suggestion of the Levant region as superior to Castile, Gener harbors an idea of racial (Aryan) superiority; a superiority that, despite facing cosmic monstrosities (the plateau, the hybrid city-monster) and genetic threats (from Jews, Phoenicians, Arabs, Castilians), still is capable of overcoming and building an alternative future.

Conclusion

In this article, I have analyzed Catalonian writer Pompeu Gener's dystopia "La coronada villa tentacular" as a tale assigned to the weird. I hope to have demonstrated how Gener subverts the traditional trope

---

77. [To create] "a race great for its energy, for its elevation and its depth; a race that tends to elevate life to an intensity, to a superiority unknown today, and which does not waste said energies in works of decadence, in *sub-Byzantinisms*, as the majority do of the other peninsular races, already exhausted from the immense effort they made in the Renaissance to impose Catholicism and the absolute monarchy on the world, which turned its eyes with love to Hellenic humanism." Emphasis in the original.

of the Castilian plateau as the optimal spatial representation of an essentialist notion of *Hispanidad,* underscoring the perils of its exclusionary, predatory nature. At the same time, I have aimed to show how Gener's own proposed revision of *Hispanidad* and the Castilian plateau reproduces the racist connotations of those traditional tropes, as he affirms the racial superiority of Catalonians over Spaniards– Catalonians whom he sees as the real human beings in the Iberian Peninsula. In using the concept of the "weird" popularized by H. P. Lovecraft, and its exploration of non-anthropocentric creatures that threaten human beings' dominant status in nature, I have shown how the racist ideology in his weird tales is reproduced in "La coronada villa tentacular" as well. Moreover, Gener eventually reproduces the exclusionary nature of the Castilian plateau toward other landscapes of the Iberian Peninsula, since he exalts the superiority of the Levant region over Castile and Catalonians over Spaniards.

Works Cited

Álvarez Chillida, Gonzalo. *El antisemitismo en España: la imagen del judío, 1812–2002.* Madrid: Marcial Pons Historia, 2002.

"Azorín" (José Martínez Ruiz). *Obras completas 1959–1963.* Volume 1. Madrid: Aguilar, 1959.

Bennett Jane. *Vibrant Matter: A Political Ecology of Things.* Durham, NC: Duke University Press, 2010.

Brown, William, and David H. Fleming. *The Squid Cinema from Hell: "Kinoteuthis Infernalis" and the Emergence of Chthulumedia* (*sic*). Edinburgh: Edinburgh University Press, 2020.

Burleson, Donald R. "On Lovecraft's Themes: Touching the Glass." In *An Epicure in the Terrible: A Centennial Anthology of Essays in Honor of H. P. Lovecraft,* ed. David E. Schultz and S. T. Joshi. New York: Hippocampus Press, 2011. 139–52.

Caja, Francisco. *La raza catalana: el núcleo doctrinal del catalanismo.* Madrid: Encuentro, 2009.

Crosson, Dena. "Ignacio Zuloaga and the Problem of Spain." Ph.D. diss.: University of Maryland, 2009.

"The Cultural Significance of Cyberpunk." *YouTube,* uploaded by Jonas Čeika—CCK Philosophy, 3 DOI: www.youtube.com/watch?v=Nvor7hhDKTs. Accessed 20 January 2024.

Frye, Mitch. "The Refinement of the 'Crude Allegory': Eugenic Themes and Genotypic Horror in the Weird Fiction of H. P. Lovecraft." *Journal of the Fantastic in the Arts* 17, No. 3 (2006): 237–54.

García Fernández, Javier. "Los intelectuales del 98 español en la configuración de la cuestión meridional: descolonización, narrativas del post-Imperio y génesis de la andaluzofobia." *Revista Letral: Estudios Trasatlánticos de Literatura* 27 (2021): 270–84.

Gener, Pompeu. "La coronada villa tentacular." In *Del presente, del pasado y del futuro.* Paris: Sociedad de ediciones Louis-Michaud, 1911. 115–23.

———. "La cuestión catalana." *Nuestro Tiempo* 29 (1903): 705–19.

———. *Heregias.* Barcelona: Imprenta de Luis Tasso Serra, 1888.

Giner de los Ríos, Francisco. "Paisaje I." *La Ilustración Artística* No. 219 (1886): 91–92.

———. "Paisaje II." *La Ilustración Artística* No. 220 (1886): 103–4.

Gómez Gutiérrez, Juan Luis. "Francisco Giner de los Ríos, la Institución Libre de Enseñanza y su labor como 'descubridores' de la sierra de Guadarrama." *Indivisa: Boletín de Estudios e Investigación* 16 (2016): 29–63.

González Trueba, Juan José. "El legado de Giner de los Ríos y la Institución Libre de Enseñanza (Geografía, naturaleza y cultura en España)." *Ábaco* 90 (2016): 45–55.

Haraway, Donna. "Capitalocene and Chthulucene." In *Posthuman Glossary*, ed. Rosi Braidotti and Maria Hlavajova. London: Bloomsbury Publishing, 2018, 79–83.

Hashimoto, Yorimitsu. "Spectacular Tentacular: Transmedial Tentacles and Their Hegemonic Struggles in Cthulhu and Godzilla." *Between* 10, No. 2 (2020): 57–88.

Jameson, Fredric. *Archaeologies of the Future: The Desire Called Utopia and Other Science Fictions*. London: Verso, 2005.

Jarvis, Timothy. "The Weird, the Posthuman, and the Abjected World-in-Itself: Fidelity to the 'Lovecraft Event' in the Work of Caitlin R. Kiernan and Laird Barron." *Textual Practice* 31 (2017): 1133–48.

Johnson, Brian. "Prehistories of Posthumanism: Cosmic Indifferentism, Alien Genesis, and Ecology from H. P. Lovecraft to Ridley Scott." In *The Age of Lovecraft*, ed. Carl H. Sederholm and Jeffrey Andrew Weinstock. Minneapolis: University of Minnesota Press, 2016. 97–116.

Joshi, S. T. *The Weird Tale*. Austin: University of Texas Press, 1990.

Joy, Eileen. "Weird Reading." *Speculations* 4 (2013): 28–34.

Keller, Céline. "The Utopian Impulse & Its Trouble with Postmodernity (Fredric Jameson)." *re:publica*. www.youtube.com/watch?v=Nvor7hhDKTs. Accessed 4 April 2023.

Lovecraft, H. P. *The Annotated Supernatural Horror in Literature*. Ed. S. T. Joshi. New York: Hippocampus Press, 2nd ed. 2012.

———. "The Call of Cthulhu." In *Collected Fiction: A Variorum Edition*. Volume 2. Ed. S. T. Joshi. New York: Hippocampus Press, 2015. 21–55.

Mariconda, Steven J. "Lovecraft's Cosmic Imagery." In *An Epicure in the Terrible: A Centennial Anthology of Essays in Honor of H. P. Lovecraft*, ed. David E. Schultz and S. T. Joshi. New York: Hippocampus Press, 2011. 196–207.

Marshall, Kate. "The Old Weird." *Modernism/Modernity* 23 (2016): 631–49.

Martín Rodríguez, Mariano. "La geoficción urbana o urbogonía: Recuperación de un ejemplo temprano: 'La coronada villa tentacular,' de Gener." *Ángulo Recto* 5, No. 2 (2013): 125–47.

Miéville, China. "Introduction." In *At the Mountains of Madness* by H. P. Lovecraft. New York: Modern Library, 2005. xi–xxv.

———. "M. R. James and the Quantum Vampire: Weird; Hauntological: Versus and/or and and/or or?" In *Collapse IV,* ed. R. Mackay. Falmouth, UK: Urbanomic, 2008. 105–28.

Morton, Tim. "Weird Embodiment." *In Sentient Performitivities of Embodiment: Thinking Alongside the Human,* ed. Lynette Hunter, Elisabeth Krimmer, and Peter Lichtenfels. Lanham, MD: Lexington, 2016. 19–34.

Newell, Jonathan. *A Century of Weird Fiction 1832–1937: Disgust, Metaphysics and the Aesthetics of Cosmic Horror.* Cardiff: University of Wales Press, 2020.

Noys, Benjamin. "The Lovecraft Event." Unpublished Conference Paper, 2007. www.academia.edu/548596/The_Lovecraft_Event

Ortega Cantero, Nicolás. "La valoración patrimonial y simbólica del paisaje de Castilla (1875–1936)." *Ería* 73–74 (2007): 137–59.

———. "Landscape and Identity: The Vision of Castile as a National Landscape (1876–1936)." *Boletín de la A.G.E.* 51 (2009): 379–81.

———. "Francisco Giner y el descubrimiento moderno del paisaje de España." *Anales* 27 (2015): 23–44.

Palomar, Aitana S. "La leyenda de San Jorge y el dragón." In *National Geographic Historia.* historia.nationalgeographic.com.es/a/leyenda-san-jorge-y-dragon_12574

Rodari, Florian; Prevost, Marie-Laurie; Sante, Luc; and Pierre Georgel. *Shadows of a Hand: The Drawings of Victor Hugo.* New York: Merrell, 1998.

Soros, Juan. "La ciudad tentacular en dos poemas de Émile Verhaeren y una ilustración de Frans Masereel." *Ángulo Recto* 3 (2011): 279–91.

Tomás, Facundo. "Una mirada a Blasco Ibáñez después de la modernidad." In *La maja desnuda*, Madrid, Cátedra, 1998. 11–47.

Unamuno, Miguel de. *Poesías.* Madrid: Librerías de Fernando Fe and Victoriano Suárez, 1907.

———. "Castile," *All Poetry.* allpoetry.com/Castilla.

VanderMeer, Ann and Jeff. "Introduction." In *The Weird: A Compendium of Strange and Dark Stories,* ed. Ann and Jeff VanderMeer. 2011. New York: Tor, 2012. xv–xx.

Verhaeren, Émile. *Les villes tentaculaires, précédées des Campagnes hallucinées.* 1893 and 1895. Paris: Mercure de France, 1917.

Verne, Jules. *Vingt mille lieues sous les mers.* 1870, Paris: Bibliothèque d'éducation et de récréation, 1871.

Waugh, Robert H. "Landscapes, Selves, and Others in Lovecraft." In *An Epicure in the Terrible: A Centennial Anthology of Essays in Honor of H. P. Lovecraft,* ed. David E. Schultz and S. T. Joshi. New York: Hippocampus Press, 2011. 230–55.

Žižek, Slavok. *Disparities.* London: Bloomsbury, 2016.

Zuloaga, Ignacio. "Vista de El Escorial," c.1905? www.tate.org.uk/art/artworks/zuloaga-view-of-the-escorial-n01357

The Igloo

Maureen O'Leary

Hardly anyone went to school in person anymore since online learning started, but Jenny's parents were professors who remembered the old days so fondly that nostalgia was more real than reality. They taught their classes from their computers at home, but Jenny they made go to school. Ruth, one of the few other students, was the only one who listened to their teachers when they actually showed up to teach. Jenny carried reading from home for the no-teacher days, once bringing an encyclopedia of faery tale creatures she was into when she was little. She cracked it open, releasing the paper's toasted vanilla scent, and suddenly there was Ruth beside her.

"Tell me a story," Ruth said. She rested her chin on Jenny's shoulder as if they were already friends, her breath warm on Jenny's cheek. She watched as Jenny flipped through the pages and put her hand down on the one about the Glaistig, the creature with a goat or deer's legs and a woman's upper body.

"I've heard of her," Ruth said. "She lives around here."

Jenny thrilled at this. She didn't argue that the Glaistig was just a story. Instead she nodded, as if what Ruth said could possibly be serious. Jenny loved the Glaistig. You could leave her bowls of milk in exchange for looking after your kids. She was a vampire, but she only drank off of unjust men, hanging their guts on branches. With one finger Ruth traced the drawing of the woman's silky dress. Her glinting hooves. The bloody viscera dripping on snow.

"She's a badass," Ruth said.

On Friday Ruth slid into the empty desk beside Jenny in Integrated Sciences. There was no teacher present. No other students. She took out the faery book in hopes that Ruth would scoot her desk closer, which she did, and they huddled together for warmth over the Glaistig.

"My uncles and aunt are taking me to the mountain to hunt trees tomorrow," Ruth said. "You should join us."

Jenny shrugged one shoulder to hide her excitement and agreed, though she knew her parents would never allow it. In the decade since the New Winter, the mountain had become dangerous. Melted permafrost caused volcanic eruptions beginning in Iceland that covered the sun for the entire planet. *For years we were afraid of burning. Now we are in a perpetual winter.* This was what the Integrated Sciences teacher loved to say on repeat when she bothered to come to school. The teacher sounded like the pastors at church. Her pastors sounded like her parents. Adults loved saying things everybody already knew.

Jenny lied and told her parents she was hanging out with a church friend. They were trying to build a second greenhouse and were happy to have her out of the way. Their neighbors tended similar makeshift gardens they learned to build from online videos. They needed to grow more food. Jenny left them hammering at wooden beams her father salvaged from the dump, their hands reddening in the growing wind.

She walked alone to the boarded-up Dollar Tree where she waited until a green van rumbled up to collect her. The van ran on cooking oil, and the smell reminded Jenny of her empty stomach. The door slid open and inside two men in the middle seat shared a marijuana cigarette, the smoke curling like incense. Ruth's Uncle Cade was driving, his wife Alexis riding shotgun. The uncles in the middle were Declan and Jackson. Jenny nodded hello, acutely aware of her own face, wishing she had a book to hide in.

Ruth always seemed full where Jenny felt empty. Jenny and the few other kids who went to school sat in the cafeteria like skeletons in worn out parkas, usually with nothing to eat. Ruth had broad shoulders and solid legs. She brought baskets of produce and boiled eggs to share sometimes, food that disappeared so fast there wasn't anything left. Despite this generosity, most people, Jenny's parents included, looked down on Ruth's family. Ruth's house was set back from the road and three generations lived under one roof. The uncles were always working on their vehicles in the driveway, heads under a hood, dirt under their fingernails. They kept gardens in their front and back yards. They kept more chickens than anyone else could manage, and a few cows and goats as well.

Jenny's parents said that Ruth's family didn't know how to live. They lived like immigrants. Like hillbillies. But Jenny's parents were broke from paying mechanics to keep their one car barely running. Their potato plants wilted and their chickens kept dying. Jenny hardly remembered a time before the New Winter, but her parents clung to their longing for the days of backyard swimming pools, green lawns, and supermarkets filled with food.

Now the power went out after four in the afternoon every day. Now there was a grocery shortage. Now the sky was ash gray, the air chilled as an iron grate.

Uncle Cade turned onto a dirt road. Everyone knew the mountain was dangerous. Weather systems were unpredictable. Deer hunters were known to disappear. There were rumors of cannibals living in the woods. Jenny wasn't afraid, not with Ruth there. Not with Ruth's uncles and aunt singing along to the radio.

Jenny's parents only listened to classical. They looked down on rock music. They looked down on people who didn't go to their church. They looked down on people who didn't have online jobs. Ruth's greenhouses were lush as jungles, the product of a long history of eschewing lawns for garden beds, even before the New Winter. Jenny's parents picked Ruth's family apart over dinners of watery soup. Ruth's family sold their goods at the farmer's market under the freeway, their table laden with honey and cucumbers and bunches of spinach and loaves of bread. Their prices were fair, but Ruth's family was loud and laughed too much and smoke clung to their long hair. They were like Vikings.

"They aren't our kind of people," Jenny's father said, and her mother murmured agreement, her spoon clanking in her empty bowl.

Ruth reached for Jenny's hand across the van seat and asked her uncle to turn up the music. Jenny let her hand be taken, her heart bursting. She wanted to be able to sing along with the radio, but she wasn't familiar with the song. She didn't know the words.

The van bumped along, the engine humming agreeably. Jenny's head buzzed from the uncles' weed. The snow piled higher the further up they drove. Jenny remembered that her mother said that when she was a girl, her parents took her on car rides for special play days at the beach, or the mountains, or the snow. Before the New Winter there was packaged food, and new cars, and stores so large they were called Big Box. That was before volcanic ash blocked the sun and tipped the world into an eternal winter that refroze the ice caps and cooled the seas and created vortexes of cold air that sat over North America like a punishment.

They stopped and got out in a clearing, and the uncles went to quick work building a fire. They invited Jenny to sit before the blaze and Aunt Alexis tucked a wool blanket over Jenny's legs and Ruth covered Jenny's shoulders with a big fleece-lined denim jacket. Uncle Cade lit a propane burner, and before long Jenny was sipping a mug of honeyed milk. Ruth handed her a sandwich oozing with butter and honey, and Jenny thought of the cows and goats that grazed on the hill behind Ruth's house. Their neighbors complained about the noise they made, and they complained about the smell. They complained about the bee boxes too, claiming they were a hazard in a suburb. What if they swarmed? What if they stung someone?

The uncles stood around the fire with hacksaws at their feet, sipping from home-brewed beers in amber bottles.

Uncle Cade looked at the sky. "Thinking we've got two hours max."

"Weatherman said clear until midnight," Jackson said.

"Doubtful," said Cade.

Ruth cupped her hands over Jenny's ear and whispered. "Uncle

Cade knows everything. Seriously. Ask him something."

"I can't think of anything," Jenny said, too shy of the uncles to meet their eyes.

"Uncle Cade," Ruth called out, "what deer species live on this mountain?"

"Coastal black tail." No hesitation.

Jackson wanted to argue. "Not mule deer?"

Cade shook his head. Aunt Alexis glanced at Ruth, a smile playing on her lips. "Hey, Cade," she said, "how long are deer pregnant?"

"Coastal black-tailed normally breed in November and December," he said. "The average gestation period lasts one hundred and eighty to two hundred days. The doe gives birth to one fawn or twins in the spring."

Ruth and the aunt spit laughter while the uncles argued over Cade's facts. One hundred and eighty days was barely six months; no way was gestation that short.

Uncle Cade gazed into the fire. "Look it up when we get home," he said. "Or better yet, let's bet on it first."

"Let's find a pregnant deer and ask her," Declan said.

"That would be rude," Jackson said. "Can't ask a lady that."

Jenny realized then that she didn't know the sound of her parents' laughter. Creamy milk coated the roof of her mouth. She was not used to having a full stomach. Her eyes felt heavy. She must have dozed because the next thing she knew, Aunt Alexis was leaning over her, a hacksaw in one gloved hand, a bowl of milk in the other. "We're just going up the hill," she said. "You two want to come along or stay by the fire?"

The sky had grown steely. Ruth said they'd stay in camp. Aunt Alexis nodded and placed the bowl of milk under a tree by the fire. Jenny rubbed her eyes. She wondered if she was dreaming.

The adults trudged off, their voices and laughter carrying through the trees. Ruth tossed another log into the fire. She stamped her feet. "Let's build an igloo," she said.

"I don't know how."

"I'll teach you." Ruth helped her stand. They cut blocks from the icy snowbank. Hunters would have to use snowmobiles after the next storm, if there were any deer left. People who never thought to hunt their own food now took gun in hand to feed their families. Jenny's parents didn't, but their neighbors did, despite the rumors of bad men in the woods.

Building an igloo was fun. Ruth smoothed the bricks and showed Jenny how to place them. They built walls and sealed the top with smaller pieces until they had a fort big enough to house them both. They crawled inside, breathless from the work.

Ruth said she was hungry. They returned to the fire where Ruth set two more logs and grabbed two more butter and honey sandwiches.

"Are you sure your family won't mind me eating all their food?" Jenny asked through a mouth full of sweet bread.

"Girl, two sandwiches is not all our food," Ruth said.

Tiny snowflakes began to flit and spit into the fire. "Why do you like me?" she asked, regretting the question immediately but really wanting to know. Ruth had everything and Jenny had nothing.

Ruth tilted her head, her gaze as intense on Jenny's face as the fire's heat. What did Ruth see when she looked at her? Maybe she saw that Jenny was too weird to be friends with, and there stretched before Jenny's mind long days in quiet classrooms, no one to share her books with. There would be no more bread and honey. No more songs and smoke and uncles who were funny and an aunt who was kind. The sky seemed to be lowering to the earth as the snow fell harder on their heads.

"You have the best stories," Ruth said, as if the fact were obvious. When she laughed, Jenny laughed too, light-headed with relief. How wonderful it was to be friends. They had their igloo, and their stories, a fire, and bread. These two girls on this cold mountain, at least they had each other.

Just then a truck pulled into the clearing, frozen snow crunching under worn tires. A man got out and both girls looked to the forest. A hot hope rushed in Jenny that the family would in that moment barrel down the hill and greet the stranger for them because he was no good. There was in his face a pinched hunger.

He went to the van, sliding open the door and going inside.

"That is not yours, asshole," Ruth said. Jenny grabbed her arm. Whispered that they should run.

From within there was the ripping of a paper bag. The rattle of bottles. The snow was thickening. Every second, heavier than the last. The man came out holding a beer and a loaf of bread.

"Where'd you get this?" He raised the bottle.

"We made it," Ruth said. "There's a lot of us. You better get going."

"I don't see anybody but you." The man tore at the bread. Took a long swig. His face was barely bearded and he was stick thin. He would be no match for the uncles and the aunt with their burly shoulders. But they did not come down the hill now.

"What is this?" The man toed the milk under the tree. "You got so much to spare you can waste it?"

He threw the empty bottle into the fire and crouched before the bowl. Ruth and Jenny shuddered. Fat flakes stuck to the ends of their hair. They watched as the man drank the milk down in one long gulp.

"You'll be sorry you did that," Ruth said.

The man lunged at Ruth. He clamped his hand around her throat, so quick that Jenny didn't believe what was happening. Ruth flailed her arms. Her knees crumpled and the man straddled her body on the snowy ground. Jenny covered her mouth like a monkey committed to speaking no evil, though this was a time for her to climb onto the man's back, to scream into his ear, to do something, to do anything. But paralysis overtook her limbs. She watched as if from a great height as the man bounced on Ruth's stomach and her friend screamed. She thought of her father, poring over his books in the candlelight. How disappointed he would be that she was there, how baffled by her disobedience. She thought of her book full of faery tales about karmic comeuppances on the greedy and the cruel. Her father once admitted that they didn't need the church as much as they needed these stories, but as the climate worsened they went to church every Sunday to hear warnings about demons coming alive in men's hearts. They went to sit in pews with their neighbors, everyone's stomachs growling, their heads bowed as they prayed for relief, and for hope. For color, for warmth, for a little bit of joy.

The bad man tightened his knees around Ruth's ribcage. He fumbled with his belt. Jenny felt the pain in her own sides. The terror in her own ragged breathing.

Ruth raised her eyes to Jenny's, wide with terror, tears freezing on her lashes. *Help me*, she mouthed.

As if unlocked from a spell, Jenny moved. In the whiteout snowfall she grabbed a split log off the pile and slammed it on the back of the man's head.

The man tottered over. Jenny pulled Ruth out from under him, and there was a flash of green by the fire. Jenny turned, her arms around her friend. A large doe, her belly fat, emerged from between the trees.

Ruth stumbled against Jenny's body, almost knocking her over. "Get in the igloo," Ruth said, her voice as dark as the sky.

They scrambled through the narrow entrance and curled toward each other, trembling. Outside, there was a long animal cry, a call like nothing Jenny had ever heard.

Ruth grabbed Jenny's coat, pulling her closer until their breaths were the same breath, their hearts one heart. Her teeth chattered violently. Jenny knew which story to whisper into Ruth's ear as the wind whistled through the trees, and there was the animal call again, and the horrible screaming of the man.

There was a spirit in the woods with the legs of a deer, who fed on the blood of traveling men, who protected children for nothing more than the gift of a stone bowl of cream left behind while the adults went to forage for food.

The man's burbling shrieks rose to the treetops, then went silent. Ruth pressed her fingers to Jenny's lips. An obscene smacking broke the quiet, and moans of such pleasure that red heat crawled along the back of Jenny's neck.

In time, the slurping was done and careful steps began circling the igloo. Circling and circling while the girls clutched each other until the steps faded and there was only the hush of snowfall. Jenny stayed vigilant until the uncles and aunt returned, cursing.

Aunt Alexis called for them and Jenny answered. The aunt ordered them to stay inside the igloo, all humor gone. There was nothing funny now. There was the grunting of effort, the swish of something heavy being dragged over snow.

Finally Aunt poked her head in. She brought her hand to Ruth's face, cupping her jaw. "We got caught in the storm. I'm so sorry."

Ruth shook her head as if to say no harm had come to her, though Jenny thought it had. They crawled out of the igloo and Jenny expected bloody snow, and guts hanging from branches. But a layer of white covered the campsite. The fire was out. The van was packed and running with two large fir trees strapped on top.

The uncles were subdued on the drive home. Aunt Alexis turned the radio on low and the uncles hummed along in quiet reverence. Jenny reached for Ruth's hand, and when Ruth rested her head on her shoulder, Jenny breathed in the scent of campfire smoke in her friend's hair, hopeful that there could bread and honey and fire and these friends, this warmth, this rising joy.

A Curse Aroused

Scott J. Couturier

Within the tomb:
Rustling of flaxen embalming bandages,
Creaking of sinews dry as sand.
Eyes withered to wrinkled sacs
Stare from orbits sunken & lidless,
Sarcophagus opening with eerie scrape.

Without the tomb:
Ringing of chisel & stab of spade,
Nocturnal delving by thieves
More rank than Mirai's jackals,
Wrapped in leprous cloth grave-stolen,
Hungry for gold & lapis, silver & myrrh.

Within the tomb:
Millennial malevolence at intrusion,
Curses of Pharaonic malice
On parched tongue behind rictus grin,
Lipless & distorted mien,
Shambling thing robed in wrappings moldering.

Without the tomb:
Covering-stone is sundered, thrust aside:
Crypt's mouth gaping wide on darkness musk-scented,
Faint remembrance of balsam & flowers
Smelt for but a passing second before
An unclean, evil fetor flows forth,
Accompanied by thud-shuffle of nearing footfalls
Sounding dully in aeonic dust.

Within the tomb:
Too late for roused vengeance to be averted,
Kingly lich of seven-foot-stature
Lurching down hieroglyph-glamored halls,
Spells for the Underworld graven in obsidian
To endure beyond even eternity's measure of years.
It emerges from interment, a monster of fright,
Spreading mephitis of deadly plague-spoor stink.

Though would-be robbers panic & flee,
Leaping atop camels & riding pell-mell
Through vastness of moonlit desert wastes,
Each is followed back by a fat black fly
That infests their tent with noisome drones.
All within a mere month's time will die.

The Third Horn of the Moon

Mark Howard Jones

> "But I hate the Moon and its horrible stony stare,
> And I know one day it'll do me some dreadful thing."
> —Robert Graves, "I Hate the Moon"

In the disfigured street outside, the approaching darkness was already chasing the people away. He hadn't had a customer for hours. Things were difficult and books were now a luxury rather than a consolation, it seemed.

Glancing up at the clock, Bedford saw with relief that he would be able to close up in twenty minutes' time. He had considered moving his business away from this part of town now that it was in decline. But there was his wife to think of.

He busied himself with mundane tasks, rearranging things and putting a particular book aside to make sure he remembered to take it with him when he left. The customer who had ordered it by telephone had paid a handsome sum for it. Bedford needed to post it to him as soon as possible.

The clock hand had crept forward another seven minutes by the time the shop door opened. Bedford looked up at this intrusion, which was unusual this close to closing time. A man of medium height stood just inside the door. The man had curly, slightly crinkly hair and wore a long dark coat. His eyes never seemed to stay still from second to second, constantly searching his surroundings for threats or clues.

As the man walked towards the desk, a dim beam of dust-laden sunlight appeared to follow him, dancing listlessly through the tangle of his hair. Then, as he drew closer to Bedford, the light seemed aware of its mistake and swiftly abandoned his sombre presence.

Bedford put on his best "can I help?" smile and waited.

"I'm looking for a copy of *Methodologies of the Makers* by Ambrose Cranford. In the original Jewelled Serpent edition, if you have it." The man's eyes glittered with a bilbliophiliac lust that Bedford saw often.

After a quick search of his catalogue, Bedford looked up. "I'm sorry, we don't have any editions of that book in stock at the moment," he said, making sure to add a hint of professional regret to his voice.

The man nodded. "A shame, a shame. Well, in that case, perhaps you have a copy of *The Gulfs of Februarius Reconsidered* by Sylphia Heron-Kristalle? Any edition will do."

Again the search was fruitless. Bedford shook his head regretfully. "I'm sorry, no."

"This *is* a bookshop, isn't it?" The man's peevish tone was clearly intended to get under the bookseller's skin.

Bedford indicated the laden shelves around them with a sweep of his arm. "As you see, sir."

"Very well. The book I'm really after—the volume I *actually* want—is called *The Three Horns of the Moon*." Having confessed his true intent, the man took a step backwards, a look of near-triumph on his face as he waited for his answer.

Bedford allowed a small flicker at the corners of his mouth, hoping it appeared merely considerate and didn't give too much away. He made a pretence of consulting his catalogue once more.

After a few moments he turned to the man. "Our occult section is well stocked, sir, with both new and vintage titles. Several guides make mention of it specifically. But I'm afraid we do *not* have that title in stock!"

"But I was told that you did have a copy!"

Another shake of the head. "I'm afraid you were misinformed, sir."

"Check again! Again!" The man now seemed quite agitated, and Bedford thought it best to comply with his unreasonable demand. Again he consulted the catalogue, knowing exactly what he would—and would not—find and again turned to the man with a courteous, cold smile.

"I'm sorry, sir. I can show you our occult section, if you wish to browse for something else," he said, calmly, knowing it would irritate the gruff, untidy man.

There was a thunderstruck look on the man's face. He stared at his shoes for a moment before inspiration seemed to strike him. "At least check the author for me. Maybe your catalogue isn't as foolproof as you think ... maybe something has been filed incorrectly."

Bedford drew himself up to his full height at the suggestion, intended to imply that his professional dignity had been wounded. "Very well," he consented. "The author's name, please?"

The man nodded eagerly. "Yes, it's Magnus Tretten-Greve. Spelt T-R-E-T- ... "

Bedford cut the man off with a swift sweep of his hand. "I am familiar with the spelling, thank you, sir." Once again the catalogue was plundered for information.

"Here it is. Magnus Tretten-Greve—eighteenth-century Norwegian sea captain, explorer, and occultist. An unusual combination of pursuits." He smiled at the man, attempting to charm him. The man's pained expression as he nodded his head quickly underscored the futility of Bedford's actions.

He scanned the alphabetical list quickly. "We have another title by that author, *Benighted Bones of the Giants*, but not the title you asked for."

The man shook his head vigorously. "No, no! No other book will do."

"It says here that it's by Magnus Tretten-Greve and Salva Soksis," continued Bedford.

"She was his scryer," muttered the man absent-mindedly.

Bedford faked a puzzled expression. "His what?"

"His scryer. She would—" He stopped himself mid-sentence and glared at the bookseller. "That is *not* the book I'm seeking!"

"Well, I'm very sorry, sir, but we don't have a copy of that particular volume in stock. What more can I say?" His amelioratory smile did nothing to soothe his customer, who glared at him with something near to hatred.

"You don't understand—I *need* this book!" The man slammed his palm down on the checkout desk, sending papers and leaflets flying. He then strutted away, throwing his arms out at odd angles like a petulant child.

"Please! My daughter . . . the doctors have failed her completely. She is dying! I've been told by certain sources that this book can provide the answer to . . ." He trailed off, perhaps realising for a moment how futile his request seemed.

Then he looked up at Bedford with the expression of a man being hunted by relentless agony. "I'll give anything for that book," he muttered.

"I do sympathise, really, sir. But if I don't have the book; I don't have it. I've only ever seen one copy of it, and that was several years ago."

There was nowhere left for him to go now. The sacrifice of his wife had been disastrously ineffective, her blood having proved too impure to secure the desired result. It was then that he knew he had to find another method.

Hints in obscure corners had led him to one bookseller after another. He could still feel the stickiness of the last man's blood on his fingertips, even though nothing was visible when he glanced at his hand. The man had pretended to have knowledge he did not possess; he had claimed to have the answer. But he had lied. That was unforgiveable.

Yet the answer had to be here. Too many sources had agreed that *this* was the place where it could be found. The shop had been dealing in near-miraculous volumes for close to three decades, by all accounts.

He groaned, softly. "All right, wait . . . wait. You people usually understand *this* best of all. I said I'd give you anything, and I will." Reaching inside his coat, he withdrew a large wad of banknotes, held together with several ageing elastic bands.

Bedford glanced down at the pile of grubby notes that the man had placed in front of him. He sighed slightly.

"You must understand, sir, that it isn't simply a question of money. Even if we had the book in stock, which we don't, it's also a question of your . . . aptitude."

"Aptitude?" The man's voice had the dismal quality of a stone being dropped into water from a height.

Bedford nodded slowly. "Yes. We can't simply let anyone purchase these volumes that you mentioned. Especially that particular book. There has to be some assurance that you are able to use it without any ill effects arising from the use. You do understand, I'm sure, sir?"

The man's face grew even darker, though he was reassured by the bookseller's tacit admission as to the power of the volume he sought. "No, I don't. You're acting more like a pompous librarian than a bookseller. What do I have to do to prove that I'm *worthy* of seeing this supposedly dangerous volume?"

Bedford smiled. "My wife *may* be able to help you. This is really much more her area of expertise."

At this news the man nodded enthusiastically. "Please fetch her!"

Bedford shook his head slowly. "My wife has a particular vocation. Some have called it a gift. This requires that she resides in very particular circumstances."

The small man bared his teeth in frustration. "Very well. Then how *can* I speak to her?"

"Follow me. Quickly, if you please. I'll be closing soon."

The man grabbed at his arm. "You can't close before you've sold me the book!"

Only when the bookseller gazed down at the man's strong fingers did he remove them from Bedford's sleeve. "Please. I've already told you—" He abandoned his explanation suddenly, realising that the man was in no mood to listen. Instead, he gestured impatiently. "Quickly!"

Plucking a loose button from his coat, the man began to follow Bedford, then paused for an instant to sweep the money back into his pocket as he passed. *No sense in wasting it,* he told himself, wholly intent on disposing of Bedford if he proved to be yet another disappointment.

With a few steps he was at Bedford's side. "My name is Arden. Edgar Arden," the man suddenly confided, unbidden. "You may have heard of me."

Bedford turned to him, smiling blandly. "It's this way." He indicated a door with peeling paint, hidden away at the back of the shop, next to the office.

Unlocking it, he said to Arden in a low voice: "I'll go first. Stay close to me." Behind the door was a steep staircase. The wooden stairs were uncarpeted and, as Arden brushed against the wall, a fine white dust coated part of his sleeve.

He fussed at it ineffectually as he ascended, almost bumping into Bedford, who had stopped suddenly. Arden found himself on a narrow landing, just a few steps wide. He shuffled sideways in order to stand next to his host.

Bedford smiled, inserted a key into the wooden door before them, and, unlocking it, swung the door inwards. Arden stepped sideways to enter the room, fully expecting to be followed by Bedford.

"I hope that you find what you're looking for," muttered Bedford before closing the door quickly on Arden. Turning to go back to his books, Bedford's steps faltered for just a moment or two on the stairs before continuing his descent.

Arden looked around the dimly lit room. It was icy cold, causing an involuntary shiver. Slow, dusty sunlight barely illuminated the perfectly square space.

It seemed as if all the silence in the world had been crammed into the room, filling it like an overstuffed piece of furniture. Arden's lungs found it difficult to decide whether the air was either very thick or absent altogether.

Some slight movement in a corner of the room made him jump. He didn't dare step forward, but he leaned over as far as he could and peered into the gloom.

Standing just an inch or two away from the deep corner of the room was a woman. She barely moved as her shadow-shrouded head turned ever so slightly in his direction.

Her almost skeletal form was covered by a simple shift dress in some dark colour. His spirits lifted a little when he saw the quarter-moon symbol picked out in gold on the woman's dress.

The woman herself was barely there, it seemed to Arden. *Perhaps she is desperately ill,* he thought, and suddenly felt ashamed of making any demands on her and her husband. God only knew what they'd been through, or were still going through.

Any feelings of shame were replaced by a memory of his daughter, running round and round his legs until dizzy, then clinging onto them as if they were the last solid thing in the world. She was the reason he was here, not this peculiar woman standing in the corner.

Her face was not clearly visible, as if she wore a mask of pale shadows, yet her eyes possessed an extraordinary clarity. They held him momentarily before he dragged himself away, unsure of where to look next. He had no idea what her husband had done to her, or asked of her, but in her fugitive gaze lay the ghost of the woman she used to be.

Both courage and a certain callousness were called for, Arden decided. "Excuse me. I—I was told by your husband . . . Is there to be some sort of test?"

The woman turned part of the way towards him. "Test?" Her voice seemed to come from somewhere near the ceiling. "No test, no."

Arden shuffled forward a few steps, unsure of what sort of person he stood in the presence of. He no longer felt in command. A dryness filled his mouth.

The woman's wandering gaze didn't promise much in the way of intellect, he thought, but maybe she had other abilities that weren't quite as obvious. He was aware of the sibyls and prophetesses of various cultures: they may not have been well-educated but they were adepts nonetheless. He hoped this woman had similar talents.

Eventually he managed to splutter through the dryness. "I—if not a test, then what?"

When she spoke it was with a ghost of a voice, something lost and almost forgotten. "The Goddess has been generous . . ."

He nodded, uncertain exactly what she meant. "The eclipse is next week," he muttered.

"An eclipse is not propitious." Her winter words chilled his heart. They sounded like the sea, hungry and devouring, dashing itself against the shore.

He forced himself to stare at her unsettling eyes once more. "But I've been told . . ."

Now her voice was hardly a whisper that he was forced to strain to hear. "You've been *told* . . . the wrong things. Mouths opening and closing, minds opening and decaying . . . But Ceridwen may find a place for you in her cold, dust-filled heart. If you believe strongly enough."

She indicated a table just under the grimy window. He couldn't imagine how he hadn't noticed it on first entering the room. On it lay a large book bound in a worn, dirty-looking leather binding.

He could just make out the gilded quarter-moon symbol shining feebly beneath the filth on the cover. His hands longed to open the book, just as his mind hungered to devour it, to find the answer he sought.

Yet just the few steps across the room to reach it felt like a trek across a vast plain, sun-blasted, pale, and empty.

Gazing down at the book at last, he could pick out more details on the cover. Some words were visible just beneath the layer of grime. The author's name was not as he'd expected. "But that's my name. How can that be? What—?"

Suddenly she was at his side, causing him to convulse slightly, eager not to touch her. Reaching past him with her thin hand, she opened the cover, seemingly unconcerned about the dust and mould covering the gritty leather.

Her mouth was at his ear, intoning enticing information.

"Stolen from the heretics library of revVen, buried these many centuries beneath the dust of the Sea of Tears," she said blandly. Then she withdrew, leaving the book to his eager attention.

"The revelations of Tanit are without end. The coming lunation is critical." He heard her fragile words, but his mind brushed them aside, too entranced by the treasure before him.

Some spider-scratched words were scrawled across the otherwise empty first page, near the bottom. He reached down to run his finger under the words, hoping somehow that this would open his mind to a greater understanding of the puzzling letters.

The instant he touched the book, he felt an unbearable sense of being entangled in the dim past; of having somehow participated in events unremembered yet still potent. Unclean. His instinct was to snatch his hand away, as if he had touched something toxic, but he forced his fingers down, splaying them out across the surface of the grimy paper. He struggled to remind himself that this was what he had sought so fervently.

He stared at the words, struggling to read them. But their meaning was just outside his grasp. Baffled by the impenetrable shapes, he dared to let his fingers stray to the page edge, grasping it firmly enough to turn it, despite its age.

Something resembling a dim mirror met his gaze, reflecting his face. Or a version of those depressingly familiar features, at least.

"Extraordinary!" He exhaled the word instead of saying it. Carefully, slowly, he reached down to touch the surface. It felt like ordinary paper beneath his fingertips, yet his touch started faint ripples moving across its miraculous surface.

When he next focused on his own reflection, his face wore the expression of a bemused idiot, so he quickly composed his features.

The page now appeared to be a hole and mirror at the same time. Its swimming darkness showed him who he was and who he didn't want to be but was being forced to become.

His mind contorted, wrestling with what his eyes showed him. He tore apart what he knew of himself, not wanting to believe what the reflection showed him. He clenched his eyes shut and reached for the page. It seemed far heavier than it should, but he finally managed to turn it.

Slowly opening his eyes, he breathed a small sigh of relief that the dreadful illusion was at an end.

The following two pages were black, entirely covered with ink. They contained no images or words whatsoever. "What? Is this some sort of a trick?"

"To call you a lunatic is an insult to the moon. Keep looking," said the soft, empty voice behind him. "There are no altars to Selene here."

He couldn't think what she meant but perhaps the next page . . .

"Go closer." Her voice was like frost in his ears, chilling his fingers, creeping across his heart. He trembled slightly as he detected a faint smell resembling cigarette smoke and rotten sardines rising from the pages, like incense from an ancient and obscene place. He gagged slightly. "Oh god . . ."

"Make no prayers to Kuu. She will not hear your words."

Steadying himself on the edge of the table, he stared down into the book. "But—but how can this help my—?"

"I never promised you help. You have put your faith in the chattering of fools." Her voice was drenched in midnight, her face eclipsed by the moonlight seeping in through the grimy windows. It had become dark too quickly, he thought. There was no time.

"The moon. The horns of the moon . . . I felt . . ." He became aware suddenly of how empty his words had become. He was just filling a hole with words.

"They *are* real," she said in a a voice that now sounded merely indifferent. At these words his spirits lifted slightly. "But they are not for you!" The words came from a million cold miles away before her whispered promise again brought them within distance of his numbed fingers. "I can show you if you want."

Desperation pushed aside any desire to know what might lie behind her change of heart. He could hardly breathe, gasping out the single word "Yes!"

She reached past him once more, turning the delicate page to reveal something that might have been a map. Or a puzzle. Or perhaps just random scribbling by whichever deranged hand had made the book. Her finger hovered over the meaningless scratches for a second before withdrawing. Had he missed it . . . had she been pointing something out to him? If so, he had been too slow to apprehend whatever it might be. He stared again at the cruel meaninglessness of the scrawled design.

"Rigantona may smile upon your plight. Or she may not. There is one road you can travel . . . but you cannot follow me. I tread the way alone but it is not a path—it is too broad, too long and too deep to be a path—but I *do* tread it alone. No man can follow me."

She raised a pale hand and pointed the way with a ragged-nailed finger. "Your way lies here. Turn the page." Obediently and with a sense of relief, he steeled himself for the shock of touching the thing and tried to turn the page using just his fingertips.

It was as if he was looking down into a narrow pit. Dimly he could make out shapes that had once been men, their dried husks lying one on top of each other. They looked desiccated and disjointed, as if they had lain there for hundreds of years. A layer of dust seemed to hover over the terrible sight, rising so very slowly.

Were there messages carried in the dust itself? Perhaps flickering traces of some ancient broadcast lingered on, atomised and floating before him. Mocked by these messages in an unreadable language, he felt numbed. For a moment he imagined small phantom fingers slipping into his palm and squeezing gently.

Life had hollowed him out—his dying daughter's defiant smile; his family turning their backs on him; his endless, sleepless search for an elusive cure. All these things felt like a code that he was too dim-witted to penetrate, or even apprehend fully.

Somewhere far off a bell began tolling, its tones long, low and sonorous. Religious rites always left him cold but somehow this bell had a timbre that seemed important, even vital. He sensed the woman moving behind him. "The third horn is the one that pierces your heart," said the frozen whisper.

He struggled to take his eyes away from the appalling sight before him, as the topmost figure shifted slightly to look up at him. He saw its eyes, emptied and desperate, as it met his gaze. Although it didn't seem possible, the room grew colder, the light dimmer.

He felt a sharp point an inch or two to the left of his spine, directly in line with his heart. Through the grime-caked window, the twin horns of the quarter-moon shone down clearly on his face as its third horn began to pierce him.

Downstairs, Bedford gazed out through the glass at the pale, mottled eye of the moon as he locked the shop door, thanking whichever god was watching over him that day that it wasn't looking at him. An unnatural cold seeped down through the ceiling, settling on the spines and page edges of the ancient volumes filling the shelves, freezing them in place.

> From *The Meditations of MonaMeni* in the latter section of
> *The Three Horns of the Moon,* Column 13, Tri-verse 7.

The daughter of the night spent her days basking in the light of her older brother, Sunnen, and knew the magnificence of his love every night. But she saw his greater regard for the empty creatures who walked in his light upon the Earth below and said to herself: "Are not these worms more beloved of my brother than I? He bestows upon them the warmth and light that is denied me. They are small and vile and vexatious things, not worthy of his great love or such generous gifts. I will make it so that some of these maggots worship me and I shall use them for my own ends whenever my radiant face shines upon them. And they shall forever be my prey."

Setebos to Caliban

Wade German

> Hoping the while, since evils sometimes mend,
> Warts rub away and sores are cured with slime,
> That some strange day, will either the Quiet catch
> And conquer Setebos, or likelier He
> Decrepit may doze, doze, as good as die.
> —Robert Browning, *Caliban upon Setebos*

"Decrepit may doze, doze, as good as die?"
Thou miscreation, open up thine eyes
And deeply drink the darkness all around:
Look up, O Caliban: behold the moon
That glides upon the night, a spectral corpse
From out the silent mansions of the tomb,
Surrounded by a floating horde of ghosts—
Or so the cloud rack seems, O simpleton,
From where thou sittest, like some grotesque monk,
In silent meditation on the shore,
Alone, as always, when the evening falls.
Such morbid imagery that fills thy mind,
Turning itself to things divine: to death
And gods, to ghosts and corpses, poet-like!
Look up, O Caliban: behold the moon;
Embody me therein to ease thine awe
And give this voice a source, a cold white shape,
To whom, as anyone, thou mightest speak.
Easier that, than try to comprehend
The strange black essence of the very night
Communicates directly to thy mind,
The first and final time it speaks to thee,

Last of a mutant line, a thing morose,
Sequestered there, vile, stupid and enslaved.

The nighted island sleeps; thou art awake,
Discerning shapes in shadow as in dream.
What matter if I come to thee in dream?
Thrice thou shouteth my name, summoning me,
Not knowing three time thus I am evoked.
Dost thou not know that I am with the dead,
And that the dead would duly have their sleep?
Thou dost not know the things that thou shouldst know;
And think a lumpish sea-beast Prosper snared
To form poor Caliban for drudgery,
But that is error: listen very well
O melancholy mooncalf, know the truth:
Thy mother was the last to worship me.
Old Sycorax was wise and kept my rites,
But understood the uselessness to teach
Her progeny, thus drifted to despair,
And when she died, I died along with her.
Thou wonderest just who her suitor was.
What imp of the perverse had moved her mind
To summon up thy father from the deep?
Ill-gotten knowledge, knowledge ill-conceived
That led to thy conception, cambion!
In fact, thy father was part cuttlefish,
A demon hatched in slime beneath the sea.
How strange the strength that bore thee, Caliban!
A witch without a midwife, on her own
And unfamiliar with abortive arts . . .
It was thy birth that built up her despair.
And now, with no one else with whom to speak,
The madness of thy mother in thy mind,
Thy crude imagination runs amok:

Such attributes hast thou attached to me!
Confused, uncouth the angles of thy thought,
Dim creature wallowing in ignorance
And making shadow puppets in a cave,
Squaring the circle with its brain contused!
A formless omni-this and omni-that,
A strange creator far beyond the world,
Outside of comprehension, noumenal,
(Though thou art right: I did not spawn the stars;
Beyond benevolence, malevolence,
Thou seest me as neither good nor bad).
Let me inform thee, dreary Caliban:
I class thee with the creeping, crawling things,
A beetle climbing on an endless wall
Upwards, as if perchance to take a peek
On some high rampart to the other side.
And what if thou beheldest black abyss;
Saw that beyond was chaos, undefined,
That nothingness now stared back into thee
With undiluted, cold indifference?
But thine imagination fills the void,
And moulds for me an image, floods the dark
With alternating eidola: at times
Thou thinkest me made of moonlight, wind and teeth,
Or as some ogreish giant in the clouds;
At other times a thing invisible—
Believing everywhere and all about
My presence may be found, if unobserved,
In marks thou hast interpreted in dirt . . .
Am I unstable, fluid, flowing in flux,
A thing dependent on which mood is thine?
Am I a vast black mirror to be filled
With thy reflection, grinning and grotesque?

The grave that flesh is heir to swallows all;
I saw some goodness waiting in the grave.
Sycorax died, and so I died with her;
I, too, now rot in something like a shroud.
The stirring of the worms had long-since ceased
In me, until a maggot—Caliban—
Began to blindly grope within my skull
And writhing, mumbled now and then my name,
Robbing me thereby of my well-earned sleep.
Thus have I come to thee, the first and last;
Until this moment, I thought not of thee.
Begone, O misbegotten one, begone;
Go back to backwards-rolling of thy dung.
Thou art a being I abominate.
I cast thee out, consider me no more,
Let not my name ooze out thine evil lips
And thereby conjure dead things from their sleep.

Ramsey's Rant: Musical Musings

Ramsey Campbell

At a recent bookshop event a kindly reader complimented me on the musical expertise she felt I'd displayed in *Fellstones*. I had to protest that I was and am merely an enthusiastic dabbler and layman—an amateur, in the French sense as well. Her comment set me thinking of my journey into music, a decidedly discursive process. I hope it provides enough diversions to be worth a read.

We begin with a mute and monolithic item—the radiogram, a combined radio and gramophone, that sat in the front room at 40 Nook Rise throughout my childhood. I assume it was one of the pieces of furniture my mother brought from home, insisting they must oust those my father had kept as remembrances of his mother's life. It was the size of a small desk, but if it ever emitted a sound in my lifetime, it soon fell terminally silent and was covered with a cloth to signify its passing. A succession of portable radios, in those days frustratingly erratic when it came to tuning stations in, took the place of one of its functions, but the house did without a working turntable until I turned ten or thereabouts. An ad in the *Liverpool Echo* offered a gramophone for a sum pretty paltry even then, and with free delivery too, and so either I or my mother—possibly both—paid the price.

The player proved to be housed in a leggy cabinet several feet high, into which one inserted a handle to wind up the mechanism, vintage indeed. Within the cabinet a niche contained a handful of 78 rpm discs: a popular Rachmaninov piano piece, the adagio from the Moonlight Sonata, Liszt's third Liebesträume and so forth. While I played those over and over, I confess my preadolescent pref-erence—I blush, I burn, I shudder, while I pen the damnable atroci-ty—was for the likes of Tommy Steele and Cliff Richard. The

Goons joined my collection too, not least their scatological song that was banned by the BBC (surprisingly so, since the broadcaster allowed equally transgressive gags and sound effects on the team's weekly show).

None of my pop obsession should be directly blamed for my floundering as a performer into the field. While at primary school I acquired a plastic ukelele my mother persuaded me I played well—not only that, but well enough to perform for an audience. To begin with I believe those consisted of polite although no doubt covertly pained neighbours, but I somehow ended up convinced I should go on stage for the school concert that ended my first term at secondary school. I believe the sight of me attempting not to drop the cordless ukelele while assassinating some of Lonnie Donegan's skiffle hits passed into legend. Disconcerted though I was by the flood of mirth that assailed my performance, the show had to go on, and doggedly did. At the next year's concert a guitarist friend Paul Ennis and I topped the bill as Campbell and Company. By now I too had a guitar and a cord to hold it up, but little skill. It hardly helped that since we were cleared out of the classroom while attempting to practice, we rounded out the concert unrehearsed. Our last song was "Frankie and Johnny," cut short by an understandable onstage intervention from the show's producer. Perhaps Captain Beefheart might have found some interest in our performance, since I was playing in a different key from Paul.

To some extent I was involved in official musical activities. In my first year at that grammar school I was confronted with plainchant, a species of music (with the luminous exception of Hildegard von Bingen) I find possibly even more boring to hear than to perform, though I was required back then to do the latter. My halting bid to read the blocky score apparently qualified me for membership in the choir, about which I recall little other than a performance at a school prizegiving of passages from *Prince Igor*, where my unstably adolescent voice reduced me to miming the music, less like a vocalist than a fish. I was also briefly involved in the school orchestra, having learned a simple examination piece for the cello, which let me pretend I could read scores rather than simply remember the music. I got out as soon as I could.

The BBC roused my first real enthusiasm for (to use an imprecise term) classical music, when an edition of the Sunday lunchtime record request show Two-Way Family Favourites included "Tempus est iocundum" from Orff's *Carmina Burana*. By the time I succumbed to its seduction I'd forgotten what had been announced, and wrote to the BBC for information. Armed with the title, I had recourse to a record shop in Liverpool, only for my request to be met with something very like contempt by a shop assistant (who did however deign to recommend the Eugen Jochum version, still a leader in a crowded field). To be fair, in my middle years I came to dismiss the work myself, but I've rediscovered its charms since.

On a lunch break from my civil service job when I was sixteen I went to see the Beatles at the Cavern. The acoustic rendered them more deafening than musical, and I didn't experience them again until I saw the two Dick Lester films. I found their songs mildly entertaining, but remained unconvinced of more until a review of *Revolver* in the *Village Voice* (to which I subscribed for Andrew Sarris's film reviews) made large claims for them, though falling short of Tony Palmer's grotesque assertion that they were the finest songwriters since Schubert. I heard much to enjoy, and the *Sergeant Pepper* album took even more of my fancy, but the white album came as a disappointment—too many songs too trivial to be redeemed by sonic inventiveness, at least to my ear.

Films sent me on my next quest. Finding Beethoven's 7th once I was haunted by the use of the adagio in Jacques Demy's *Lola* gave no trouble, but locating the Mozart that recurs throughout Agnes Varda's *Le Bonheur* proved to be a different matter. I had recourse to the music library, where I displayed the extent of my ignorance by borrowing a disc of Mozart's clarinet concerto, even though the two soundtrack pieces by the composer are scored respectively for quintet and for woodwind. It took me years to identify the clarinet quintet and the Adagio and Fugue, not least because the latter had been orchestrated for the film, but by then I'd immersed myself in the concerto and a great deal else of Wolfgang. Serendipity has long been my friend.

My classical journey gathered momentum in the late sixties, propelled by several advisors. Let me not diminish that of Rosemary Prince, my fleeting fiancée of 1967. She was a flautist who, as I recall, had studied with Atarah Ben Tovim. She introduced me to the music of several composers who have since become beloved, not least Britten, although our first encounter with his *War Requiem* (which I've come to place among the greatest English choral works) was conducted by the ponderous Charles Groves, who displayed an apparently habitual penchant for taking breaks not provided in the score. Similarly, a performance of Bach's *St Matthew Passion* (among my favourites of my favourite composer together with Beethoven) failed to engage me much, not least in the absence of a printed libretto to help me understand the proceedings. My first encounter with Debussy's *L'après-midi d'un faune* might have put me off for life. Involved in a concert as a flautist, though not the soloist, Rosemary coerced me into reading the entire Mallarmé poem (in a stumbling French mumble and then, as not much of a relief, in English) as a preamble to the hapless audience. Happily, I later learned to relish Claude's work.

Where might Rosemary be now? Enjoying her music, I hope, as performer and aficionado. Other advisors of mine have gone on to higher things too. Barry Forshaw is a celebrated expert on crime fiction, who in the sixties worked at Beaver Radio in Liverpool and often recommended recordings: for one example of many, I owe my experience of Berio's Viola Concerto (alas, no longer in the catalogue) to him. His colleague Alan Price (these days a noted poet and online essayist) soon moved to Circle Records, Mike Roberts' shop dedicated to classical and jazz. I still recall Alan introducing me to Mahler's 3rd (the Leinsdorf version), which was a revelation and the start of a lifelong commitment to the composer. These days Andy

Brown of Psychamok in Wallasey does his best to guide my stumblings through the mysteries of rock, though Matteo Carnio was first to recommend the Residents (check the official video of "Gingerbread Man," that unsettling song cycle, for a taste).

In 1967 I worked at Liverpool Central Library, where in the staff canteen I often saw an intensely introverted young woman reading music scores as most of us might read a book. When I was moved to the music library I sometimes encountered a barely teenage reader, if he was even so old, as awkwardly precocious as I'd been at his age. His loans were of scores too. Years had to pass before I grasped how significant serving Simon Rattle had been, and his sister Susan was the reader in the canteen. Meanwhile, my months in the music library offered the option of unlimited borrowing of discs, of which I took vigorous advantage, greatly expanding my sphere of experience: Penderecki's *St Luke Passion*, Messiaen's *Turangalila*, Ives' Fourth Symphony, Ligeti in quantity . . . We received the *Gramophone* each month, and recommendations in the column on pop sent me in search of Jefferson Airplane and the Incredible String Band and the United States of America, among others. They're still with me.

All this and the subsequent considerable collection I haven't space to specify might lead the reader to expect more music in my tales than can be found. "Never To Be Heard" plays with it, as does "Concerto in Five Movements" (yes, I know those are rare; that was rather the point). I can only hope *Fellstones* does my amateur enthusiasm justice. Perhaps a column looking in detail at favourite works might help? Readers dismayed by the prospect should make their protests heard—in chorus, by all means.

The Phantom Bus

W. Elwyn Backus

[Backus (1892–1979) was an American writer who published six stories—two of them serialized short novels—of horror and science fiction in *Weird Tales*. This story appeared in the September 1930 issue.—ED.]

1

Out of the vagueness of the half-dawn a dark bulk loomed to the accompaniment of a dull rumble. To Arthur Strite, waiting for his regular bus—the big, orange six-forty-five to the city—this nondescript contraption which usually preceded it by a minute or two seemed more like a ghostly coffin than a public conveyance. Its sweating black sides glistened oilily in the gray light as it passed him. A single dim incandescent lamp seen through the windows silhouetted stiffly nodding heads against the background of a dingy interior. Then the black bus was gone, swallowed up in the swirling December mist and fog.

As always, a feeling of odd disquiet possessed Strite with the passing of this conveyance—a fleeting impression of mystery, strangely repellent and defying description; of ill omen. What manner of passengers it carried or whence and whither it traveled, he did not know—and cared less. Yet, queerly enough, the affair had increasingly irritated and disturbed him ever since his moving to Emerymont three weeks before.

"Just an old junk-heap that loops out through Norwood and back over this direction," a fellow commuter said in answer to his question. Until this morning Strite had refrained from what he deemed the weakness of a query about this thing. For he had hesitated to give definite shape to his senseless disquiet by admitting any curiosity, even to himself. "I believe a couple of death-traps like that one comprise the company's entire rolling-stock," his informant finished.

"Oh," said Strite, mentally categorying the bus line with several that operated a sort of cross-country service between outlying sections of Cincinnati. Of course, he reflected, *some* concern had to serve this need. But he was conscious of a feeling of relief that he did not have to use that service.

Arthur Strite was boarding in Emerymont with the Ransons, not because of any liking for the make-believes, the rabble of bourgeoisie and scandalmongers that peopled the little suburb, but because he did enjoy the shrubbery and lawns and the quaintly designed houses, despite the crazy butting of garbage-can-studded back yards against living-room windows of adjoining homes. He minded his own business, displaying no curiosity in the neighbors or affairs of the place—which was one of the reasons why he had not discovered sooner the purpose of the bus line mentioned.

The night of the same day he had asked about the bus, he found himself pondering, with some intentness in the midst of an absent-minded perusal of the evening comic sheet, on the dingy conveyance that passed him each morning. Why should that silly bus thus intrude itself into his mind? He smiled self-indulgently and turned over to the sports page. The thing actually was becoming a nuisance! And for no logical reason. What should it matter to him how uninviting, how disagreeable a box on wheels those people rode in every morning?

Nevertheless, he dropped off to sleep thinking about the ghostly bus.

The same thing began to be the rule on the nights that followed. Always that ridiculous feeling of indefinable dread would come over him, would cling tenaciously to his thoughts from the moment he happened to think of having seen the shadowy bus that morning. He had half a notion to hail the confounded contraption some morning and see where it took him, just to dispel all this absurd air of mystery about it which had so unaccountably fastened upon him. Though perhaps there was some reason for his strange obsession after all. Not quite one year before, his fiancée, Doris Tway, had been killed in a terrible bus crash. He remembered the crumpled remains of the fatal bus, which he had seen afterward, vividly. It, too, had been black and shabby. An odd girl—she had always said that if she left first, she would return for him. Her idea of a joke, of course, but unusual.

In spite of his notion about hailing the other bus, Strite did not ride it—not for several weeks anyway, although its daily rumbling and jangling approach, made more eery by the shortening of the days, had driven that impression of weird mystery deeper than ever into his waking thoughts. Waking, because, so far, the dark bus had troubled him only during the evenings before he retired.

However, there came a night when he dreamed that he obeyed an impulse and boarded the strange bus!

He was conscious of a sickly odor as he entered the rickety door, which had slid back with a softness in strange contrast to the outward clatter of the conveyance. The vizor of the operator's cap was pulled well down over his face as he leaned over his levers. Strite felt the bus begin to move. Oddly, there was no vibration, none of the jarring rattle and bang he had expected. He might have been on a river barge, for all the motion he could feel. Startled more by this unnatural quiet than he could have been by the loudest of banging or jolting, he raised his eyes toward the occupants of the bus. Perhaps it was the strange effort this act seemed to impose upon him; at any rate, he awoke in that instant, seized by unreasoning, incomprehensible terror!

It was an hour before his taut nerves had relaxed enough to let him drop off to sleep—and not before he had vowed to ride that bus in fact the next morning.

2

Strite did not ride the black bus the next morning. It was nearly seven o'clock when he opened his eyes from a troubled sleep. This meant that he would be late to the office where he worked, on the other side of the city. Of course he missed his regular bus, and, with it, the other. Too, the daylight put a different aspect upon things. It would have been ridiculous, after all, to board a bus bound for another part of the city merely to humor a crazy impulse.

Yet, when that night came, Strite hesitated to go to bed. He told himself that he was hopeless, a fool and a coward. Then he undressed and resolutely turned out the light.

His hesitancy had not been unfounded. Again he found himself boarding the mysterious, sweating conveyance with its leaning operator and strange, illusive odor. And again a sudden agonized awakening.

But this time he saw the other occupants before he awoke. They all—there were six of them—had their eyes closed as they sat nodding slightly with the almost imperceptible swaying of the bus. There was a repellent something about those faces, other than their closed eyelids, that struck a chill into Strite's heart. He wondered whether they were just weary, like him, or—

A cold finger touched his wrist. He managed to turn and face the operator. The latter, his face still hidden, was pointing to the fare box. Of course, these ill-built, ill-kept buses *would* reverse things by demanding their fare when one entered. He readied into his pocket for a dime, and in that moment caught sight of a seventh passenger, seated in front on the other side. The operator's head and shoulders had partly hidden her from him before, despite her slender tallness.

As his fingers found and automatically brought forth a dime, he observed that this passenger's eyes were not closed like the rest— that they were pale gray and staring at him. They were like—oh, God, it couldn't be—Doris! But it was—it was! How could he have failed to recognize her sooner, despite her position on the other side of the operator? Now he could understand why this bus had drawn him so strangely, irresistibly.

As he stared back at her, speechless with amazement, her eyes left his face, turned toward the windshield. Her pale lips twitched oddly, as if, mute with fear at what she saw there, she sought vainly to scream.

Then abruptly the spell was broken. She leaped to her feet, throwing one arm across her face in a gesture of one warding off some fearful harm. A shrill, hysterical scream pierced the quiet of that closed space like the stab of a knife!

That cry jarred Strite back to consciousness with a suddenness that jerked him upright in bed.

As he sat there trembling with the realism of his dream and that agonized scream, he became aware that he held something tightly in one closed hand. A fresh chill passed through his body at the familiar feel of that something. He needed no light to tell him that it was a dime he clutched—the dime he had been ready to drop in the fare box of his dream!

3

Of course he found that the coin evidently had fallen out of his vest when he sat on the bed while undressing. In fact, he usually kept some change in his vest pocket so as to have it handy for tips, newspapers, and such. Perhaps the accidental finding and touching of that coin in his slumbers had even started the train of thought that had made him dream of the fare box—and the other things. But there was no more sleep for Strite. After tossing about for the rest of the night, he got up about five o'clock.

This morning he was determined upon one thing. He would ride the black bus—"the phantom bus," as he had come to term it privately—this morning, and kill for once and all this persistent subconscious illusion that had taken root in his mind from the seed of his first absurd impression of the rickety conveyance in the eery light of half-dawn.

Once more his intention was to be defeated, however. The black bus failed to appear before the six-forty-five, though he had arrived at its stop more than a quarter-hour before it was due. He even waited for it ten minutes after his regular bus had gone—only to learn later that the other line finally had been discontinued.

His first reaction to this information was an overwhelming relief. No longer would he be reminded by this shadowy rumbling hulk each morning, of things he wanted to forget.

But on the heels of this thought came the realization that the very discontinuance of the line had removed all chance of his ever killing the illusion if the latter continued to trouble him.

That day at noon as he walked along a downtown street a peculiar odor halted him. There was an illusive, dread familiarity about it. He was before a florist's open shop, and a great bowl of tuberoses, those once choice flowers for all those departed, was set out in front. He knew now where he had smelled their scent before—on the phantom bus of his dream.

4

Once again Strite was in the phantom bus—in his subconscious mind. This time he knew exactly what was coming. He seemed powerless to change a single detail of it all. The pause just inside the doorway as he forced his gaze up to where the six passengers sat in plain view, their eyes closed, in death-like weariness or worse. The icy touch of a finger on his wrist, the reaching for a coin, and the discovery of the slender, tall girl up front. Doris!

At this point the sequence of events suddenly galvanized him into a feverish alertness for the next thing. As Doris' hysterical scream rang in his ears, he was abruptly released from the grip of immobility. He turned quickly and looked out of the front of the bus.

What he saw there made him throw up his hands in an involuntary gesture similar to her own instinctive gesture of terror. He heard the brakes squealing shrilly—felt the bus skid on the sleet-covered road even as he caught a side glimpse of the operator's face—saw with sudden added horror that half the face was missing. Beyond that fleeting glimpse, he had time for no further examination; for just ahead a heavily loaded truck was emerging from a narrow bridge-end, blocking their way. Then a terrific, rending crash. . . .

5

The six-forty-five bus was four minutes late on account of the icy condition of the roads; they had been that way for two days. A little group of commuters on the roadside were talking in subdued tones, for once unmindful of the delay as they waited.

"Personally," a pompous, red-faced man was saying, "I believe Ranson killed and—mauled—him for attentions to Mrs. Ranson."

"But Strite didn't appear to be that type," objected a young member of the group. "Nor is Mrs. Ranson the sort who would encourage him. Besides, consider the condition of the body. Why, Ranson or no one else could have so mangled another—to say nothing of leaving it in bed and persistently claiming that he didn't know how it happened, except that he and his wife were awakened in the middle of the night by a frightful cry—and found him that way! No, I say there is some deeper mystery about the affair, the nature of which we haven't suspected."

The big, orange-colored bus hove into view at this juncture, interrupting the discussion for the time. Presently they all had boarded it and found seats at various vantage-points. A little distance along the road one of them pointed out to his neighbor a twisted and splintered mass of wreckage at the foot of an embankment of the narrow bridge they were just then crossing.

"Lucky it jumped off when it struck—didn't even delay us yesterday when we followed a few minutes after it was discovered."

"Queer thing about how it got there," said the other. "Nobody witnessed the accident, and the defunct bus company's officials swear that the last they saw of their 'death trap' was when it was locked away in an old garage on the other side of Norwood. Can you imagine any one swiping a can like that for a ride? But the present-day young coke-head will grab anything for a joy-ride."

"No queerer than that—that mess inside the wreck—as if some one had been crushed like—well, like poor Strite, for instance. Yet they could find no trace of a body!"

A Schizophrenic's Diary

Aditya Dwarkesh

The Farm

The dying yellow light illuminating various modestly sized stalls on the ground glowed from naked bulbs strung together by exposed wires. It was 5 P.M. and already pitch black: such were the winters here. Garbage lay strewn on the grass across the ground; thick smog made it difficult to breathe. The paradox of dirty country air was one among many found here. My exhales produced dense plumes of mist; and so with each breath, winter reminded me of and affirmed its hold over this land.

Book fairs in this small town never did boast of a large attendance, but the level of apathy on display this time made it plain that this horse had been beaten dead. All that took place now was a grotesque attempt at reanimation which everyone would perhaps be better off without. There were at best eight or ten people, browsing the stalls haphazardly, knowing nothing of interest would be found by them.

The town was many hours away from any city, on the edge of nowhere. Where I lived was another half an hour north of the town, in the middle of nowhere. I was beginning to regret my decision to make the journey here and see the vulgar exhibition of decay that this book fair had turned out to be.

A drunken couple stumbled out. I realized that I had been standing unmoving for long enough to attract a few funny looks, and began moving toward the closest functioning stall. Each one looked as forlorn as the next.

A thin man sat on the ground, seemingly hiding himself from the world behind the towers of damaged and forgotten books he was selling. Wrinkled skin and white beard. He leaned against one of the bamboos propping up the small stall and smoked something.

I began looking through the titles, before realizing that most of them no longer had any discernible title—it had been erased by the passage of time. One of them, perhaps, had never been given a title; it was just a handwritten diary.

I asked the man to take it out for me; for it was sandwiched in the middle of the tower, and I was afraid of having it all collapse in my clumsiness. He glanced up at me and airily waved his hand in a manner that I understood to indicate that I should remove it myself.

I could have sworn the tower started quaking even before I made a movement. And I needed to give it only the gentlest of tugs before half the books stacked above it came crashing down all over the damp and dirty soil. The man examined the situation before him, and I prepared myself for his admonition. But he merely turned away wordlessly and went back to smoking that untold substance.

I withdrew and rubbed my hands together. They had started getting numbed by the cold. If I were to check the temperature, it would read a completely reasonable 14 degrees Celsius. It was always 14 here in winters, but it never felt the way it should. The chill went all the way to the bone. Where I lived, devices could not be relied upon: Not for the time, for the light began leaving at midday; and not for the cold, for one would be shivering regardless of the temperature. No causal explanation could make sense of the soul of this place.

I bent down to undo some of my damage and rearrange the books.

"Let them be."

The voice was ragged and metallic. I turned toward it. He still hadn't looked at me.

Old regional music was wafting from a radio, presumably hidden somewhere inside his jacket. It was so tinny and soft that I had not even registered its presence until now. And now that I did, I could not understand any of the words that were being sung. Nor did they appear to gravitate toward or suggest any discernible human emotion. It was as if they were being sung by nobody, out of nowhere; as if the music had always been there, and would always be hovering around this region, long, long after all book fairs were past.

I stood back up and picked up the book that had originally caught my attention. But before I could browse through the pages, the same voice uttered:

"If you want to read this one, you must buy it first."

It was only because there was nobody else around us that I could be certain the voice belonged to the man on the ground. He cut a strikingly despondent figure, crouched on the ground, consuming as well as consumed by his substance. It seemed as if nothing could have provoked him out of his reverie and into human speech. And yet, I had.

My grasp over the local language—which I could still neither read nor write—was rudimentary at best. Perhaps I simply misunderstood.

"I'm just seeing—"

"If you want to read this one, you must buy it first."

At last, he was looking at me. His voice had acquired an almost startling sharpness. My eyes met his, and I saw in them senseless violence and righteous anger. Seeing that it was in my best interests to put the book back and put some distance between myself and him, I began doing so. But this didn't please him either. He had made up his mind about somehow offloading it onto me.

"You have to buy this now."

"Why?"

He stood up with some effort. "You cannot leave without buying this."

I realized what he was playing at. Everyone around here was always trying to swindle you and make a quick buck out of you. It was tiresome and sickening, and I no longer had the energy to stand my ground against it. Conceding frustratedly, I resolved not to come for this again next year—if, that is, the whole thing didn't cease altogether by then.

"How much?"

At my submission, his demeanor changed. He took a moment to register it and then collapsed back down on the ground. I took a few small steps backwards, his erratic behavior making me warier.

He waved a hand to signal that I leave and went back to his smoke. At my hesitation he repeated: "Take it."

I grabbed it and left. I was unable to endure him any longer. The music played on in the stark silence that followed.

On my way back by means of the shoddy local transportation, the smog was so thick as to render visibility practically nil. The roads were illuminated by streetlights sparse and dying, and peppered with abandoned stalls that had never seen a proprietor, forgotten gates that appear to lead to nothing, and an occasional signpost made inscrutable to me by an unknown language. The only thing around for acres was farmland that was no longer used.

The vehicle's lights briefly illuminated something that was once a dog and now but a smattering of decaying fur, carpeting the middle of the road, probably a victim to some truck with unknown destination and unknowable purpose. Somehow I could still hear the old, crackled music. I realized that it had not been from any radio inside the man's pocket; it must be coming from huge speakers somewhere far off. Another mystery: I could only wonder who was partying in these empty farmlands on this cold, moonless night.

I stared at this fragile diary in my hands. It was clearly something the man in the fair simply wanted to get rid of. Perhaps there was something wrong with it. The whole interaction had left a bad taste in my mouth, and this book being its outcome, my confused thoughts provoked within me the desire to dispose of it as quickly as I could. I had to resist the impulse to simply fling it out of the vehicle.

All this was simply irrational thinking, and it lost much of its power when I entered the familiar security of my living quarters. My residency was located inside the premises of a science institution, where I had been posted for a temporary year-long position.

With some curiosity I searched the book's pages for a name and found none; but saw, to my surprise, an address written down—an address that was none other than this institution's.

This coincidence demystified the object for me to a significant extent. I was not particularly interested in being subjected to the humdrum preoccupations of some student of this place—although how it ended up in that dilapidated stall posed an interesting question. As I was also intrigued by the possibility that the author may be someone I have had acquaintance with, I began reading that shabbily handwritten and tattered diary of a stranger.

The music seemed to be getting louder.

The Diary

11 June

I want to keep this diary as a record of my deteriorating sanity. Not because I think such a record may help me in some chimeric future—the nature of my existence is far too radical to ever allow any help to reach me—but because I am still capable of recognizing that the manner of this deterioration is, in fact, a thing of profundity par excellence. By a thorough examination of this deterioration, one may acquire the vision needed to look into the heart of the world, see the sculpture hidden by the veil, the face behind the mask, the truth under the lie.

I no longer recall when I first started hearing their voices and seeing these visions. And for the longest time I knew not what they meant.

The first question a disembodied voice provokes is one of ownership. If it has an owner to be spoken of. My imagination would run wild, invoking a variety of spectral creatures, cursed souls, and infernal ghouls attempting to communicate to me from some netherworld. But the truth of my condition was far more damning.

Today evening, after work, I went to the supermarket. I had to go at least once a week, but it was an ordeal I hated. This was one of the most common places for me to have severe attacks of my condition, and as a result, being there imparted a heavy psychological strain upon me.

My kitchen had been missing some sauce. I turned into an aisle stacked with rows of bottles of it. I wanted something hot. Most people here weren't too big on spicy things, although I did spot some almost devastating-looking sauces. I finally settled on a slim bottle that contained some reasonably threatening-looking sauce with a label that screamed "Hot Pepper Sauce" in a bright red font against a yellow background.

Nothing happened when I picked it up.

I moved into the aisle with rice. Basmati rice was the most appealing to the palette, but it was also more expensive than most others. I wasn't particularly picky about food, and jasmine rice was relatively cheaper.

Which one?

All laid out on the shelf in front of me. All threatening to chatter untold tragedies their creation was witness to into my ear. All waiting to overwhelm me with the humanities their production suppressed.

I took a deep breath and reached out for the two-kilo packet of jasmine rice. I was on the precipice of a chasm.

I grasped the packet. Nothing happened.

I picked it up and put it in my cart. Had people been observing, they would have noticed the subtlest of unnaturalities in my movements, induced by a deep and omnipresent anxiety.

For those prone to hallucinations, the purported task of psychiatric medication is to ground the victim back to reality. But what of those unfortunates, such as me, for whom those hallucinations constitute their only window into reality?

Soon I was nearly done. I just had to get my stuff billed and pay. I started putting everything on the counter one by one. I noticed that the cashier was the same girl who had billed me when I was here last week. She had colored her hair pink. As she scanned my things, I thought about asking her what her name was.

Then again, maybe I didn't need to ask her at all. Maybe I'll end up knowing in that other inexplicable way. On an impulse I grabbed from one of the racks near the billing counter a green packet of ch—

A lone man with a hat is softly singing to himself, and his gruff yet sweet voice is drowned in the animalistic hum of a huge machine. The cold evening sun of the North glints on its metal. He's deciding what to buy his son for his birthday. He remembers that he had been asking for a watch for a while. That would make a nice gift. Not a very expensive one, though; boy wasn't yet responsible enough for that. He remembers how he learnt the meaning of responsibility in his own childhood, and all the fearsome beatings he had incurred from his father during the learning process. No, he would never do that to his own son. I'll make my fair share of mistakes as a father, but it won't be the ones made by mine. In the time it took for these thoughts to pass him by, seven rows of potato lay uprooted by the harvester.

There is a moment of disorientation when she walks through those glass doors, having done so countless times that week. The analysts had just finished their training session and went into their separate booths. She grasps the door handle and recollects the features of the samples. Two and four had the largest difference in oil content. Someone gives an instruction to dim the lights in the booths. The practice was a recent innovation, when findings last year reported how much of a psychological bias the visual stimulus can induce. It was soon becoming an industry-wide standard. Now: if they reported a difference more in terms of flavor rather than texture, it was trouble.

A drop of rain takes a glitch-filled path down a glass window. High up above the city in one of those dystopian glassy skyscrapers hosting numberless anonymous workplace cubicles, an air-conditioned room divorces its occupants from the battering of the elements outside, cocooning them in comfort. The room has also been sheltering an endless argument; raised voices are juxtaposed with the smell of stale fruit. One of the people in it is taking a nap; he now wakes up with a jolt. That part of his self, dominant in his college days, which had wanted to create something of genuine value for the world, which had housed some artistic drive, had long since ended its existence. He once again interrupts the conversation with his preferred hue of green for the item at hand, offering a lazy, offhand justification. It was all posturing. Nobody pays him any attention. He might as well not have been there.

Skip, skip, skip, skip, ah, Zeppelin, perfect. It's a long drive ahead. The truck pulls out of the warehouse. On the way out of the complex, he crosses numerous other office complexes. Once in a while he looks at them wistfully, wishing he was educated enough to be able to breach that impenetrable barrier that lay between him and white-collar work. Life could have been so much more comfortable, money would have come so much easier. Of course, he is grateful for what he does have. Trucking is far from the worst job in the world. And since last year, he worries a little less about taking care of their parents. His brother, at least, seemed destined for a brighter future. He recalls with pride the way the kid now toils in his little room, studying for hours on end.

She begins unloading the carton onto the shelves, thinking, all these packets of shit for stupid unhealthy pricks who keep on eating junk. She knew she should be grateful she even managed to get a job, given her legal history. Women prone to fits of psychotic rage as intense as hers found themselves ending up inside a prison more often than not. One day she would sit and figure out where this endless rage came from. But for now, as hard as she tried, she simply couldn't dredge out that gratitude from within. Not when the job was something as pointless as this one. She was fond of remarking edgily that she'd really rather starve than have to go through this to put food on her plate. Saying it out loud helped her cope with the realities of her life. A green-colored packet slips and falls. She glares at it angrily and flings it back on the shelf.

For some length of time I had been able to resist an understanding of what was happening to me. But I know now that this world has been shaped such that the distance between any entity symbolic of a productive climax and the people who made it what it is is far vaster than one fathoms; the terrain cultivated between them poisonous beyond comprehension, such that not even the bravest cartographer dares map its geography in its entirety.

There can be no compromise. A way of life coexistent with symptoms of such an order is a mirage, one I chased for many years before finally recognizing its treachery and accepting the finitude of my sanity in the face of such trials. The world is a spiderweb with no mother, and each string of silk is an endless, complex narrative of madness. Every life around me was fragmented down to the bitter end, and these shards broken out of our beings only found a perverse unity in these humdrum objects that we helplessly to come together to create.

I now understood the fearsome unity my hallucinations formed, always bound together into a fatal significance and made incarnate by that which lay in my hand at that moment.

A packet of chips.

13 June

I was forced to use for warmth this brown woollen blanket, but its powers had been reduced to the purely physiological; it no longer gave me that soporific sense of comfort that it is one's birthright to demand from a blanket, for the revelation of how distant and quietly violent its birth was engendered an inescapable alienness to it. Equally cruel was the transmutation of my yellow night lamp from warm and comfortable to jagged, unknown, vaguely threatening; all these aspects being related to the scattered knowledge of its genesis that had been forced upon me. No longer was it a recourse for me on unnerving nights; indeed, it had become yet another source of discomfort in a room populated by them, by objects from the abyss of everydayness. Elements from the vast, cold world outside had penetrated into my chambers and clung onto things in it, reminiscent of parasites that have corrupted their host so deeply that one no longer knows where one ends and the other begins. In anything I turned my attention to, I saw the essential *strangeness* of the object, made all the more fearsome by its unassuming manner. Nothing was free of this sickness. The bottle of water I used to quench my thirst had the most terrifying story to tell of them all, and I had to fight off the impression of rancidity it gave the water held within every time I wanted a drink.

The true horror of it all lay in its mundanity.

The longer I live, the more torturous must my existence become, for with the inexorable passing of time, more and more of the world around me and the things in it were stripped to their disgusting nakedness. The difficulty a trip to the supermarket presented to me was an undeniable indicator of the fact that I was slowly but surely becoming incapable of functioning in society. But there was no need for me to dwell on how doomed my future looked; the present was foul enough.

Novels were a form of escapism that often worked for me. But unfortunately, even stories cannot escape the necessity of having a material medium in order for me to receive them. It is this materiality that was inescapable. Today's evening had begun with me listening to some folk music and reading a book in the living room; but as I turned one fatal page, the airy vocals of the song started acquiring a harsher, more vengeful tone to them, jarringly different from what it had been like. And as the music seamlessly transformed into the sounds of a heated argument, I began sensing a certain rage in the gaze of the letters printed on the book; a rage expressed artfully in the curves and edges of the script. I was being exposed to an argument that had taken place in the publishing house over the choice of typeface, I realized.

I tried to focus on my breathing and ground myself back into the present. Unsuccessful. The din of the quarrel turned into the sound of a power tool gone rabid, and it was with mounting distress that I sessed that the paper of the book's pages had begun feeling hot, pulpy, *fleshy* . . .

Somewhere, a now-mutilated lumberjack had had the most horrific moment of his life in the process of putting together what I was now enjoying it in my warm, sunlit room. He and I, our lives intersected opaquely at this singular miserable point; such is the loathsome way of life we lead today.

Some museums preserve once-used weapons of murder and humiliation. Axes, knives, guns, handcuffs. One is invited to watch them from afar, with the beast kept safely sealed inside its glass cage. The idea of actually doing the forbidden, reaching out and grasping such a tool, fills one with a morbid thrill and righteous disgust. But I had no need to enter museums to feel the presence of such vehicles of suffering. Murder lies latently in everything around us; it is only for me that it is so often stripped of all indirectness. The bag and the wallet are no less venomous than those knives and guns and handcuffs.

Our intuitive revulsion toward these latter betrays a fundamental fact, a fact hidden expertly by most others. It is only out of convenience that we believe objects to be essentially memoryless, incapable of holding onto any authentic trace of its past lives and the impingements affected upon it. They remember the hopes and the fears of which they were the instruments, and they reflect them back onto us.

For the most part, objects remain silent, and we confuse this silence with the muted stare of an amnesiac. But I have been chosen, and for me they deign to forgo the depths of this silence; out of the subterranean depths of its hidden values this book now whispers and gibbers endlessly to me.

And so it was that by the end of the evening I had been driven to hurl the book into the trash, for I now knew that it was the source of lifelong torment for a traumatized family somewhere in the North, the knowledge of which made me feel infected by its touch.

This book here is not from without. Quite literally, a portion of someone's flesh and blood had been consumed in its production, and I was looking at this mutilated piece of him. Every single thing around me exists as it does only by having robbed a million different souls.

15 June

I went for a walk near the lake today evening. It was the only place where all the pain wrought by the absurdity of my life was numbed. My love for its natural beauty was not vulgar, for I had ceased wishing to extract from it the most splendorous sight, the most breathtaking vista, some economic maximum of pleasure; I merely sat on the earth and let the time roll over me, watching as the soporific, golden-yellow rays of the evening sun upon the bark of the trees endowed them with a strange and beautiful color beyond the known palette.

On some evenings the vastness of the sky over my head was so overwhelming that it was as if even the birds flying high above me were in some ambiguous space between the earth and the sky, failing to reach that heavenly canopy of the sky itself, which in turn persisted as the backdrop.

The lake was a moody creature. On most days its beautiful, dynamic surface would be shimmering, reflecting the temper of the sky—sometimes a clear blue, an empty canvas, yet not any less beautiful for its emptiness; sometimes the inverted image of that fascinating painting created by the elements, constituted by the clouds. Clouds coming in streaks racing across the sky, in balls floating along placidly; clouds in other, more ambiguous landscapes containing within themselves a threatening gray castle and leaving almost no empty space on that great blue canvas. All these stories would be reflected perfectly on that surface, disturbed only by the occasional bird chugging along one of those inverted clouds.

But on other days, as if overcome by the superabundance of its own life-giving powers, the lake would be choked by vegetation that had grown on and was floating upon it. That surface that was earlier defined by its unwavering commitment to yielding, and its ability to swallow whole anything that chanced upon it, seemed now to be replaced by something more solid. And yet, the occasional ripple that managed to penetrate through its thickness would betray the fact that this ground was no ground at all; that it was still unwaveringly fluid by nature. These vegetated chunks of water distorted the sky and inspired little interest from the flocks of birds, who restricted their movement to cleaner zones; and being shunned by the birds gave these areas every appearance of dead zones on the lake, in contradiction to the biological fact of their life.

Tall leaves of grass surrounded it by the border, dancing in the twilight wind, whispering secrets to one another. Occasionally, from somewhere inside their kingdom, one could hear the honk of a goose. Each honk betrayed only vaguely the location of the birds; the grass was tall enough to shield them from visibility. The cumulative effect of these disembodied honks was that of a concert whose musicians were scattered at some arbitrary locations and were unable to see or hear each other, thereby playing their instruments discordantly, in disagreement with the rhythm of their partner.

The clouds that fed the lake that fed the soil that fed the trees, with the sun hugging them all with life. No opaque connections and no nebulous arrangements: All was laid bare; nothing was lacerated. Whereas the nakedness I see everywhere else horrifies, here it brought forth waves of peace. Insofar as places such as these preserved this mystical quality of theirs, that queer appearance of a thing hitherto unseen by human eyes, I was safe from the torture defining my life.

Today was a good day, for my surroundings weren't waiting, knife in hand, to strike my psyche at the opportune moment.

20 June

I went on another lakeside walk today—but my surroundings failed to absorb me into them and halt my racing mind like they usually did.

I kept imagining and reimagining what it would be like if, one day, for no reason at all, I stopped feeling the peace and happiness I did on my evening walks. Sadness is most terrifying precisely when it is acausal, when it shows up with utter disregard for the material conditions of one's existence, striking at the most paradoxical of moments. What if, one day, by a fundamentally stochastic event, I simply ceased to feel how I usually did by the lake? This is a sadness that cannot be reasoned with or rationalized away; you have no choice but to submit to it. The world around me was unceasingly, against my will, revealing to me its conflicted and confounded chains of causation. Surrendering to such a sadness would, then, be a final act of defiance.

Such were the thoughts running through my mind when something on the grass caught my eye.

It didn't so much catch my eye as arrest it, threaten it into submission. I wavered hesitantly in the distance, taking in the malevolence of the aura emanating from the object I as yet could not even see clearly; whose existence was still merely a black void on the grass, attached to a vast space of possibilities, each of which uniquely filled in the rest of its appearance. I sensed the arrival of another one of my seizures, certain to set onto me were I to approach the thing; it would scream its stories into my ears as I listened powerlessly. And yet, this was not what made it feel so threatening.

I circled round it without going closer, in order to get a better look from another angle.

It seemed to be a miniature tower of some kind. It looked jarringly out of place in the middle of the grass; and yet, the way it sat on the earth spoke in a certain way, and I felt as if it had been here many aeons before the grass and the trees, which only later grew around it. It spoke in a language I could not understand, but from the tenor and tone of which I sensed antiquity. The intensity of its blackness went so far as to drain its immediate surroundings of color—or so it seemed to me. It did not glint in the sunlight; to the contrary, it appeared to suck it into a black gorge it held within.

I saw now that it wasn't a tower at all. It was a model of some kind, to be sure, seemingly made of some plastic; but it was something out of the mind of an architect driven insane. From a center of symmetry emerged four wings that coiled into themselves and one another as Möbius bands; throughout the span of these wings, inscrutable designs or perhaps hieroglyphics were carved out, suggesting arcane spells and evil runes that may have been used to reanimate the corpse of Escher, who alone must have been the artist behind this.

In my curiosity toward examining these details, I had, without realizing, gravitated paralyzingly close to it; had I stretched out my hand just then, I could have touched it with the tips of my fingers. This knowledge came with a submission toward my fate: surely, after such an strong level of engagement with it, it was too late to escape. It had already grabbed me by the neck and drawn my ear close to its slavering mouth. All that was left now was for it to begin speaking, and I prepared myself for another acrimonious onslaught of pathetic information that would, if nothing else, lay rest to my fantastical ideas about its origin.

I swayed in the wind for another moment. And just when I decided that I might be able to get out of it this time after all, I felt that familiar, dreaded distortion of the world around me.

The grass around the object started dying rapidly—or so I thought, for I saw it drain of its lush green color and turn brown. But it didn't stop there; from a paler and paler brown it became white, and then, impossible as it may be to understand my meaning, it began to be drained even of the *white*—yes, giving way not to transparency, nor to blackness, but to something simply bereft of any color and even the possibility of any color. I was left stranded in a sea of anemones that refused to participate in one of the necessary dimensions of perceptual stimulus, sending my head spinning.

My foray into the unknown had only begun. It was now the shape of the blades of grass, thin, flat, and sharp, which began twisting and turning, disintegrating, not taking on an impossible geometry but simply refusing to have anything to do with geometry at all.

Contrary to my expectations, there was no hallucination. Rather, I was being transported to a place wherein the very *possibility* of perceptual stimulus had ceased to exist. Distortions themselves can only occur on the backdrop of being situated in an undistorted world, but what I was being forced to face up to was the prospect of utter worldlessness.

Not even black, which is a color; not even silence, which is only the absence of sound; not even emptiness, which cannot exist without space. I had been taken someplace beyond and outside of all thought, somewhere our everyday dualities cannot even begin to arise. A sterile and inhospitable space, to be imprisoned in which meant a fate worse than death—for even death is rendered meaningless in the absence of life.

From out of the depths of its silence, what it said to me was far more radical than anything I had heard so far. What I was looking at was alien to its core, and could not have been borne by this universe.

That was my first encounter with this unnamable object. Something about it compelled me to take it home. The horrifying emptiness of its origin felt like a balm against the tumultuous histories of everything else in existence.

My seizures were akin to a weapon beyond my control; an axe that would not be wielded by my arm but would, rather, make the arm subservient to its endless hunger. Falling upon objects arbitrarily and splintering them into a million fragmentary lives. But I had now found something immune to its blade. An object out of nowhere, utterly ahistorical and answerable to nothing.

Undated

I have managed to muster up the sanity required to detail this final tryst with reality because of my determination to disseminate my ill-gotten knowledge, so that what I now know may be made known to others, and made known before whatever monstrosity that is to befall me takes away what is left of my shattered psyche.

After that first encounter with that tiny artefact, I had decided to take it back with me and give it a place on my table. Every once in a while after that day, I picked it up, close my eyes, and waited with bated breath to see if I would be transported to that realm of nothinghood. Dare I hope that, at long last, an antidote of some sort had fallen into my lap?

It was after a few fruitless attempts, as I reopened my eyes to see it staring back at me from its twisted center of symmetry with its mutilated and angelic wings, that I entered a vision. All that is left to do now is relay the singular memory that is to haunt me for all the nights I have left on this planet.

I was taken somewhere dark, cavernous, stifling, corrupted. Green moss-like vegetation clung to and lay scattered across the walls of this cave like a failed and forgotten tapestry. I sensed these walls pulse in and out, faintly and arrhythmically. Guttural sounds from an alien thorax surrounded me.

I sensed myself as being far, far away from any known land. Across vast oceans, through abandoned forests, past unscalable mountains, within hidden caves. On some corpse of a planet. A place nobody could ever reach, whose existence could thereby only be revealed through indirect means such as this vision. I was in the infernal workshop that produced that artefact.

For long had I desired an antidote to the axe out of control which my mind wielded; for long had I sought after a way to put back together the fragments I broke the world into. But such an antidote would be incommensurable with the way the world is today. Or would it?

The moss on the wall began glowing, and in its fluorescence illuminated the ghastly scene within this cave. I looked up to see, hanging from an invisible ceiling, bodies that had begun rotting away, although their owners were yet living. One mutilated half of a person grafted onto another's so that they may come together to sustain an abomination that, while composed of dying organisms, may yet not escape the vile grip of life.

Symptoms of a putrefying, decayed understanding of life taken to excess. Failed attempts at clinging onto something forever lost to us. Creatures pieced together senselessly, no two parts of which could be said to have belonged to the same organism. Decapitated bodies with a single dying flower in place of their head and legs not even of flesh but simply rotten chunks of garbage.

I had been given the ability to see, in the objects that populate our world, the violence engendered in their production; the way in which the *material* tears the human soul asunder. Each thing deserts its makers, who are nothing but variously positioned cogs in the crushing machinery of modern-day labor. And with each of their creations that thus escapes from them, they lose some of their humanity.

I had desired to undo these divisions and reconstruct, out of the swarm of partial voices that constituted each thing I saw, a human being in unified wholeness. But the truth is that there is no human being left to restore. There are no people in the factories, waiting to be discovered. The truth is that the world remains populated by only partial animuses. To be human is to be an anachronism.

I gazed upon the poisonous fruits of this doomed endeavor of restoration. This cave was once a medium of healing given from the heavens, something designed to produce whole and intact human beings; but it can now, it seems, do nothing but spit out manifold abominations.

The moment I returned from the vision, I knew it was special. Something felt different. A queer sensation overcame my body, provoking me to stumble into the bathroom. And as I looked into the mirror . . .

The Farm

What really upset me was how harrowingly authentic the document appeared to be. It wasn't just a matter of being handwritten in some diary. The very strokes of the pen bubbled with an unfathomable misery. It was as if, underneath every written word, there was a secret word trying to tell me something beyond the visible; a secret word animated by the jagged and flailing manner of the handwriting, screaming with pain and destitution. A master of calligraphy could not have done a better job at giving those penstrokes such an expression of anguish.

Being in its presence made me uncomfortable. Almost as if its author's disease was infectious, I was beginning to feel their being, their madness, and their pain emerge out of this inanimate object. The tale it had to tell, this obituary to life it declared, seemed too tortured to be a simple fiction. I needed to get rid of it.

I decided to go for a walk to clear my head—and to get away from it for a time. It was cold tonight, too cold to go out without a jacket. I picked mine up on the way out and looked back at the diary, lying on my table, for one last time before stepping out of the house. I felt unsafe leaving it alone in my room like that, as if it would somehow alter the nature of my living space in my absence through the pain it embodied. I forced myself to ignore these thoughts and left.

The moment I walked out of the gates of the institute's campus and onto the highway outside, I was struck by its emptiness.

The music had stopped. It was probably barely nine P.M., but without a watch it was indistinguishable from the wee hour of two past midnight. Everyone had sunken into their homes; nobody wanted to be outside and engaging with this dusty, empty patch of the world for longer than required.

Lining the road were a few huts, and, every half a kilometer or so, a small apartment building. The only people ever to require that kind of accommodation here were those temporarily hired by the institute for some work. As a result, most of these buildings remained empty year-round. Some of them had been abandoned as lost causes and fallen into disrepair. Streetlights were also far and few, but I thought I saw some light coming from one such building somewhere further down the road. It was one that I had hitherto assumed was one of the abandoned, but the light looked to be a sign of life. I started walking in that direction.

Authentic or not, the diary felt like a scream of pain; pain of a kind so novel and unimaginable that one's first reaction to it would likely just be dumbfounded confusion. And all this, written by someone from this institute? Maybe I walk past this person every other day without even realizing it.

I shivered and briefly looked around me. There was nobody in sight. Looking ahead again, I saw that the light was coming from a window in the building. It was the only one illuminated. I imagined the rest of the rooms were all, as usual, dark and empty.

I thought about asking around tomorrow to see if I could figure out who had authored this pamphlet. Perhaps their own individuality and identity was as fragmented as they felt everything to be, and nobody would be able to pinpoint any one person as the author. Perhaps it simply spontaneously arose into existence out of a million muffled screams of subhumanity.

It was cold enough for me to be able to see my own breath. In the sole illuminated window of the apartment down the road, I saw a vague shadow stir—shiver? For just a moment something about its outline struck me as unfamiliar, something *uncanny*.

The moment of unfamiliarity when we see something afresh lasts for but a second. Once our vision gets habituated to it, we forget entirely how mysterious it first felt to us. The road one walks on for the first time is perceived in a manner almost unrecognizably different from the way it is perceived on our hundredth walk.

In like manner, the moment of mystery with the shadow, wherein it appeared to be taking up dimensions incommensurate with the human body, lasted for but a moment; my senses eagerly restructured it as something comfortably humanoid, and I could thereon not even remember the strangeness of that first glance.

My thoughts drifted back to the diary. Most inscrutable of all was, no doubt, the suggestion of a cure gone wrong at the end. I could scarcely even fathom this profound disease that they were suffering from, let alone understand what a cure may be and where it could go wrong. But it was clear that there was some object of temptation, some delicious fruit with poisonous and horrific aftereffects; a failed antidote that they had perhaps nearly opened the door to, out of utter desperation.

Although there was no year given with the dates, its author must have been around here not too far back if it had been up for sale in this year's book fair. I didn't much like the idea of being in proximity to someone this deranged. There was in me an irrational fear of somehow catching their mysterious and intolerable ailment, like an infection.

But if only I had known that I was closer to them than I could have ever imagined.

It was then that I froze in my tracks. I was closer now, much closer to the apartment with the light; and that light had just flickered off and on. But in that moment of darkness the shadow changed.

Oh, yes, I could only imagine how wretched such an ailment would have made me. I would have been willing to try anything, anything at all, to avoid being stuck with such a fate; even—dare I say it?—any accursed antidote alluded to, no matter the consequences . . .

It changed, and I recalled the final few words of the diary as I beheld what took its place.

. . . and as I looked into the mirror, a gaunt, fleshless, limbless body staggered in front of me; a thing that could not have been human. An upright arm sprouted from where its face should have been, and I beheld in my place a mangled carcass supplanted with life.

Ruins of Carcosa

DJ Tyrer

A name carved in stone
Windworn and weathered
Like the ruins
Amidst which it stands
Strange, cyclopean
Shattered, silent, still
Save for a lynx
Two bright eyes
Blazing in the darkness
Surprised in mid-step.
A figure moves
From shadow to shadow
Tall, tattered
Terrifying
Unseen, an enigma
A memory
A mystery
A past and a future
A symbol and a sign
A cipher
Embodied by the stone
All that remains
Dark and shadow-strewn.
Here you stand
Alone
In lost Carcosa.

The Three Versions of Ramsey Campbell's "Made in Goatswood"

S. T. Joshi

Ramsey Campbell's first short story collection, *Demons by Daylight* (1973), is a seminal volume in modern weird fiction. What makes the stories in this volume so distinctive is, first and foremost, their style—wondrously supple, atmospheric, dreamlike, even hallucinatory. Some seem like pure nightmares, while others seem like the effects of a drug-delirium (although Campbell's experimentation with drugs dates only to the early 1970s). Conjoined to this—and, really, scarcely distinguishable from it—is the tales' intense concentration on a single character's moods and sensations as he or she encounters the bizarre; combined with the first feature, the result is a frequent inability on the part of the reader—and, indeed, the characters—to distinguish illusion from reality or to determine whether the weird event has actually occurred or is merely in the mind of the protagonist. Thirdly, it is the tales' forthright addressing of modern issues—class and religious conflict, sexuality, gender confusion, the terror of random crime. It is this quality that made *Demons by Daylight* so revolutionary in the field and so different from the stale vampires and mad scientists of the enfeebled Gothic tradition.

It is not well known that some drafts of the *Demons by Daylight* stories date to as early as 1963, when Campbell was only seventeen—and a year prior to the publication of his collection of Lovecraft pastiches, *The Inhabitant of the Lake and Less Welcome Tenants* (1964). These drafts, to say nothing of their final versions, most of which were completed by 1968, show Campbell striving to evolve a new style and tone that eschewed mere imitation in order to convey the complex network of ideas, moods, and images he now wished to convey. These drafts will now be published in a new edition of *Demons by Daylight*, forthcoming from PS Publishing.

The final story in the book is "Made in Goatswood," and its key position highlights the story's importance to the volume as a whole and to Campbell himself. The first draft dates to 1964, when the story was titled "A Garden at Night"; the second draft was written in 1966, and the final draft—the one that was published in the volume—dates to 1968. Comparison of these three drafts illuminates Campbell's growing mastery of his medium and his increasing skill at saying—with subtlety, complexity, and emotive power—the things he wished to say.

The basic premise of all three versions is the coming to life of the three stone gnomes that Terry Aldrich has purchased for his girlfriend, Kim Francis. But beyond this core conception, the drafts are remarkably different. "A Garden at Night" runs to 3800 words. After Terry has presented the gnomes to Kim, it becomes apparent that she does not care for them, as they are physically ugly: "their noses were longer and more hooked than she remembered from her childhood story-books; their grins more evil, their eyes larger and buried deeper, and the wickedly sharp teeth she did not recognise at all." Her tentative decision to place in her back yard, away from public view, leads to an argument, as Terry accuses her, "And how many other presents have you felt that way about, anyway?"

The animation of the gnomes is handled with some subtlety. As she finds herself alone in the house—her mother has gone out (her father does not appear in this draft, although he does in the final one)—she "thought she heard footsteps ascending the stairs; regular stealthy creaks." On a later occasion, Kim, on the first-floor landing, sees that "a face leered at her from the floor at the landing end . . . a grinning face with menacing deep-set eyes, its muscles stiffly shifting." At last, the full horror of the situation becomes evident: "And then she screamed, for knife-hard claws were catching hold of her, cutting into her defenceless flesh, thrusting her forward into a nauseous jerky plunge, head first down the stairs . . ." We later learn that Kim has become a "slightly imbecilic girl" who now works in a brothel at Fitzroy Street—a conclusion anticipated at the beginning of the tale, when a friend of Terry's, Phil, tells him about the area: "Why, it's worse than Willis Road in Brichester—prostitutes, queens, the lot . . ." It is worth noting that this draft cites not only Goatswood but other cities in Campbell's invented Severn Valley, including Camside, Brichester, and Temphill (but not Severnford).

"A Garden at Night" would be considered a competent weird tale if it had been written by anyone other than Ramsey Campbell, and if the later drafts did not exist. In light of them, the story is just a horror story, with some attempt to highlight the discord between the chief protagonists but with little indication of the causes of that discord. In particular, the focus of the two later drafts—the religious differences between Terry and Kim—is not mentioned at all, except for Terry's flippant characterization of the gnomes ("There'll be a hot time in Pan's forest on Tuesday," suggesting that the gnomes are a symbol of paganism). This draft, as with the others, makes a point of stating that Kim was ignorant that the time of the story's events is close to Midsummer's Eve.

The second draft, now titled "Made in Goatswood," is fragmentary: we are missing the opening section. The draft as it stands is 4767 words—and the full version certainly exceeded 5000 words and may have come close to 6000, since the extant text begins with the gnomes already in place in Kim's back yard. Here the religious subtext is made evident right at the start, as Terry "told himself that if religion required faith in primitive beliefs, then pagan nature-worship would be just as valid." This comment aligns Terry with the gnomes, but the rest of the story pushes the religious element far too strongly, as Terry, Kim, and her mother debate the subject at excessive length, especially the relationship of religious belief to sexual expression. (Terry, clearly wishing to engage in sex with Kim, hurls an accusation at her: "The way you make it sound, religion and sex just aren't compatible.") There is also a needlessly long discussion of films that Kim and Terry see, which adds little to the overall thrust of the story. Even so, a passage portraying the gnomes attacking Kim is grimly effective:

> Then cruel hands gripped her soft flesh and lifted her into a jerky vertiginous plunge down the stairs. The hands cut into her. They carried her down the hall, struggling; the ceiling lurched far above, and as the back door passed over her her head cracked on the stone step. She began to weep. Inverted faces grimaced stiffly all around her in the moonlight. They dragged her through the hedge; she tried to hold on to the roots, but the claws crushed her fingers. A knife-blade of grass slashed the edge of her eye. Through a growing blur she glimpsed the swaying trees of Oak Gardens closing in. "Terry!" she sobbed again.

This draft also ends with Kim becoming a prostitute.

The final draft of the story, standing at just under 5200 words, is worlds apart from the earlier ones. Now, the element of religious conflict has been seamlessly integrated into the narrative. Terry makes no secret of his unbelief: "he'd accepted a hostile universe, he couldn't be expected to do more." That single word "hostile" not only suggests Terry's acknowledgment of the lack of a benevolent deity but also hints at the violence that the gnomes will inflict upon Kim. At the outset he is convinced that the gnomes will bring Kim's garden "back to nature." Meanwhile, the first image we see of the interior of Kim's house is this: "Behind her in the hall an angel hung, eternally elevated." Kim's mother, becoming involved in the religious dispute between Kim and Terry, says tartly, "All this godlessness that's going round can cause nothing but unhappiness!" This line too perhaps has a double meaning, unwittingly alluding to Kim's fate. The gnomes themselves are described evocatively: "The eyes were grey globes set deep in pits; the noses were hooked like those of childhood witches she'd leafed over; the mouths grinned, revealing pointed teeth." It can be seen that this passage is a substantially more subtle expression of the idea found in the first draft.

Here too, Kim's squeamishness in regard to sex is highlighted, but in a way that advances the supernatural element of the narrative.

As the two of them are snuggling in her house, she thinks someone is watching. Terry becomes annoyed (Kim had made a similar comment in an earlier session outdoors), snapping, "Don't tell me this is a subtle Catholic objection." He is referring to a crucifix on the wall, but in fact there is a strong likelihood that it is the gnomes who are watching the couple.

The climax of this draft is extraordinarily powerful, embodied in a single imperishable sentence: "The grey stone silence inched toward her." Campbell has now jettisoned the unseemly suggestion that Kim has entered a whorehouse; but he adds the even more disturbing hint that the gnomes may have sexually violated her and taken her virginity. The conclusion—where Terry "made the sign of the cross" before re-entering the house—may imply that he has now become reconciled to Kim's (and, especially, her parents') religiosity, but it is an open question whether he himself has shifted his views significantly.

First drafts of other stories in *Demons by Daylight* are likewise revelatory in demonstrating the remarkable leap that Campbell made in these critical years of the 1960s, evolving from a competent pastichist to an author with powerful messages to convey and the literary artistry to convey them skillfully and evocatively. That he has continued to evolve in the subsequent half-century, producing vital and dynamic work right up to the present day, is a testament both to his longevity and to his relentless desire to refine his talents with each passing work.

The Wild Hunt

J. G. Maybrook

Is that a stranger passing by my door?
You'll catch your death of cold on such a night;
The wind is rising fast upon the moor,
And many hours remain till morning light.

There isn't any inn with rooms for hire
For many miles around; so you'd do well
To come inside and sit before the fire
And hearken to the tale that I will tell.

One wintry Christmas Eve, an hour before
The clock struck twelve, I rose and started out
Upon the path that cuts across the moor,
The only soul upon that lonely route.

Most dismal was the land through which I passed,
Yet nonetheless my heart was filled with mirth,
For I was on my way to midnight mass
To celebrate our Holy Savior's birth.

So on I went—the path I scarce discerned—
When midway through my journey there befell
A sudden, strange event; for as I turned
My eyes unto the heavens, I beheld

A curtain woven all of shining light,
Which vast, yet unseen, hands appeared to draw
By slow degrees across the face of night,
While from below I watched in silent awe.

I'd seen this once before, I soon recalled,
When yet a lad of only seventeen;
Aurora Borealis it is called,
And hereabout but rarely is it seen.

A most auspicious sign, no doubt, thought I,
For just as on the night that Christ was born,
Light shines in darkness, and the very sky
Rejoices, turning midnight into morn.

Yet as I gazed entranced upon the sight,
Elation turned to utter fear; for there,
Above the snowy hills now gleaming white,
A pack of hounds was running through the air!

Across the phantom curtain there outspread,
Those fearsome hounds pursued their unseen prey,
All bounding, dashing, leaping as they sped
With neither rest nor pause upon their way.

Then, lo! behold! astride a stallion's back,
A man in hooded cloak, his hair unshorn!
Upon his mount he towered o'er the pack,
And as he rode, he blew a hunter's horn.

From lowest vale to highest mountain height,
The winding of that ancient horn did sound;
And as it died away, the ghostly light
Grew dim, and darkness settled all around.

Now wholly lost to fear, I ran and ran
Until I reached the church where, all that night,
I said my prayers while trembling like a man
Whose mind is shaken by an awful fright.

And thus it is that now you find me here,
A haggard man with features gaunt and grim
Who dares not leave his dwelling out of fear
That some relentless foe is stalking him.

Hark! Even now I hear the awful sound
Of baying hounds intent upon the chase;
The time has come at last when I am found
And meet my dread pursuer face to face!

The Worm Death

Joshua Green

1

On the first night, I spent a great deal of time writing in my vellum-bound journal.

A scream poured out from an open window two houses over. I crouched before closing my logbook. My other hand rested firmly on the .44 Magnum revolver attached to my hip.

My eyes were fixed on the house in question. I listened for the crack of flesh, a thousand whips. Whatever lived in that house would soon live alone. I would not put my raven, Aurora, at risk. Nor would I put Zara in harm's way. She was my brightest student.

"Heal, not kill," Aurora said, flapping her wings, landing on a wooden beam that stuck out from the Morton house.

"Very good," Zara whispered with a smile, nodding to Aurora. "Edgar, her speech is improving."

I raised my hand to quiet Zara, used mindspeak to calm Aurora. *This is different,* I thought to her, thinking of the pages I had written describing the state of the town. *This is the first time I've ever been worried about her.*

Zara will learn, Aurora thought back. *The Worm Death is here.*

I appreciated Aurora's intelligence, was glad that she could speak freely to me due to our shared mind. Her common, spoken speech was abrupt, but it was something she continually worked on.

The house fell into silence, one pregnant with horrors I knew Zara wasn't ready for. There was no question someone had just died, that the Worm Death had claimed yet another victim. There was no joy in this town, but it would be wrong to say that I wasn't relieved. The town doctor, June Morton, was still alive, evidently immune from the disease.

Rising to my feet, I turned and looked at the Morton house in front of us. It loomed high above the other homes. The strong hickory beams supported a large porch. After making my way up, I rapped quickly on the front door before stepping back. Immunity against a malicious contagion was never a certainty, though I did trust June's assessment.

The door creaked open, revealing a gaunt-looking woman with a pale face. She wore an apron soaked in blood. For a moment I thought I had the wrong house. June was no longer the strong-looking woman I once knew. She was haggard, her face emaciated. She was not pleased to see us, the lines in her forehead forming deep canyons of annoyance.

"I do not need Gatmer's help," she said, glancing behind her for a moment. When she turned back around, her face was softer, perhaps more kind. "The town will survive without the use of magic. It will certainly survive the night without interference from the university."

I wasn't so sure, though I understood her concern. I had been sent by the University of Gatmer to investigate the Worm Death, to help heal the sick where possible. The white, tattered cloth wrapped around the base of my gray hat was proof of this. I was here to heal, not kill. But news of a university-trained Hunter was rarely ever welcome. I was oft viewed with dismay, as part of an order that dealt with profane knowledge and secret words.

"Dr. Morton, we are only here on inquiry," I said. "I do not plan on staying long."

"We?" Dr. Morton said, curiously.

I motioned for Zara to come close. She hurried up the steps and planted herself right beside me. "This is Zara. She's my student."

"It's good to meet you, Dr. Morton," Zara said. "I admire your works, especially *Principles of Surgery* and *Surgical Technology*. I reference them quite a bit in the field when Edgar lets me travel with my books."

"Oh?" said Dr. Morton. She looked at me then. A hint of a smile formed around the edge of her lips. "For her sake I will let you in. And because of her you may call me June. The town isn't safe for a child her age. I assume you brought the bird?"

I half expected Aurora to flood my thoughts in anger at such a derogatory question, but nothing came.

"She and I are one," I said. "We do not leave one another. It is prohibited."

"I see," Dr. Morton said. "I will not—"

"Aurora will stay outside," I said, lifting my hand. "She is to keep watch."

At this, Dr. Morton nodded and stepped aside for us to enter. I could hear Aurora as she flew for higher ground.

I will be above you, she thought. *On the roof.*

Be safe, I thought back, stepping across the threshold.

But Zara would not follow, for she had seen, before I had, the gore that awaited us in the house.

2

Zara was accustomed to death. She had lost her parents three days after her eleventh birthday to a sickness that had claimed half her town. With nowhere to go, she had packed her own bags and traveled north across rough terrain to the University of Gatmer's doorsteps. She would have been turned away by the Keepers had I not been out in the garden picking some of Gatmer's flowers. I try not to think about what would have happened to her if I had been anywhere else. She was small in stature with dirty blond, curly hair. I had been astonished that she had made it to Gatmer on her own.

I stared at her now with similar sentiments. She was a few months past thirteen. I didn't view myself as her father. No, that was something she would never have again. But I did think myself responsible for her well-being, both physical and mental.

"It's different from the books," Zara finally managed to say. Both of us were leaning over the corpse, studying the various lacerations and contusions that ran up and down the torso. The body was a mess of red and purple. I winced as the outline of a worm made itself apparent within the forearm, slithering about before retreating back up into the shoulder. "How can we be sure the skin won't break?" Zara asked.

June was busy taking notes in the corner. "In your medical textbooks, Zara, what is the proper name of the organism that causes Worm Death?"

"Mastigomorpha," Zara quickly said. "It means 'whip form.'"

"Correct," June said, still writing. "However, many years ago my colleagues and I voted to rename the Mastigomorpha. Of course, we will rectify your outdated knowledge by updating the textbooks whenever Gatmer gets around to a revising. Moving forward, the proper name of the organism is Glassomorpha."

"Tongue form," Zara said, not missing a beat. "Why?"

I watched as June put down the pen to look at Zara. "Because, while the worm does flail and whip and lash about, infecting and injuring and killing all in its path, we have found that its primary function is a tongue."

My brow lowered at June's words. Aurora must have sensed my anxiety, for she spoke to my mind without delay. I calmed her and in turn made an attempt to calm myself. I had visited a few towns afflicted by the Worm Death before, once even with June. This was before her exile. Up until now I had believed that the Worm Death was just another contagion that resurfaced every decade or so, an unfortunate and disgusting disease that worked to replicate and destroy all in its path.

"But how would you know this?" I asked, stepping back from the body. I motioned for Zara to do the same. "The worms emerge from the mouth to lash, but it was assumed that it was just the path of least resistance."

"Would the anus not be closer?" Zara asked.

"We assumed as well, Edgar," June said, ignoring the child. "But mostly because they were impossible to study. Though this year we have been able to . . . hold . . . those infected by the Worm Death in confinement for examination. At first, nothing of merit was found.

But after a few months Arthur Weadon, a colleague of mine, found that subjects would utter a single phrase. Yoth-Mthog."

The body moved at the uttering of the phrase in what I assumed were hundreds of worms working together in tandem. I watched as the throat expanded, much like the swelling of a frog's vocal sac.

"What is wrong with them?" I asked, my hand on my revolver. "I have never seen this."

"I am currently observing the life span of the worms. I've sealed the esophagus and trachea of this victim. I've left the anus unplugged, to answer Zara's question. They are not interested in going down, so to speak. Only up into the mouth. There is no need to worry. While the Glossomorpha are dangerous, they are quite harmless when confined."

I relaxed a bit, despite my newfound concerns of June's methodology. "You killed this man," I said. "Killed him before the worms grew. Then let them grow within his dead body."

"I'm sorry, Edgar," June said. Then she looked at Zara. "Take note of this, young one. Edgar has always been a bit soft."

"It isn't right," I said. "I could have helped him. You know this."

June rose from her chair, collecting her notes in the process. "As I said before, Edgar, this town does not need magic to survive the night. I have already sealed those who showed early signs of infection. Come morning, those who have been afflicted by the Worm Death will be burned on a pyre."

I could hardly believe June's words. While we hadn't talked for quite some time, I remembered her as kind and merciful—even bright-eyed. But the June in front of me was hard and lacked remorse. She seemed no longer burdened by a desire to heal the sick.

"Yoth-Mthog," Zara said, still staring at the corpse.

The body churned in response, the stomach distending far beyond what was natural. I could hear the sloshing of the body's organs within. Even when confined the worms caused destruction. I feared June was wrong, that the skin would soon burst, setting loose a hundred worms to seek a new host.

"Do not utter that name again," I said.

Zara looked at me, eyes sharp with desire for knowledge. "Name?" she asked.

June was silent.

"Yes, Zara," I said. "It is a name. One that is hardly ever uttered, even amongst Gatmer's professors."

"What does it mean?" Zara asked. Her eyes floated back and forth between June and myself. Still, June remained silent.

"I do not know," I said, my gaze falling to the ground. "There are universities that predate Gatmer, ones that have taught the language. But those schools are no longer standing. Most places ignore teaching on the Peripheries."

"The Periph—"

"Old gods. Strange ones," I said. "But I will not speak any more of this. Not here, Zara."

I lifted my gaze and turned my attention to June. "Are there any still living?" I asked. "Any that you have sealed that are still alive?"

"It is possible," June said. "Despite sealing the windpipe, I've witnessed individuals stay alive for up to eight hours after. I have not been able to study the phenomena adequately, although—"

"Take me to them," I said, turning for the door.

"I will not!" June said. I didn't need to turn around to see the anger on her face. "Besides, I did not keep a tally, nor did I keep time. I sealed many bodies. I will not—"

"By the end of the week I will have every available Hunter in the region at your doorstep, Dr. Morton. You will take me to them."

At this, June sighed, moving toward the door.

We stepped into the cool night together.

3

Despite the stench of death that drifted from every which way, the cold air was a welcome presence. Zara and I followed June from house to house while Aurora flew above. Many houses lacked doors, and there were obvious signs that they had been bashed or kicked, either from looting or foolish family members looking to bury their loved ones. We checked very few of these. In one house we found a woman weeping over a corpse. She screamed at us until we left. Her grief was great.

The second house with a bashed door was rigged with a live trap, a small piece of rope that would trigger a hail of gunfire when bent. June told us that ten years ago, during the last Worm Death, many looters would rig abandoned houses in hopes of luring fellow opportunists to their death, allowing them to take all they had gathered. After the rigged house, we decided as a group only to go where June was certain a sealed body was. And from there, the door must have no signs of having been disturbed.

An hour or so passed before we found a house June was certain remained untouched. This house was small, most likely one bedroom with a small living space. It sat alone at the end of a short trail that led through the woods. I determined that this was the reason why it remained in its current state. It wasn't far from town by any means, but it was easy to miss.

The chimney, Aurora, I thought.

Without hesitation Aurora flew from my shoulder, landing on the brick.

A moment passed. The three of us waited in silence.

"No. Thing," Aurora said, cocking her head to the side. "No. Words."

Zara smiled. She always loved when Aurora spoke aloud.

I climbed up the steps. June followed. Pressing my ear to the door, I listened for anything unnatural. I closed my eyes, let my mind seep more into Aurora's. It allowed me to hear from her vantage point on the chimney as well as my own here on the porch. I stayed this way for quite some time. I truly didn't want to risk Zara getting hurt. The extra precaution felt necessary.

"It is quiet," I said. "I don't think the worms have broken through, if they are there at all."

"I've told you before, Edgar," June said. "I have sealed the Glossomorpha. They are harmless when confined."

I grabbed the handle and pushed the door open. The house was dark. The trees that surrounded us let in very little light. Before entering, I opened one of my small pouches, which held a fair amount of white flower petals from Gatmer's garden. Without speaking, Zara opened one of her pouches and brought me the remains of a witch moth. The tiny corpse and paper-thin wings were weightless in my palm.

"May I try?" Zara asked. I looked to her. Both arms were outstretched, palms facing the sky. I nodded and handed her a single white petal as well as the witch moth. A moment later she was squishing them together, bringing her folded hands to her lips to whisper words that only Gatmer's flowers ever heard.

Light emanated from Zara's clasped hands, and she released the light out in front of her. The transmutation had been successful. She had created an orbfly with her words, a white petal, and the moth.

"Can you control it?" I asked. Her eyes seemed to dart about in confusion. There was no doubt her mind was struggling to comprehend the awareness of another conscious being. But it was a good first step in the principles of binding, the mind amalgamation that she would one day seek with a creature of her choice.

Zara didn't speak. The orbfly flittered about like a mote of dust caught in the wind; but a moment later it began to move steadily, almost purposefully. A smile broke across her face.

"A disgusting thing," June said from behind us.

I ignored her, instead keeping my focus on Zara. I watched as she commanded the orbfly forward. Bright white light filled the entrance of the small home.

"Thank you," Zara said, looking to me.

I nodded in return.

We slipped into the home together. June was the last of us to enter. The house was in disarray. Clothes littered the floor as well as shards of broken glass and ceramic.

"It was like this when I arrived," June said. "I don't believe it has been looted."

"It seems the victim was in a panic then," I said. "Where did you leave them?"

I turned to face June. She was pointing somewhere off toward the left side of the house. Zara commanded the orbfly to move, and we followed cautiously.

Sure enough, a woman lay half naked on the floor in what looked to be a small study. She was in front of an oak desk. Papers were scattered about and an unlit lamp was leaning against the wall as if it had been stumbled into.

"Who is this woman?" I asked, kneeling at the body. Her breasts were exposed, revealing the subtle rise and fall of her chest.

"Her name was Annabel," June said. "She was a record keeper for the mayor."

"This woman is still alive," I said, bringing my hands to her throat. I felt for any sort of hardness caused by June's sealant. "How?"

"What I use expands after a few hours. I've found that this is the easiest way to seal a victim and prevent the worms from emerging."

"Can it be removed?" I asked.

"Well," June started, "it does generally take seven hours before fully hardening. But I don't believe it would be something worth doing. There may be irreparable damage to her voice. She would never be able to speak again."

"Can you remove it?" I asked, turning around to face her. June's countenance was hard. Her forehead crevices returned.

"It's not a matter of *if,*" June said. "I simply will not. I have brought you to the body, Edgar. I have done as you asked to keep Gatmer pleased. But I will not participate in whatever profanity you're thinking of conjuring. I will not take part in the ruining of her body."

"Please," Zara said.

It struck me in that moment that Annabel could be her mother, for they looked strikingly similar. Of course, Zara's mother had died years ago. It couldn't be her. Zara's parents had been older. But I could see the pain on Zara's face, the faint connection she felt with this almost-dead woman.

"Please," Zara said again, this time turning fully to look at June. "You may not agree with Gatmer. But we can help. Edgar can help. I know he can. Let him try to help. Please!"

June was silent for a moment as she seemed to regard the words of a child. Zara was convincing. Almost adorable. I watched June's face soften.

"All right," June said. "Just this once. Even if I'm able to do it at all. But I will not be held responsible for what happens to Annabel."

June moved to the body and knelt down. Removing her sack, she rummaged through her surgical supplies and set to work. I kept close to Annabel's body and helped position the head in a way that would be helpful to June.

"I forgot to tell you," Zara said, "I had a nightmare last night."

"Oh?" I said, looking to her. I could see June enter the throat at the edge of my vision. "And what was it about?"

"A serpent of great power," she replied. "It was devouring the world from below."

"A dream about the Deadlands. There must be a warning totem nearby."

"A warning totem?"

"Yes," I said, checking on June's progress. I could see the body beginning to spasm from the invasive procedure. "It is very rare to dream of such a place, especially with no prior knowledge of it. There are those who serve the great serpent and its vicars. They raise totems in areas to ward off potential intruders. There must be one nearby."

"Are we safe?" Zara asked, her eyes wide in terror.

"Never," I said. "But no harm should come to us from that cult. I have dealt with them before. They prefer to remain hidden."

"You have dealt with them? When?"

"Many years ago. They stole the body of my wife from the grave, sacrificed her in a changing pool near Dulwich."

"I didn't know that. What was her—"

I felt them before they struck, emerging from Annabel's throat with such great force that her entire neck bent upward, pointing to the sky. I was too slow and Zara was too close. I moved my head out of the way as a worm flew past my face. I could hear June swearing as she rose to her feet, backing away from the body as a worm flogged Zara in the stomach not once, but twice. Aurora was in a frenzy outside and I could do little to calm her.

I screamed Zara's name and pulled out my revolver, pointing it at Annabel's contorted and frenzied face. But I couldn't do it. I couldn't bring myself to shoot this innocent woman. And so I moved quickly, securing my revolver in its holster and drawing out my knife. I dove on top of Annabel and grabbed the base of the worms that were pouring out of her mouth. They were like a clump of violent, wet noodles in my hand, but they were solid enough to grasp. I thought about cutting them, but remembered June's words, that they were only dangerous within a host. I pulled with all my might, not knowing if I was sending Annabel to her true death. At first they resisted, no doubt grasping at organs and bone and muscle. But they soon relented as I continued to pull and heave with all my anxious strength. A moment later I felt them loosen. I fell backward with them in my hands, still flailing but with noticeably reduced effort.

There were more worms, I was sure of it, more that lived dormant within Annabel's body. But for now we were safe.

Zara, Aurora thought to me.

I dropped the gray worms on the floor. They wriggled about, trying to whip and harm despite their inability to do so. Zara was on the ground with her hands on her stomach, eyes wide. There was so much blood.

I frantically crawled to her, laying my hands on her stomach, putting pressure on her wounds. But they were too great, too large for me to deal with on my own. There was no time for magic, no time to fumble for a flower in my pouch with bloody hands that would only ruin any chance at proper transmutation.

"June!" I screamed, turning my head to find her. She was on the ground tending to Annabel, working diligently on her throat. I assumed she meant to seal her once more.

"June! Stop!" I said again, this time more forcefully. She looked to me with anger in her eyes, ones full of judgment. "Please," I said, moving to reveal the shock on Zara's face. "She's dying. Please!"

"They are both dying, Edgar," June said, turning away. "They are both dying a horrible, miserable death because of you."

I felt so small. June had been right the entire time, correct in her assessment of the town, right in saying that she did not need Gatmer's help. I was a failure, a complete fool for thinking I could bring a child to a place like this.

I looked to Zara. Her eyes were still wild with shock, moving about as if searching for her mother. She would only find me, a man of perdition. I rubbed my hands through her hair, hands full of her blood.

The air whispered a name.

Yoth-Mthog.

It was the worms, the ancient tongues. They spoke the name of their god as the wind came from under the door to usher Zara's soul away. Knowledge from a mentor poured into my mind, one that spoke of resurrection and an old pact. I recalled Yoth-Mthog's search for a host, and a man who had lost everything to the god of tongues.

But the man who had made a pact had received back what he had lost.

I made my decision quickly. I could feel the change in the air, the spirits of the Deadlands coming to claim what was rightfully theirs. There was little time to perform the necessary ritual. There was little time to speak to the god of tongues.

I cleared the floor quickly, pushing aside all papers and broken things to the side of the room. I lifted the rug and pushed Annabel's body aside, ignoring June as she yelled my name. The hardwoods beneath would suffice, and I felt for a pouch that I vowed never to touch. Opening it, I removed its only occupant: a petal of ash with a thin red streak. One of Gatmer's rarest flowers, infused with the blood of our first priest.

What are you doing? Aurora asked, speaking within our shared mind. She must have felt the chill down my spine. I had never held this particular petal before. The pouch had been given to me by a professor.

I was tempted to lie, but there was no such thing as a lie between us. *I am summoning,* I thought. *Please do not interrupt.*

I placed the petal on the floor. June was already in another room, no doubt to escape what she believed was profane. I quickly grabbed one of the dead worms nearby and cut off a very small portion of what I believed was its head. Then, taking the butt of my revolver, I began smashing what was left of it into tiny bits, infusing its guts with the gray petal whilst using a small portion of white and red petals from another pouch on my chest. I hoped Zara's blood wouldn't ruin the process. But I had no choice. The fire would have to be great, but temporary. Only Gatmer's flowers could engulf the wet worms. Candle flame alone would not be adequate.

Taking the knife from my belt, I cut a small incision on my left hand. The blade was clean, but I did not have time to disinfect my hands. I would have to live with any potential disease, though this seemed hardly a worthwhile thought given the situation.

After squeezing some of the blood and allowing it to pool in my hand, I dragged Zara's lifeless body to the middle of the room and placed the crushed worm and flower bits onto her belly. I could feel the presence of the Deadlands here in this room, but they did not take her. Her spirit somehow remained, even though her body had given up. I could feel them, as though the spirits of the dead were watching me work. As if Yoth-Mthog himself were watching in anticipation.

I thought of the words that only Gatmer's flowers would ever hear, spoke them aloud to my clasped and bloodied hands before placing them on the crushed petals, allowing them to hear what it was I had to say. Fire erupted from Zara's stomach. It engulfed only the offering. Smoke billowed in its place as the spirits of the Deadlands fled. I could feel them leaving, but the gooseflesh on my neck did not relax, for I could feel a more sinister thing coming, a being of great power and words.

Something approached my mind. It was a feeling I had only felt once before, back when my mind had first joined with Aurora's.

Words filled my head from a language I did not understand. Closing my eyes, I brought the shape of the words into focus, allowed them to sink deep into my heart. I could not derive the surface meaning of what was being spoken to me, but I could feel their revelation.

I knew Yoth-Mthog had accepted my offering. While there was a dangerous undertone to the words in my mind, I did not feel afraid. I allowed my heart to lurch toward Zara in an attempt to communicate my desire for her to live. I focused on my emotions and less on the presence rattling my mind.

"Your desire is for the child to live," said a chorus of whispers.

These words had been spoken aloud. I opened my eyes. Zara's body was covered in worms. I could not see her, but I knew she was still there. It was as if the smoke had spawned the creatures.

"Yes," I said, careful not to say too much.

"Then you know, Edgar." These words echoed all through the small house, a cacophony of whispers and utterances foreign to this plane of existence, natural only to the Peripheries.

"I have heard," I said. "I have heard of the man before me—the one who made a pact with the god of tongues. But the stories were never specific. The story has been retold many times and mostly not told at all."

No words came forth for a moment, only an idle noise from the worms, much like the sound of a trickling stream. Active, yet somehow dormant.

"The bird," said the worms. "The One Who Speaks."

My heart fell deep into my stomach. Was this the price I had to pay? Must I trade the life of Aurora for the life of a child?

"I cannot," I said, tears welling in my eyes. "She is as much me as I her. I would have used the ash-strewn flower for her as well."

The god of tongues seemed to regard this for a moment. The same idle trickling of wordless sounds uttered from the mass of worms that still pooled on Zara's body. But then the pile seemed to move, shift in shape as if making way for something else.

A lone worm emerged from the pile, upright in stature as if confident, or perhaps controlled by the god himself. It reared its ugly head even more, posturing itself against the gray light pouring through the windows, seeming to claim victory over Zara's lifeless body.

The mass of worms spoke, but I did not listen. I already knew what must be done, what the god demanded. And so I stepped forward, cautiously, and knelt before Zara. The noise that clamored against her body was almost deafening; but I still, though hesitantly, reached out and allowed the worm to crawl upon my hand.

"Open," said the worms. Even in my stupor I could not ignore the word. The sound grated against my mind and skin. But I obeyed, opening my lips as the gray worm slithered into my mouth. I threw my own head back, unable to breathe, eyes wide in fear as my throat clenched. I could feel the veins in my neck as they protruded from my skin. I spoke things that should never be said as the worm made its way into my chest, into my lung. Finally it nestled and lay still within my body where it rested.

When I looked back at Zara's body, the worms were gone, engulfed in the ritualistic flames as promised by the one that gave me the ash-strewn flower. But another promise had been fulfilled as well. Where there had been pooling blood and an open gaping wound, there was now skin, untouched and unharmed. Zara's eyes were open, wide with surprise as if she had seen the spirits of the Deadlands, which I supposed she had.

I moved closer to her and checked the torn cloth around her stomach. "Are you hurt?" I asked, moving one hand under her head.

My other was on her ribs, checking her breath. "What do you feel?"

"I feel nothing," she said with shallow breaths.

"What did you feel? What did you see?"

Zara didn't respond, and I silently berated myself for asking the question. I knew what lurked in the corner of every room. I have seen the spirits of the Deadlands before, wisps of what was once human, the tendrils of damned souls and long faces with no other thought but to reach for those who are dying. Even now, there were spirits in the house, around Zara. They could not touch her. Not any longer. But their anger . . . I felt their anger, their—

"Nothing," Zara finally replied.

She was lying.

But it would have to be a conversation for another time.

4

We sat silently within the confines of June's house. Night had fallen over the town, the cries of those grieving seemed to soar through the sky like a great bird of prey. Occasionally we would hear the cracking of whips from far off. June was not naive. As good as she had been, she had not been able to seal every single person. People would continue to die throughout the night.

"I have failed," I said, twirling a spoon in a cup of lukewarm tea.

Aurora sat perched beside the fireplace. After much discussion—and mostly begging from Zara—June had allowed Aurora within the house, with the promise that she would stay silent. And she had remained silent, even within our shared mind. I supposed she felt the worm was an intruder, that it could hear the soundless words we spoke.

"You have," June said in rebuke.

"He has not," Zara said, nibbling on a piece of bread. "He saved my life."

"Child, you will someday die," June retorted. "He has saved you from nothing."

"Remind me of your profession, Dr. Morton? If Edgar did not save me, then you have never saved a soul in your life."

I looked over to Zara. Her eyes were unusually hard for her predictably pleasing demeanor. June didn't respond. Silence filled the house.

"I failed," I said, setting the cup down on the table in front of me. "I did not heal a single person, and I do not believe getting you killed and creating a pact with a god for your resurrection is anything other than an act of desperation succeeding a foolish choice."

The worm churned within me, somewhere deep in my chest. The god had given no indication as to the worm's use or the importance of it within me. I had simply accepted the request under the declaration that it would bring Zara back to life. And she was back, wasn't she? Unharmed and more aware of the spiritual realities that surrounded her. I knew of very few who lived to see the spirits of the Deadlands.

"Foolish or not," Zara said, "I am still grateful. Very grateful to be alive and to be your student. Now would you stop being so melodramatic? We have a problem, Edgar. You have a worm in you."

Her cheerful demeanor made me smile.

"Can the god hear you?" June asked. She rose from her chair and looked out the window. There was a great wailing happening a few houses down. Moonlight poured through the aperture.

"Little is known about him," I said. "But I don't believe he can be in all places at once." I paused, trying to think as I continually swirled the spoon in my cup. "His attention is focused elsewhere. I can feel it. He is focused on the town, on the thousands of other worms. But when the night is over I'm afraid his sole attention will be on me."

Zara rose from her chair and made her way to June's window. "Then we don't have a lot of time. June, are you able to remove it surgically?"

"No," June said. Her eyes never left the dark. "There's a reason I seal the bodies. The worms move, and the more they move the more destruction they cause. I'm not going to guess and open up Edgar's stomach to find that it moved into his lung."

"Think, Dr. Morton," Zara said. "There must be a way. Something you know. Something you've talked about with your colleagues."

"My. Kind."

I looked over to Aurora. She was still perched beside the fireplace. There was light in her eyes. She had been silent in my mind ever since the worm's intrusion.

"Please explain, Aurora. As best you can."

I ignored the look of disdain from June.

"Song. Bird. Feel worm."

Zara came and sat by the fire. She was much better at interpreting Aurora's broken speech, and far better at speaking in a way that was encouraging rather than condescending. "Songbirds, Aurora?" Zara said. "What about the way they feel for worms?"

Aurora often dissociated herself from her species. Not necessarily out of pride, but because she had truly become something else altogether when our minds became one.

"Feet. Ears. Feel vibrate."

"Ah," I finally said, adjusting myself in the chair. "You can feel the vibration of the worm with your feet." I smiled and stifled a laugh with my hand. Of course it would be something entirely natural, something as simple as a bird finding a worm in the dirt.

"I could help." June said from the window. Her gaze finally left the other houses and she moved quietly back to her chair. We all sat together, huddled around the fireplace. "If the bird can find the worm we could try and surprise it. But Edgar . . ." She paused, her eyes softening. "It would be quite violent. This would not be a careful surgery. I would need to open you up quickly before it moves. Would you be able to grab the worm once we are in?"

It took a moment for me to realize she was talking to Aurora, as June refused to speak her name.

"Yes," Aurora said. "Grab. Beak."

June shook her head and looked to the fire. The worm writhed within me somewhere in my chest. Then I felt it no more.

"Are you sure about this?" I asked. I looked to Aurora. "My heart is beating, my blood pumping throughout my body. There are a million sounds within me. Are you sure?"

It was a ridiculous question. But the entire predicament was ridiculous. Of course she could. The earth was filled with far more sounds than me.

"Yes," Aurora said with firelight in her eyes. "Yes."

"June, you will have to work under a spell."

I said the words more matter-of-factly than I wished.

"Excuse me?" June said, shuffling in her chair. "I will not."

"There is no other way," I said. "If the worm feels threatened by your tools it will leave for another place in my body. Instead of working quickly and violently as you said, you will need to be slow and thoughtful, careful not to spook it."

"What about the pain?" Zara asked.

"What about?" I asked.

"Well," Zara started, "it might not be wise for June to administer anything to you, lest the worm get spooked as you say. It might recognize a change in your body, in your blood."

I hadn't considered this, but Zara was right. I would need to sit silently while June opened me up.

"I still haven't agreed," June said, crossing her legs. "I do not want to participate in this profanity."

"More. Death."

I shifted my gaze over to Aurora. I opened my mouth to speak, to help clarify her words to June. But I quickly closed my lips, realizing she had made perfect sense.

If June refused, more death would follow. I was due to become a surrogate for the god of tongues. Once he was done with the town, his gaze would be fully on me once more.

"Fine," June said in reassignment. "Just this once. And then you will leave. You will all leave."

5

What is the color of silence? This was a question I posed to Zara only a few months ago, on a walk within Gatmer's gardens. As a student she didn't have unfettered access to Gatmer's flowers but was allowed to pick a few under my watchful eye. In the garden she had responded that she thought silence was black, a representation of nothingness. It was then that I kneeled and put my fingers between one particular flower, one that only seemed to grow on cloudy days.

"Silence is light, blue like the sky," Zara said, picking through my pouch. My shirt was off, Aurora sat upon my chest. Her claws were sharp against my skin. "Silence is pregnant, fuzzy with possibility."

She ran her finger across the petal to examine it for any impurities. June was somewhere behind me, sharpening her tools. Dawn licked the darkling sky beyond the window.

"We will need to go back to Gatmer right away," Zara said. "Some of your flowers are growing stale."

I opened my mouth to speak, stopping when Aurora flexed her talons. She wanted me quiet.

I watched Zara work, peeling the petal into many parts before dispersing them around me. Before lying on the table, I expressed worry that the worm might feel the silence, that it would simply burrow and hide somewhere deep within me, unreachable. But we determined together that this was a risk worth taking. None of the options were good.

"The flowers burn slowly," Zara said. "But not so slowly that we should take our time, Dr. Morton."

"How long will I have?" June replied, moving a set of tools to a table nearby.

"Maybe a few minutes," Zara said.

June paused, looking at me before resting her gaze on Zara. She looked embarrassed. "How . . . exactly does it work?"

Zara looked to me. I nodded and allowed Aurora to continue working.

"There is a lengthy explanation," Zara started, "but for the sake of time, I will say that the petals of this particular flower are connected. I will place the five petals around Edgar's body, two near his head, two near his feet, and then one more I will hold before setting them on fire. The connection of the petals will create a bubble, so to speak, which is why I will hold one of the petals alight above his body. But be warned, June: while they burn slowly, they will not burn evenly. The one I am holding will be lit last so as not to break the bubble."

"Ah," June said, her eyes darting the other way. Though her curiosity had been obviously satiated, I could tell she was annoyed. "Well then. Bird, are you ready? Zara?"

Aurora bobbed her head. Zara nodded as well. I watched Zara as she moved to the fireplace before coming back with a fire poker. With it she lit the petals one by one. Then she stood on a chair and lit the one in her hand last, holding it far above my body.

Silence erupted around me as Aurora used her feet to sense the worm's vibrations. I was surprised at how difficult it was to perceive anything meaningful at all. I could feel my blood, my heart, my stomach acid as it gurgled. But at the same time, everything was dull. Sound is the consequence of vibration—that much I knew. But I could not for the life of me feel anything that mattered. It was as if everything within and around me were connected, vibrating impossibly and soundlessly together. Despite this, Aurora was good, able to separate and pinpoint with deranged accuracy the vibration of the worm. She stepped around my body carefully before placing her beak between my lower left rib, signaling to June where the worm rested.

I felt the cool of the antiseptic before June's blade, which surprised me more than it hurt. My senses were barraged with every sort of feeling, and for a moment I thought that I was speaking these thoughts silently aloud. I closed my mouth and remained still.

Aurora was perched upon my stomach while Zara stood unmoving on the chair. All eyes were on the gaping wound.

There was commotion and incredible pain when Aurora struck me with her beak, a chaos that I could only read on Zara's face. I felt Aurora digging within my ribs. I hoped she didn't breach the intercostal muscles. But a moment later Aurora's head emerged, crimson as if soaked by bloodlust, dripping with my very life. She was flapping her wings, pulling greatly with all her might as June worked to stop the bleeding. All this I saw and never heard, though I was beginning to feel everything. Something was wrong, and something was coming. I could feel it in the air, in the cool retreat of night and arrival of dawn.

The god of tongues had come—his focus was on me in full.

A haggard wind blew in through the window. It snuffed out the fire before turning its attention on the rest of us. This wind was tired and insatiable, sick with the death it had carried all night long. The silence broke when it knocked Zara to the ground. Rising to my feet I tried to assess my surroundings, but my ears screamed in protest.

Chaos was all around me.

I first looked to June, who was backed into a corner with bloody hands, scalpel held out in self-defense. I followed her gaze to the floor where Zara held the worm, which was now partially wrapped around Aurora's body. It had grown a considerable amount, so much so that I wondered how it had ever been in me at all.

"Edgar!" Zara screamed. "Edgar, you have to do something!"

Her words startled me out of my thoughts. "Aurora," I said to myself, running to her. I grabbed the knife from my belt and knelt by Zara. My vision was cloudy from the loss of blood.

"It's too strong," Zara said. "I can't get it off her. Kill it, Edgar. You have to kill it."

I moved the knife toward Aurora's body. I would have to be careful, lest I accidentally cut her.

"Start the fire," I said, taking the head of the worm from Zara. Below me Aurora seemed to go limp.

"What?" Zara asked, rising to her feet.

"Start the fire!" I said again, cutting off the worm's head. "Hurry!"

Zara grabbed my pouches as I continued to try and pry the worm from Aurora's body. She was suffocating before my eyes, and no matter how much I tried to speak within our shared mind she would not respond.

"You cannot die," I said, tears welling in my eyes. I managed to get my fingers in between her body and the worm, but it only seemed to tighten. Moments passed. I was losing blood and consciousness, my grip growing weaker by the second.

And then there was fire. Brilliant, radiant fire. I reached my hand toward it. Toward Zara. "Throw it," I said, my words beginning to fail. "Throw it!"

Through starry vision she came and took the worm's head from my hand, throwing it into the fireplace. I could feel the worm go limp under my fingers. But it was all too much. I had lost an excessive amount of blood.

Then everything went black.

6

I remembered the first time I met the raven:

It came to me after fleeing a fight with my sister, upon a high cliff overlooking the ocean. I was cold, but the water sparkled. I didn't yet know that my parents had been murdered, that my sister was hiding in the brush just beyond the tree line outside our home. I didn't know anything yet. Nothing of mind amalgamation, nothing of my future with Gatmer. I only knew the silliness of childhood squabbles as the raven croaked from a dying tree. I had wondered, then, if the bird had fled her sibling like me, if together we were looking over the cliffside for anything other than shared annoyance, or if there was a reason for our disquieting stillness.

But then I saw it, if only for a moment. It was in her eyes, in the way she croaked. Perhaps she had seen what happened to my parents, had followed me all the way to the ocean. Perhaps she had seen some futurity, some convergence between us in the way only she could.

She followed from above when I left, rested upon the hanging boughs outside my home as I consoled my sister, never left us even after we were captured by the cicada kings.

When I finally found Gatmer after losing my sister, the raven was still there, perched upon the nearest tree, as if she had sat upon every branch that had ever been born from my life.

7

"Breathe."

I heard the word before I saw anything at all. Aurora sat perched upon my chest, her head cocked, listening for signs of life. "I will move if you let me," I finally said, using my hands to push off the ground.

My ribs throbbed in pain. It took a moment for me to inspect myself. I had been properly sewn together. The stitches were well placed.

"We almost lost you," Zara said from behind. "When the worm died, everything fell apart. June was infected. She'd been infected this entire time. Look."

I turned to look, which was far more difficult than I thought it would be. June's head was gone, her body limp on the ground against the wall. There was something else resting where her head had been, some monstrosity, tentacled and wormlike, that rose out from her neck; like vines with thick branches they grabbed the wooden walls of June's home, as if trying to escape.

Zara killed her, Aurora thought to me. *You should know. She has never killed before.*

"Are you all right?" I asked Zara.

"Yes," she said, throwing her pack around her shoulder. "But we should leave. Report all this to Gatmer. I was able to stitch you up, but it wasn't clean. Infection might set in."

I smiled, but not out of happiness or joy. No, all this was terrible. The town was in ruins. June was dead. I had almost lost

Aurora and Zara both in one night. I smiled because I was proud of Zara. She was good when everything wasn't. She had saved me despite the fact that I had put her in harm's way.

"Thank you," I said, carefully lifting the shirt over my head. "Thank you, Zara, for everything. And to you as well, Aurora."

We left at midday, under a hiding sun. The air was cool and inviting. Nothing screamed, for all was dead.

But we were alive, and we had much to report.

Lucidity Subsides

Lee Clark Zumpe

We worship at the altar of an unknown god,
     a cruel and ravening divinity,
     faceless and incomprehensible,
     flanked by pious, white-robed priests
     and an entourage of bloodletters.

We surrender dignity for moments of clarity
     and fleeting fragments of memory;
     but each day lucidity subsides
     and reason recedes into the dim borderland
     between experience and illusion.

We commune with the nothingness of being,
     yielding to the voracious appetite
     of some unfathomable celestial being
     or to the uncontainable gluttony
     of the intensifying void within us.

From Boz to Bedeviled:
Madness and Mystery in the Urban Gothic of Dickens, Poe, and O'Brien

John P. Irish

> Whoever battles monsters should take care that he doesn't become one in the process. And if you stare for a long time into an abyss, the abyss looks into you, too.
>
> —Friedrich Nietzsche, *Beyond Good and Evil*, §146

> The shadow is a moral problem that challenges the whole ego-personality, for no one can become conscious of the shadow without considerable moral effort. To become conscious of it involves recognizing the dark aspects of the personality as present and real. This act is the essential condition for any kind of self-knowledge, and it, therefore, as a rule, meets with considerable resistance.
>
> —C. G. Jung, *Aion: Researches into the Phenomenology of the Self*, II. The Shadow

In the literature of the nineteenth century, the city emerges not merely as a backdrop but as a central figure—a living, shifting landscape that mirrors and distorts the minds of those who move within it. Charles Dickens (1812–1870), Edgar Allan Poe (1809–1849), and Fitz-James O'Brien (1826/8–1862) each confront this urban space from different narrative and psychological vantage points, tracing the transformation of city life from observable reality to a metaphysical enigma. While Dickens's "The Drunkard's Death" in *Sketches by Boz* positions the narrator as a moral observer cataloguing social decay, Poe's "The Man of the Crowd" plunges the observer into epistemological crisis, and O'Brien's "Broadway Bedeviled" collapses reality entirely into delusion.[1] Across these three stories, the figure of the flâneur[2] evolves—from detached witness to obsessive pursuer to hallucinatory victim—while the city itself shifts from a legible social landscape to a weird and self-reflective abyss. This essay examines how each author progressively destabilizes the urban gaze and narrative authority, moving from realist moralism to psychological fragmentation to ontological collapse. As madness, monstrosity, and the supernatural increasingly blur, the city becomes not only a stage for horror but an active agent of it—ultimately revealing that the greatest terror lies not in what can be seen, but in what can never be understood.

Urban Spaces and Literary Forms in the 1830s–1850s

The cities of London and New York in the mid-nineteenth century became a growing fascination for literary writers. Positioned be-

---

1. These stories are connected in compelling and intricate ways. *Sketches by Boz* marked Dickens's first major foray into publication, achieving considerable success and distinguishing itself through its focus on urban observation and the flâneur as central narrative figure. Poe expressed particular admiration for the collection, offering an unusually favorable review in the *Southern Literary Messenger* and recommending it to the American reading public, noting especially the Gothic elements embedded within the sketches. O'Brien's connection to both Dickens and Poe is especially noteworthy. After departing Ireland in 1849, he spent nearly three years in London, actively participating in its vibrant literary and social scenes before relocating to New York. During his time in London, O'Brien published one early horror story and two poems in Dickens's periodical *Household Words*. His tale "Broadway Bedeviled" stands as a direct homage to Poe's "The Man of the Crowd," echoing its themes and structure while introducing his own distinctive stylistic and psychological inflections. O'Brien frequently drew inspiration from Poe's work, often imitating and reimagining it in a manner uniquely his own, thus weaving a rich intertextual dialogue between the three authors.
2. *Flâneur* is a French term popularized by Charles Baudelaire and referring to a man who wanders through an urban landscape and comments upon what he sees.

tween the waning Romanticism of the early nineteenth century and the emerging realism of its latter half, many writers found themselves caught within this transitional period, often blending elements of both literary movements. In many respects Dickens, Poe, and O'Brien exemplify this liminal phase in literary history. Murray Baumgarten captures this idea perfectly: "Realism in . . . [this] time was magical, for the city was a fairy-tale come to life, grim, exhilarating, and transformative. To describe this urban world was to create a new Bible, encompassing heaven and earth, and all that lies between" (106). All three writers were firmly embedded within the urban environment, and their narratives are saturated with explorations of city life and its myriad complexities. Charles L. Crow observes: "As the forests recede, the importance of cities grew, and the urban gothic became popular" (380). As major metropolitan centers, both London and New York provided ample opportunity for these authors to observe the full spectrum of urban experience. As pioneering figures, their sharp-eyed reportage and journalistic precision, combined with imaginative storytelling, offered readers something distinctive, resonant, and unmistakably urban. For all three writers, the city was both a source of fascination and a site of horror—a space that revealed as much about the self as it did about the world around it. In the cities, Fred Botting notes, "our own darkness is often there to meet us" (133).

The growth of cities in the nineteenth century was driven by a number of interrelated phenomena: natural population increase, the migration from rural to urban centers in search of economic opportunity, the influx of immigrants seeking new lives,[3] advances in

---

3. Some scholars have claimed that O'Brien—despite being an Irish immigrant—was intolerant of Irish and other immigrants. This view appears to stem largely from a public feud with *New York Times* assistant editor Augustus Maverick, who in 1858 falsely accused O'Brien of plagiarizing William North's work in "The Diamond Lens." The dispute escalated in the press, and after O'Brien's death Maverick continued to disparage him, alleging he was "absurdly ashamed of his Irish birth." Maverick's statement was based on a statement originally made in North's novel *The Slave of the*

transportation that facilitated relocation, and agricultural innovations that reduced the need for rural labor. Both the United States and England experienced massive urbanization during the first half of the century. In 1840, the population of the United States was approximately 17,000,000, according to the U.S. Census, while the 1841 census placed the population of England, Wales, and Scotland was a little over 18,000,000. Daniel Walker Howe notes: "Overall, in the years between 1820 and 1850 the sector of the population considered 'urban' . . . multiplied fivefold and increased its share of the total population from seven percent to eighteen percent—commencing the period of the most rapid urbanization in American history" (526).

This demographic transformation in both countries coincided with a shift in how individuals perceived one another. As Philip Grech observes, "Before this period, people were accustomed to easily identifying others, which allowed them to determine whether a person was safe or threatening. But these new people were largely incomprehensible—socially, economically, politically and otherwise . . . to [the] established population" (60). These anxieties, rooted in the disorienting effects of urbanization and shifting social boundaries, provided rich material for Gothic writers, who both exploited these irrational fears in their narratives and commented on the psychological turbulence of the era. As Benjamin F. Fisher comments: "Cities' vastness made perfect settings for crime and mystery" (22). It was within this historical context that Dickens, Poe, and O'Brien crafted their masterpieces of urban Gothic fiction.

Lamp, in which he claimed Fitzgammon O'Bouncer (an O'Brien persona made up by North for his novel), "secretly despised his country. . . . To call him an Englishman, was the surest way to flatter him. . . . He was an Irishman because he could not help it." O'Brien's only biographer, Francis Wolle, repeated these charges without critical scrutiny, yet there is no substantial evidence to support them. O'Brien's writings reveal no such bias, and his poetry—particularly popular works such as "The Ballad of the Shamrock" (*Harper's New Monthly Magazine,* March 1861)—frequently affirms his Irish heritage.

Unraveling the Texts: Dickens's "Sketches," Poe's "Crowd," and O'Brien's "Broadway"

Dickens's first published book, *Sketches by Boz,* was a collection of short pieces originally printed in various newspapers and periodicals between 1833 and 1836. The sketches, which depict London's streets and inhabitants, were reissued in book form under the now familiar title in late 1836. Michael Slater, in his introduction to the collection, notes: "these farcical stories, in which Dickens's literary skills can clearly be seen developing, have for their subject matter the social and material preoccupations of nineteenth-century middle and lower class life" (xii). Divided into four sections—*Our Parish, Scenes, Characters,* and *Tales*—the collection offers glimpses into a city fraught with dangers and struggles for the poor and working class, who are the primary focus of most of the stories. These pieces quickly drew attention to Dickens as an emerging literary talent.[4] The early sketches for the *Morning Chronicle*, published between September and November 1834, "represented something completely new in descriptions of London . . . [and] Dickens, the trained reporter . . . rendered the sights and sounds of ordinary daily life in the streets of London" (Slater xiii). While the sketches did not initially bring him significant financial success—many of the early publications were unpaid—they garnered praise from critics and interest from publishers. In its initial publication year, the collection was reviewed by Poe in the *Southern Literary Messenger*. In an uncharacteristically positive critique, Poe praised Dickens's wit and stylistic control, writing, "In regard to their author we know nothing more than that he is a far more pungent, more witty, and better disciplined writer of sly articles, than nine-tenths of the Magazine writers in Great Britain . . . We conclude by strongly recommending the

---

4. Paul Schlicke argues that Dickens's *Sketches* had an extraordinary contemporary impact, rapidly elevating Dickens to prominence through his vivid, realistic portrayals of urban life and boosting his career.

Sketches of Boz to the attention of the American readers" (*Essays and Reviews* 204–7).

"The Drunkard's Death," which appears in the final section of *tales*, was written specifically to close the *Sketches: Second Series*, published in 1837; it was designed "to give the book a striking conclusion" (Slater xix). The tale opens with a haunting reflection: "We will be bold to say, that there is scarcely a man in the constant habit of walking, day after day, through any of the crowded thoroughfares of London ... [who fail to experience] some being of abject and wretched appearance ... miserable wretch, in rags and filth, who shuffles past him now in all the squalor of disease and poverty" (554).[5] The narrator, Boz, acknowledges a range of reasons why individuals fall into such a decrepit state—misfortune, misery, the ruin of worldly expectations, and the death of loved ones—all contributing to lives that "present the hideous spectacle of madmen, slowly dying by their own hands" (555). The story opens with the utter dissolution of the drunkard's life: his wife lies on her deathbed, and he is left with four children to support, a task for which he is entirely unequipped given his condition. As the narrative progresses, his three sons abandon the household following episodes of domestic violence, leaving only his daughter, who herself is gravely ill. Driven by a sense of familial obligation, she struggles to care for her father despite her deteriorating health, her self-sacrifice a tragic counterpoint to his unraveling.

Warden, the protagonist and alcoholic, returns home from a day of drinking, weaving his way through the streets until he is intercepted by his daughter before entering their apartment. She informs him that one of his sons, William, has returned, seeking shelter and protection. William, now facing hardships of his own, is wanted for murder. When Warden confronts him about his involvement in criminal activity, William responds with a bitter retort: "Does it surprise you, father?"—a line that resonates with the idea that the sins

---

5. All quotations from Dickens's *Sketches by Boz* are taken from the Penguin Classics edition.

of the father are visited upon the children. After a few days of hiding, with William and the daughter, Mary, confined to their miserable attic, Warden ventures out to obtain food for the family. He begs for money in the streets and manages to collect enough to purchase a small amount of food. However, rather than returning directly home, he decides to stop for a drink. In the tavern, he is approached by two men who, unbeknownst to him, are searching for William.[6] In his inebriated state, Warden is easily manipulated into revealing that his son is hiding at home. The men follow him back to the apartment, where they arrest William, sealing the son's fate and deepening the tragedy of the father's ruin.

The story concludes with Warden collapsing into unconsciousness after William's arrest; when he awakens the next day, he discovers that Mary has disappeared. "He rambled through the streets, and scrutinized each wretched face among the crowds that thronged them, with anxious eyes. But his search was fruitless, and he returned to his garret when night came on, desolate and weary" (563). Eventually, Warden gives up the search and, unable to pay rent, is cast into homelessness. Living on the streets, he begins to contemplate the ultimate escape—suicide and death. "Never did a prisoner's heart throb with the hope of liberty and life half so eagerly as did that of the wretched man at the prospect of death" (565). Here, Dickens powerfully juxtaposes the imagery of a free man with that of one imprisoned by his alcoholism, framing suicide not simply as despair but as a perverse act of liberation. Warden throws himself into the river that runs through the city, and although his primal instinct compels him to fight for survival, he ultimately succumbs. "A week afterwards the body was washed ashore, some miles down the river, a swollen and disfigured mass. Unrecognized and unpitied, it was borne

---

6. The text draws an even more explicit connection to the themes found in Poe's and O'Brien's stories: "Two men whom he had not observed, were on the watch. They were on the point of giving up their search in despair, when his loitering attracted their attention; and when he entered the public-house, they followed him" (561).

to the grave; and there it has long since mouldered away!" (565–66).

Building on his admiration for Dickens's early work, Poe engaged deeply with *Sketches by Boz*, frequently reviewing Dickens's writings and singling out pieces such as "A Visit to Newgate" and "The Black Veil" for their haunting effect. This critical engagement reveals Poe's fascination with Dickens's urban vision.[7] Poe's story "The Man of the Crowd" was published in two different magazines in December 1840, the *Casket* and *Burton's Gentleman's Magazine*.[8] Poe's story is one of his more well-known urban Gothic tales. Structurally, the narrative unfolds in two major parts: an initial section in which the unnamed narrator provides background and context, followed by an extended chase sequence that dominates the story, which has been the focus of much Poe scholarship. Stephen Fink observes that "Poe scholars have tended to focus on the character of the narrator more than on the old man himself, and in doing so they have analyzed the various ways in which the narrator is limited, inadequate, or unreliable" (17).

Poe's story opens with an unnamed narrator who is convalescing in London from an unspecified injury or illness. Although never explicitly stated, it is often assumed that the narrator is American. One evening he sits in a coffee shop and watches pedestrians pass by the window, initially positioning himself as a neutral observer of the city. As the narrator observes the crowd, a particular figure suddenly seizes his attention: "suddenly there came into view a countenance

---

7. Stephen Rachman offers an interesting analysis of the notion and concept of plagiarism, which he applies to Poe's indebtedness to Dickens's *Sketches of Boz*.

8. T. O. Mabbott offers a detailed explanation of the publishing history of Poe's story. "The Man of the Crowd" was first published in December 1840. The story appeared simultaneously in the *Casket* and in *Burton's Gentleman's Magazine*, just after the latter was acquired by George R. Graham. Although labeled separately, the two issues were nearly identical and marked the transition to Graham's new periodical, *Graham's Magazine*, which was formally launched in January 1841. Poe joined the magazine's staff shortly thereafter.

... that of a decrepit old man ... a countenance which at once arrested and absorbed my whole attention" (392).[9] The detached observer is quickly transformed into an obsessive pursuer: "I resolved to follow the stranger whithersoever he should go" (393). The narrator details the erratic movements of the old man as he weaves his way through the streets of London. Ultimately, in an act of resignation and exhaustion, Poe's narrator abandons the pursuit: "I grew wearied unto death, and, stopping fully in front of the wanderer, gazed at him steadfastly in the face. He noticed me not, but resumed his solemn walk, while I, ceasing to follow, remained absorbed in contemplation ... He refuses to be alone. He is the man of the crowd" (396). Poe's story becomes a meditation on the search for meaning and knowledge in an urban environment, told through the lens of the hunter. While his tale has often served as source material for later writers, it was one of his most devoted literary successors who crafted an imitative narrative that stands as a worthy counterpart to the original: O'Brien's "Broadway Bedeviled."

O'Brien's story was first published in *Putnam's Monthly Magazine* in March 1857, a periodical that became a frequent outlet for his short fiction, poetry, and essays, beginning in May 1853. Initially, the story was not attributed to O'Brien by Francis Wolle, his first biographer and the earliest scholar to systematically organize his works. It was identified as O'Brien's in 2012 by Wayne R. Kime.[10] The story falls within O'Brien's middle period, a phase in which his

---

9. All quotations from Poe's "The Man of the Crowd" are taken from the Library of America edition.

10. The story is unmistakably O'Brien's. First, his journalistic series "A Man about Town" was being written concurrently with the story's publication, indicating that its themes and ideas were already occupying his mind. Second, the story closely imitates Poe's "The Man of the Crowd," a practice typical of O'Brien, who often modeled his work on Poe's. Third, it is not merely an imitation but an adaptation: O'Brien reimagines Poe's narrative, elevating it and approaching the situation from an entirely different perspective, a hallmark of his literary method. Finally, the style and tone are also consistent with O'Brien's distinctive narrative voice.

experimentation with various literary techniques and styles begins to coalesce.[11] However, "Broadway Bedeviled" resists easy categorization; it weaves together elements of the supernatural, paranoia, monomania, Gothic horror, and existential angst. This hybridity is characteristic of O'Brien's middle period, where literary innovation remains at the forefront.

"Broadway Bedeviled" unfolds in three distinct narrative phases.[12] The first section introduces the unnamed narrator, offering insight into his background and personal history. Told from a first-person perspective, the story relies on an unreliable narrator whose perceptions are deeply distorted by alcoholism and alienation. The narrator openly acknowledges his struggle with the "devil drink," a force he attempts—but often fails—to resist. Trained as a surgeon, he recognizes the catastrophic consequences of performing surgery while intoxicated and ultimately abandons his profession. However, this decision only deepens his isolation. His alcoholism has already estranged him from both family and friends, leaving him homeless.[13] In an attempt to escape his circumstances, he takes to wandering, yet his travels yield no sense of stability or belonging. Eventually, he

---

11. This O'Brien periodization is developed in my introductions to my edited collections published by Swan River Press (Dublin): *An Arabian Night-mare and Others (1848–1854)*; *The Diamond Lens and Others (1855–1858)*; and *What Was It? and Others (1858–1864)*.

12. The narrative structure of "Broadway Bedeviled" is notably uneven in its distribution (a metatextual device that mirrors the narrator's fragmented interiority): the first section (the setting and context) comprises approximately 720 words, the second (the chase) expands significantly to 1,874 words, while the final section (the dénouement) is a mere 111 words. This contrasts with Poe's "The Man of the Crowd," which maintains a relatively balanced distribution between its two narrative sections. Dickens's story is relatively even throughout the entire narrative, with no clear breaks in the story structure.

13. Compare this to Boz's comment: "drunkenness—that fierce rage for the slow, sure poison, that oversteps every other consideration: that casts aside wife, children, friends, happiness, and station; and hurries its victims madly on to degradation and death" (555).

returns to New York, though his homecoming is anything but comforting. His connection to the city is fraught with contradiction, as he describes his return in paradoxical terms: "I found myself home again, where there was no home" (156).[14] This sense of profound alienation is reinforced throughout the opening of the story, culminating in the bleak admission: "I found myself alone in New York—truly, in its most actual and painful sense, alone" (O'Brien 156).

This profound sense of isolation, however, is tempered by an unsettling yet reassuring presence—an irrational, possibly supernatural force that the narrator believes watches over him. Though he acknowledges that this feeling defies reason, he is convinced that this entity serves as his protector, shielding him both from external dangers and from committing harm himself. He clings to the belief that this mysterious presence will one day save him, speculating that it may even be the ghost of his mother. Regardless of its origin, he perceives it as a supernatural guardian, one that has intervened during his most desperate moments of loneliness and despair, preventing him from succumbing to self-destruction.

At this point the narrative transitions into the second phase of the story. After establishing the setting and providing the necessary background context, the narrator shifts focus to a night out in the city. He has spent the entire day drinking, and it becomes clear to the reader that his earlier resolve to abstain has collapsed and he is once again in the grip of alcohol. While he still perceives the protective presence that has shielded him from harm, he now senses a second, more ominous force—one that he believes is pursuing him with malicious intent. "Especially had I an overpowering dread of danger . . . holding the way in front of me, following closely behind me, and near me on either side" (158). He becomes convinced that he can identify at least some of his pursuers, catching glimpses of their whispered conversations and attempts to direct others to join the chase. In a desperate effort to evade them, he employs every trick he

---

14. All quotations from O'Brien's "Broadway Bedeviled" are taken from the Hippocampus Press edition (forthcoming).

can think of—altering his walking pace, ducking into buildings, crossing the street, entering and exiting cabs—yet nothing shakes the feeling that they are closing in on him. The paranoia intensifies, reinforcing his belief that he is being relentlessly hunted.

At last he finds himself in front of a hotel and, in a final desperate attempt to escape his pursuers, rushes inside. Sensing his intentions, the figures close in, but he breaks into a run, shouting for help as he moves through the building. When he realizes that fleeing alone will not save him, he takes the walking stick he carries and strikes one of his nearest pursuers squarely in the face. Panic mounting, he cries out to the hotel staff and guests, "Stop them! Save me!" The next moment, he loses consciousness. When he comes to, he is sprawled on the hotel floor, surrounded by people offering assistance. Blood streams from his mouth and nose, a stark physical manifestation of his ordeal.

The story concludes in the final section with the narrator attempting to make sense of his harrowing experience, suspecting that he may have suffered from *delirium tremens*. He reasons that his struggle to abstain from alcohol, combined with his indulgence that night, may have triggered a hallucinatory episode. However, as he returns to his hotel in the company of friends, he remains unconvinced that what he experienced was mere illusion. Instead, he insists that the pursuit was real, attributing his tormentors to malevolent specters intent on harming him. The final lines of the story offer a striking reflection on suffering and redemption: "Since that day, the doctrine of universal salvation has had arguments as well as charms for me. So much of hell as was compressed into that stage-trip from Madison Square to Barnum's Museum, has saved me from believing in an eternity of it" (162). This revelation suggests that his brush with terror, whether real or imagined, has fundamentally altered his perspective on damnation and salvation, reinforcing the psychological and existential depth of the tale.[15]

---

15. Another possible conclusion that one might draw from these stories is that of satire—an interpretation that would distinguish both Poe and

From Observation to Obsession: The Flâneur and Urban Psychogeography

In *Sketches by Boz,* Dickens employs a third-person omniscient narrator who stands outside the narrative action, offering a moralizing and socially observant perspective. This narrative position allows Dickens to comment on broader social issues—poverty, addiction, class divisions—while maintaining a measured distance from the psychological interiority of his characters. The city, in this framing, becomes an observable moral terrain, a space to be scrutinized and interpreted rather than internalized. The narrator adopts a voyeuristic stance akin to that of the flâneur[16]—detached, yet deeply judgmental—where individuals such as the drunkard become both spectacle and symbol of urban decay and social failure. As Boz remarks, readers are all familiar with "some fallen and degraded man, who lingers about the pavement in hungry misery—from whom every one turns coldly away," individuals who have been observed "sinking lower and lower by almost imperceptible degrees" (554). Yet while this moral gaze condemns systemic urban suffering, it also risks reducing lives to symptoms of a social pathology rather than full interior worlds. Boz becomes, in effect, a figure who hovers be-

---

O'Brien from Dickens. A noted advocate for reform initiatives, Dickens was outspoken in his support for social change, a stance shaped in part by his difficult childhood circumstances. Poe and O'Brien, on the other hand, were more critical of the urban reform movements promoted during the antebellum period. While O'Brien's work elsewhere reveals a genuine sympathy for the downtrodden and the most vulnerable in society, the final lines of "Broadway Bedeviled" suggest that the story may have been intended, at least in part, as tongue-in-cheek social satire.

16. Rosemary Lloyd distinguishes the flâneur as a figure fundamentally different from the narrators in these stories: "It's a ramble without an aim, more active than hanging out, more passive than going for a walk. It's a loitering without intent, an extension of window-shopping to cover the whole spectacle a city can offer" (138). By this definition, none of the three narrators—Dickens's Boz, Poe's obsessive observer, or O'Brien's hallucinatory wanderer—truly embodies the flâneur.

tween sociologist and storyteller, observing a metropolis not as a psychic labyrinth, but as a diagnostic chart of modern vice.

This perspective, however, is not merely a function of narrative structure but part of Dickens's broader realist and reformist agenda. As Julian W. Breslow argues, Boz is developed "as a consistent character who provides the reader with an authoritative perspective from which to view and judge the world" (127). Boz evolves from participant-observer to moral commentator, offering the reading public not just entertainment, but guidance.[17] The narrator's detachment enables a clarity of vision that aligns with Dickens's social critique, yet also signals a departure from psychological depth in favor of sociological generalization. F. S. Schwarzbach notes that what distinguishes Dickens's sketches from other urban literature is their prioritization of the immediacy and ephemerality of city life. The city, he contends, is a space of "continuous institutionalized change," where "traditional kinds of knowledge and customs no longer apply" and urban existence becomes "a new way of life" that is "self-referential" (Schwarzbach 34). In this sense, Boz's authority is paradoxically rooted in the transient, ever-shifting present. Amanpal Garcha further suggests that Boz's movements—from the suburbs to the city, and from the middle to the lower classes—mirror a disorientation that prefigures the more psychologically fraught perspectives found in Poe and O'Brien: "His formal move from narrative tale to nonnarrative sketch corresponds to a move in geography from the suburbs to the city, and a move in social milieu from the relatively comfortable middle ranks of society to the struggling lower class" (Garcha 5). As the modern city transforms, the narrator's role as observer becomes increasingly unstable, caught between moral certainty and the elusive dynamics of a society in flux.

Poe's "The Man of the Crowd" employs a first-person subjective

---

17. Michael Slater argues that Boz, the narrator, undergoes a narrative evolution—beginning as a closely tied flâneur in the early sketches and gradually developing into a more overt moral observer in the later tales, of which "The Drunkard's Death" is one.

(limited) narrator, whose introspective voice gradually dissolves into obsessive fixation. Unlike Dickens's Boz, who offers a morally authoritative, detached overview of urban life, Poe's narrator offers readers access only to his own perceptions, speculations, and psychological unraveling. Initially, the story presents a rational observer—a flâneur surveying the crowded London streets from a café window, indulging in classification and attempting to impose order upon the urban spectacle. But as the story unfolds, the line between detached observation and psychological compulsion begins to blur. The narrator becomes less a classifier of urban types and more a captive of the city's opacity, his reason increasingly warped by his obsessive pursuit of the enigmatic figure in the crowd. As he confesses, "I was at a loss to comprehend the waywardness of his actions" (395), the clarity of empirical vision gives way to bewilderment and epistemological destabilization.

The narrator's descent from rational observer to haunted pursuer marks a fundamental shift in the flâneur's role. The observational clarity that governs the first half of the narrative—reminiscent of Dickens's moral lens—is gradually replaced by visual intoxication and ontological instability. The crowd no longer reveals categories; rather, it absorbs the observer and reflects back an uncanny mirror image of his own fragmented self. The narrator becomes entangled in the very spectacle he once controlled, transformed from subject to object, consumed by the mysterious figure he attempts to follow. His epistemological failure culminates in his final admission: "It will be in vain to follow, for I shall learn no more of him, nor of his deeds" (396). The story ultimately dramatizes not discovery but the collapse of the possibility of knowledge.

Susan Elizabeth Sweeney offers a compelling reading of this collapse, arguing that Poe's story stages a tension between analytical observation and immersive experience to critique the Enlightenment ideal of visual mastery. She notes that the narrator initially positions himself behind a symbolic window—a space of detached control akin to a magnifying glass—allowing him to observe the city without participating in it: "Poe's narrator actually leaves the window through which he spies a sinister old man in order to follow him down the mean streets of London" (Sweeney 4). The first half of the story preserves a coherent visual perspective, but once the narrator enters the city's labyrinthine spaces, that structure disintegrates. Sweeney describes this as a narrative rupture: "The carefully established visual dynamic of the story's first half—in which the narrator organizes everything he sees in terms of his own vantage point, as if according to the rules of linear perspective—breaks down" (8). Time, spatial coherence, narrative sequence, and the categorization of the city become dizzyingly circular rather than hierarchically ordered. The narrator, who "seems motivated less by a desire for amusement than by a desperate need to make sense of the tumultuous sea of human heads" (Sweeney 5), fails in his interpretative mission. The story thus becomes a critique of the very act of observation, portraying the flâneur not as a master of the urban scene, but as one ultimately undone by it.

Jeremy Cagle extends this interpretive framework by arguing that Poe's narrator exemplifies a form of "transcendental hermeneutics," in which the act of reading becomes more significant than the content being read. The narrator's obsessive pursuit reflects a performative mode of interpretation—an introspective, irrational engagement with the world that parallels American Transcendentalist thought, particularly the philosophies of Emerson and Thoreau. In this sense, the narrative resists empirical understanding and instead embraces the impossibility of resolution. Cagle suggests that Poe deliberately avoids translating the irrational into an intelligible or poetic language; rather, he portrays the narrator's pursuit as a transcendent journey—an interpretive act that foregrounds the limits of comprehension and gestures toward future, more productive forms of reading. As Cagle writes, Poe "does not wish to reduce the irrational into an estimable language—even that of poetry—but rather detail the transcendent journey, or action, as a hermeneutic for further, more productive 'readings' in the future" (31).

In this way, Poe sets the stage for the complete breakdown of narrative and perception that will follow in O'Brien's "Broadway Bedeviled," where the city becomes not only uncanny but hallucinatory. Whereas Dickens's narrator maintains distance and judgment, and Poe's narrator becomes destabilized through proximity and obsession, O'Brien's narrator is fully consumed by the city's surreal phantasmagoria. Poe's story thus occupies an intermediary position—between realist urban observation and the weird, disorienting psychogeography of O'Brien—where the city no longer functions as a knowable space but becomes a self-reflective enigma.

O'Brien's unnamed narrator in "Broadway Bedeviled" is a quintessential first-person unreliable narrator, not merely subjective but clearly compromised by madness, paranoia, and delirium tremens. This narrative voice collapses the boundary between external reality and internal delusion, rendering the urban landscape a projection of the narrator's unraveling psyche. Unlike Dickens's morally detached observer or Poe's psychologically destabilized flâneur, O'Brien's narrator is fully engulfed by hallucination. The city is no longer a legible terrain of social observation; it becomes a site of ontological confusion and uncanny spectacle. The narrative perspective exemplifies weird fiction's defining impulse toward ontological instability, where distinctions between self and world, real and unreal, dissolve entirely. As the narrator confesses early on, "This was no operation of reason" (157), signaling that even his own cognitive processes are suspect. There is no attempt at systematic observation; instead, the narrator begins his tale not with purposeful flâneur but disoriented wandering: "I set out about dusk to loaf—that is the word—to kill time, to run amok down the narrow lane of a day" (157).

This collapse of observational distance marks the complete disintegration of the flâneur figure. In O'Brien's narrative, the city no longer produces urban types to be interpreted; it instead generates hallucinations that mimic observation, inverting the very act of seeing. The narrator experiences the city as a conspiratorial theatre: he is pursued by stalkers, surveilled by strangers, and deciphering signs that exist only in his fractured perception.[18] "As I walked, the scene around me whirling, upside down, in the same jumbled condition as my own mind, scarcely knowing whither my steps were tending, nor caring much" (158). The crowd is not symbolic or archetypal, as in Poe; it is spectral, elusive, and entirely projected by a disordered mind. The city has become a mirror of internal breakdown, a haunted space where psychological and physical realities fuse. The transformation and ultimate disintegration of the flâneur across Dickens, Poe, and O'Brien—from observational distance to obsessive proximity to complete absorption—marks a trajectory in which the city itself shifts from a socially readable landscape to a destabilizing psychogeography, one that reflects not just external chaos, but the interior fragmentation of the self.

Madness, Monstrosity, and the Supernaturalization of the City

While *Sketches by Boz* is often remembered for its Gothic realism and social commentary, "The Drunkard's Death" represents one of Dickens's most disturbing visions of urban decline—a descent so bleak and grotesque that it borders on the uncanny. Though the story lacks overt supernatural elements, Dickens's portrayal of madness and urban horror is unsettling in its own right. The narrative reframes the modern city as a space not of haunted castles or storm-tossed landscapes, but of decaying tenements, streets choked with anonymity, and lives quietly unraveling into despair. The figure of the drunkard, Warden, serves as a symbolic monster—transformed not by demons or curses, but by vice, poverty, and social abandonment. As Dickens puts it, such individuals "present the hideous spectacle of madmen, slowly dying by their own hands. But, by far the greater part have willfully, and with open eyes, plunged into the gulf from which the man who once enters it never rises more, but into which he sinks deeper and deeper down, until recovery is hope-

---

18. O'Brien's interest in the theatre is well documented in my introduction to *What Was It? and Others (1858–1864)*.

less" (555). These madmen become unhuman and unrecognizable; they become monstrous. Michael Hollington argues that this results in a dehumanization of human individuals within the city: this "is only one of the paradoxes of the Dickensian grotesque" (*Dickens and the Grotesque* 43). The horror here is starkly naturalistic, but its intensity—its grotesque routineness—echoes the Gothic.

The descent into madness, while not clinical or metaphysical, becomes a kind of psychic implosion. Warden's collapse is not portrayed through interior psychological depth but through the outward, cumulative effects of degradation and isolation. His madness is social, visible, and deeply embedded in the urban landscape around him. The city exerts pressure not by supernatural forces, but by the very weight of its grim familiarity. The moment of Warden's complete unraveling—when he searches for his lost daughter—reads like a passage from uncanny literature: "He rambled through the streets, and scrutinized each wretched face among the crowds that thronged them, with anxious eyes. But his search was fruitless, and he returned to his garret when night came on, desolate and weary" (563). The city offers no revelation, no redemptive knowledge, only endless repetition and anonymity. His failure to locate Mary, and his ultimate surrender—"At length he gave up the pursuit as hopeless" (563)—underscores the futility of agency in the face of urban despair.

Importantly, Dickens's portrayal of Warden's final days flirts with the tropes of haunting, even as it remains grounded in realism. Warden becomes haunted by spectral memories of his former life: "He thought of the time when he had a home—a happy, cheerful home—and of those who peopled it, and flocked about him then, until the forms of his elder children seemed to rise from the grave, and stand about him" (563). Though these are not literal ghosts, Dickens evokes a haunting psychological residue: the past refuses to die, and instead reanimates itself within the drunkard's unraveling consciousness. This spectral return culminates in a terrifying scene of psychological disintegration: "Suddenly, he started up, in the extremity of terror. He had heard his own voice shouting in the night air, he knew not what, or why. Hark! A groan!—another! His senses were leaving him: half-formed and incoherent words burst from his lips; and his hands sought to tear and lacerate his flesh. He was going mad, and he shrieked for help till his voice failed him" (564). Here, Dickens gives readers something uncanny—a horrifying spectacle of internal madness mirrored by the external grotesquery of the city.

Hollington's concept of Dickens's "new Gothic" is especially illuminating in reading this tale. He argues that Boz constructs a distinctively urbanized Gothic—one that "lays bare through the telling of suppressed and hidden 'new Gothic' narratives the strangeness and cruelty of the modern metropolis, of what have evidently become quite routine city tragedies and monstrosities" ("Boz's Gothic Gargoyles" 162). "The Drunkard's Death" exemplifies this shift from traditional Gothic trappings to the horrors embedded in routine city life. Warden is not attacked by ghosts, but by the city itself—its pressures, its anonymity, and its indifference. The banality of this horror is what makes it so effective. As Hollington notes, "the sketches seek to address the banalization of horror in modern city life, and to educate or recuperate the reader's powers of vision" (163). Dickens forces his readers to look closely at scenes they might otherwise dismiss—a man dying in the gutter, a daughter vanishing without trace—by aestheticizing them within a form that borders on the Gothic. Boz becomes the vehicle for this transformation; as Hollington suggests, the narrator is not simply a passive recorder but a flâneur who "urges the reader . . . to 'look about himself' and become a sharper observer of immediate or adjacent horrors" (Hollington 163).

Thus, even without supernatural manifestations, Dickens's story presents the city as a site of horror—social, moral, and existential. Warden's monstrosity is entirely human, yet Dickens renders it in grotesque terms that push realism to its limit. His eventual suicide—cast in imagery that evokes liberation and imprisonment simultaneously—"the hope of liberty and life" (565)—suggests that escape from the city's psychic claustrophobia can only come through obliteration. The final image of Warden's disfigured corpse, "unrecognized and unpitied" (566), leaves no space for resolution or redemption. What remains is only the modern urban abyss—mundane, grotesque, and utterly inescapable.

Poe's "The Man of the Crowd" intensifies the disquieting atmosphere found in Dickens by infusing the urban landscape with epistemological instability, metaphysical ambiguity, and uncanny horror. The story transforms the city from a site of moral observation into a psychological labyrinth—a space where the boundary between perception and delusion begins to dissolve. The narrator, speaking in the first person, begins in the position of an observer, a pseudo-flâneur watching the "tumultuous sea of human heads" (391) with detached curiosity. However, this detached gaze quickly becomes a compulsive pursuit, unraveling into obsession. Poe's city does not merely reflect despair; it actively destabilizes reason. "As the night deepened, so deepened to me the interest of the scene" (392), the narrator states, suggesting that urban observation no longer yields clarity but draws the observer into psychological murk. The narrator's descent into obsession represents a shift from external observation to internal unraveling, mirroring the story's ontological slide into weirdness.

Poe's narrative logic is fundamentally uncanny: the city hides a horror that cannot be named, a presence that cannot be explained. The moment the narrator sees the old man, he is overtaken by a metaphysical unease: "a countenance which at once arrested and absorbed my whole attention, on account of the absolute idiosyncrasy of its expression" (392). The man is likened to "pictural incarnations of the fiend" (392), but whether this is a metaphor, hallucination, or literal spectral presence remains unresolved. Poe leaves the reader suspended in ambiguity. The story's climax is not a revelation but an epistemological failure: "It will be in vain to follow, for I shall learn no more of him, nor of his deeds" (396). The pursuit leads nowhere, and knowledge collapses. The narrator is not merely a voyeur; he is consumed by the unknowable, turning the flâneur into a self-fragmenting subject. He is no longer observing types—he is confronted with a figure who defies categorization and infects the observer with his ungraspable otherness.

Poe's city, then, becomes a breeding ground for a new kind of madness—one not rooted in vice or morality but in the limitations of cognition itself. Madness is not diagnosed, but enacted through the narrator's compulsive behavior and disintegrating sense of reality. As Philip Grech argues, Poe's narrative displaces madness from an individual pathology to a structural urban condition, one driven by fear, alienation, and anonymity. Grech reads "The Man of the Crowd" as a study in social psychopathy: "I am referring to social anonymity in modern city life as it creates a breeding ground of threat, crime, fear, unfeeling, interaction, lack of familiarity, disconnection, voyeurism, and uncertainty" (56). The crowd itself becomes monstrous in its anonymity—a dense swarm of unknowable others whose very presence threatens the integrity of the self. As Poe notes, "The wild effects of the light enchained me to an examination of individual faces" (392), yet that examination yields no understanding, only further fragmentation. The urban crowd becomes a surreal entity—both real and symbolic, human and inhuman.

Jeffrey Andrew Weinstock takes this further, suggesting that the story enacts an ontological paradox: the impossibility of aloneness. The crowd, for Weinstock, represents an externalized form of the narrator's internal anxieties, and the old man becomes a mirror image of the narrator's unconscious self: "The absence of secondary confirmation encourages the reader to consider the man of the crowd not as an 'actual' presence existing in the world of the narrator but as the ghostly projection of the narrator's psyche" (59). Selfhood, in this reading, is not fixed but shaped and fractured through encounters with the other.[19] "The Man of the Crowd," then, is not just

---

19. Numerous scholars have interpreted Poe's "The Man of the Crowd" as an exploration of doubling, suggesting that the narrator and the old man are, in fact, mirror images of each other—two halves of the same fractured

a pursuit of another, but a confrontation with one's own irreducible otherness. Poe connects this ambiguity to language itself: the city is not just unreadable, but unspeakable. The failure to interpret the old man parallels the narrator's failure to articulate meaning. The city becomes a monstrous text that refuses to be deciphered.

In contrast to Dickens's naturalistic moralism, Poe offers a proto-weird vision of the city: madness becomes a collapse of cognition, monstrosity becomes symbolic and spectral, and the supernatural remains suspended in possibility. "The whole atmosphere teemed with desolation" (395)—not because of social tragedy, but because the very structures of understanding have decayed. The horror in Poe is not only in the crowd or the city; it is in the recognition that meaning itself might be unattainable. The monster may be real or imagined, but either way, it signifies the narrator's—and perhaps the reader's—unresolvable epistemological condition.

In O'Brien's "Broadway Bedeviled," the line between mental illness and urban experience collapses completely. Where Dickens's drunkard is a moral figure and Poe's flâneur a psychologically unraveling observer, O'Brien's narrator has already crossed the threshold into full-blown psychosis. The city ceases to be a representational space or a backdrop for madness; it becomes madness itself, a hallucinatory extension of the narrator's fractured consciousness. Delirium tremens structures the entire narrative, rendering the city not a site of descent but a terrain of total immersion in unreality. The crowd, once a metaphorical social body, is now spectral and phantasmagoric—a projection of the narrator's terror and internalized guilt. The city no longer merely reflects mental collapse; it performs it. The city is not just haunted; it becomes a haunting mechanism, a conduit for the narrator's madness.

---

self. O'Brien's "Broadway Bedeviled," however, complicates and even subverts this interpretation by reversing the paradigm: here, it is not the pursued who functions as the double, but the pursuer. In this way, O'Brien turns Poe's psychological logic on its head, suggesting that the self's fragmentation emerges not from the object of pursuit, but from the act of pursuit itself.

Unlike Poe's ambiguous boundary between perception and delusion, O'Brien erases that line entirely. The story is filtered through a narrator who, by his own admission, is unreliable and fragmented. As he states early on, "As I walked, men walked by my side; or I encountered them as they stood in knots on the corners; or they crossed over from the opposite side of the street, always eyeing me suspiciously" (158). The reader sees the world entirely through this paranoid lens, with no external or objective narrative framework to correct or ground the hallucinations. The narrator registers conspiracies, stalkers, signals, and coded phrases in every corner of the city. These are not archetypes or social types, but wholly imagined figures—monsters born from the narrator's deteriorating mind. In this way, monstrosity in O'Brien is not a metaphor or symbol; it is perceptual structure itself, the mechanism by which madness expresses itself through hallucinated threats.

O'Brien's urban horror is not just internalized; it is cosmic and persecutory: "Yet this fear was strangely soothed by a desire to penetrate the mystery, and to learn what it was I had done, that they should seek my life" (159). The madness here is not rationalized or moralized; it is irrational, immersive, and theological. The narrator even interprets his pursuers as divine agents: "I felt that the fiends that followed me were sent by God, and that I must abide the issue. I scorned to seek an asylum at that moment" (160). In this theological register, the supernatural is no longer metaphor; it is believed to be literal, even as the story reveals it to be delusion. The power of weird fiction lies precisely in this duality: O'Brien offers no resolution between madness and haunting, treating them as ontologically indistinguishable.

The total psychic collapse is evident in the narrator's experience of doom: "I felt myself approaching nearer and nearer to my doom" (160). O'Brien presents madness not as a narrative endpoint, but as a narrative form. The structure of the story itself is defined by paranoia, fragmentation, and hallucination. Even after the crisis passes, the narrator's memory retains the experience with surreal clarity: "I am now going to describe phantasms which, although they were the tricks of madness, I as vividly recall at this hour as though they were the realities of yesterday" (161). This lingering vividness blurs the line between recollection and trauma, between reality and unreality. In the story's closing moment, he reflects, "My abused brain had conjured up that horrid warning. And yet, that very night, walking the floor with my kind friends, I told them the story as circumstantially as I tell it now; as clearly aware, too, as I am at this moment, that my foes were spectres" (162). The acknowledgment of delusion does not dissolve the uncanny; it reinforces it. The city remains a space haunted not by ghosts, but by the mind's inability to distinguish ghosts from reality.

In contrast to Dickens's social realism and Poe's metaphysical ambiguity, O'Brien offers a fully weird vision: a city that is not merely observed but inhabited by madness, a landscape that hallucinates rather than reflects. The flâneur has disintegrated, the monster is no longer outside the self, and the supernatural is no longer a question of belief but a function of perception. This final collapse into spectral hallucination marks O'Brien's contribution to the weird tradition—a vision of urban horror where madness and monstrosity become inseparable, not from the city, but from consciousness itself.

The Unsolvable Mystery: The City as a Self-Reflective Enigma

In "The Drunkard's Death," Dickens offers what appears to be a straightforward moral resolution: the inevitable demise of Warden serves as a cautionary tale about the perils of alcoholism and personal vice. Yet beneath this surface-level moralism lies a deeper ambiguity, one that complicates the narrative's didactic function. Though the story concludes with the drunkard's death, it leaves the broader social structures that produced his misery fundamentally untouched. The flâneur's gaze, embodied in Dickens's narrator Boz, observes and documents the spectacle of decline but ultimately fails to penetrate the systemic causes of suffering. Warden becomes just one more tragic figure among many—a case to be catalogued rather than understood. As David Seed notes, "The mystery of the urban scene arises from Dickens's realization that even trained and attentive observation has its limitations" (163). The narrative recognizes the impossibility of fully grasping the social mechanisms that lead to such degradation, rendering Warden's fall not just a moral tale, but an unresolved urban mystery.

Dickens's portrayal of the city underscores its role not only as the setting for this decline but also as an active agent in it—a "machine of forgetting" that absorbs and erases individual suffering. After Warden's suicide, Dickens notes the ultimate anonymity of his death: "Unrecognized and unpitied, it was borne to the grave; and there it has long since mouldered away!" (566). The city is not simply indifferent; it is structured to overlook its own casualties. It offers no space for remembrance or redemption. Warden's demise does not lead to any transformation within the social order; it merely vanishes into the city's endless churn of human misery. As Seed argues, Dickens's London sketches reflect an awareness that "we should not think of London as a static location since Dickens constantly recognizes different aspects of change taking place" (160). Yet this change is not progress; it is flux without resolution, a dynamic instability that only further obscures individual suffering.

Even as the narrative gestures toward moral clarity, the underlying logic of "The Drunkard's Death" resists closure. Dickens's story ends with a corpse, not a conclusion—a tragedy that speaks more to the inescapability of social despair than to its causes. Warden's death may fulfill the story's moral arc, but it leaves the reader with a lingering unease—a recognition that the social horrors of the city persist off the page, unmitigated and unsolved. In this way, Dickens's realism shades toward the uncanny, not through overt supernaturalism but through the repetition and routinization of horror itself. The story contains no ghost, and yet the city feels haunted—haunted by past lives, lost families, and better futures that never came to be. Warden himself is haunted by these memories in his final moments: "He thought of the time when he had a home . . . until the forms of his elder children seemed to rise from the grave, and stand about him" (563). The city, then, becomes a spectral archive—not of literal spirits, but of failed possibilities and buried histories. While the tale moralizes Warden's downfall, it also illuminates the limits of moralism in the face of structural urban decay. As Dickens shows, the city may be visible, but it is not comprehensible—and certainly not conquerable.

In Poe's "The Man of the Crowd," the story culminates in a profound epistemological collapse. The narrator's pursuit of the mysterious figure through the labyrinthine cityscape ultimately leads not to revelation but to unresolvable ambiguity. Observation becomes futile, and the act of following is stripped of interpretive value. The tale closes with a startling admission of failure: "It will be in vain to follow, for I shall learn no more of him, nor of his deeds" (396). The narrative ends not with a deciphered mystery, but with the narrator's recognition of unknowability—a hallmark of weird fiction's emphasis on ontological uncertainty. The city no longer functions as a readable surface; instead, it becomes an inscrutable, shifting maze where the observer becomes lost in the act of looking. Poe does not offer resolution—only a deepening of mystery that reflects not just the anonymity of the crowd, but the instability of meaning itself.

This radical epistemological failure defines the central dynamic of the story. The old man is never understood, never contextualized within a comprehensible social framework. He becomes a cipher, "a countenance which at once arrested and absorbed my whole attention, on account of the absolute idiosyncrasy of its expression" (392). The mystery surrounding him is not merely narrative; it is ontological and epistemological. The old man may be a criminal, a lunatic, a supernatural fiend, or nothing more than an anonymous drifter—but none of these readings coalesce into certainty. As Noel Polk argues, Poe's tale exemplifies the alienation and disorientation of modern urban life: "Poe's narrator does not pretend to be a writer, but claims merely to be an interested observer of human types"

(553). Yet even this observational role unravels, as the narrator loses control of his gaze and becomes consumed by the object he cannot interpret. His failure is not just narrative; it is existential.

The narrative structure itself reinforces this descent into interpretive disarray. The city becomes a metaphor for the narrator's interiority—a complex, elusive space in which clarity is only a mirage. Ray Mazurek suggests that Poe's story is as much about the limits of artistic perception as it is about the mystery of the city: "It is on one level about the mystery of human existence in a horrifying urban environment; on another, it is a tale about the unreliability of its narrator, who is unaware that his own illness colors his perception" (25). The story, then, becomes a narrative about narrative—one that dramatizes the failure of interpretation and the self-reflexive instability of perception itself.

Poe's crowd, unlike Dickens's study of urban characters, resists classification entirely. It becomes monstrous not in form, but in function; it absorbs the observer, distorting perception and destabilizing identity. The narrator is not merely following another; he is circling the boundaries of his own unknowability. As Mazurek argues, the story "turns in upon itself," structured by "images of doubleness and descent," revealing "the unreliability of the narrator and the ambiguity of the text" (25). The city, like the crowd, resists totalizing meaning. It becomes a metaphorical text with no key—a space where the individual's attempt to understand others is mirrored in the failure to understand himself. Ultimately, Poe's story proposes that the city is not merely a backdrop, but a psychic labyrinth—one in which identity, meaning, and even perception disintegrate into a self-reflective void.

In O'Brien's "Broadway Bedeviled," resolution arrives not through comprehension, but through madness. The narrator eventually reveals that his entire narrative was the product of delirium tremens—a psychotic episode, not an intelligible mystery. Yet this revelation offers no catharsis or narrative clarity. Instead, it foregrounds the core logic of weird fiction: understanding is not withheld to be revealed later, but made structurally impossible from the start. The story is framed not around a solvable problem but around an experiential collapse of reason and perception. The narrator may admit that his ordeal was hallucination, but that recognition itself is not wholly reliable. As he says in a chilling moment of self-awareness, "I am now going to describe phantasms which, although they were the tricks of madness, I as vividly recall at this hour as though they were the realities of yesterday" (161). The line between delusion and memory remains blurred, and the story ends with no stable ground beneath either narrator or reader.

In this way, O'Brien pushes the motif of urban unknowability to its extreme. The city no longer merely eludes understanding; it becomes the unreliable narrator itself. Architecture, shadows, street-lamps, and crowds are not passive background but active agents in the hallucinatory spectacle. The city performs madness: it conspires, gestures, whispers, and pursues. As the narrator insists, "As I walked, men walked by my side . . . always eyeing me suspiciously" (158), and "I felt the fiends that followed me were sent by God, and that I must abide the issue" (160). The urban environment absorbs the narrative voice and collapses into it, so that the city is not merely a reflection of paranoia, but its very source and structure. The city itself becomes hallucinatory. Even the story's rationalizing gesture, its conclusion in diagnosis, cannot retroactively stabilize what has been narrated. The mystery was never external. It was internalized from the beginning, and even the apparent solution only confirms the instability of perception and identity.

Moreover, the city in O'Brien is not merely unknowable; it is generated from the narrator's fractured subjectivity. The crowd does not conceal the answer; it is the symptom. There is no fiend to be unmasked, no crime to be discovered—only the internal collapse of the self, projected outward onto a cityscape that offers no distinction between real and imagined menace. O'Brien writes, "The scene around me whirling, upside down, in the same jumbled condition as my own mind" (158), and "I felt myself approaching nearer and nearer to my doom" (160). The crowd becomes not an object of analysis, but an emanation of breakdown—a phantasmagoria conjured by a mind that cannot trust its own perceptions. Even after the moment of supposed clarity, the narrator's recollection remains vividly detailed and emotionally charged, refusing full dissociation from the unreality he once inhabited.

"Broadway Bedeviled," then, stages the weird city as a narrative vortex—a space where epistemological failure is not just a thematic element, but the very form of the story. As such, it exemplifies what weird fiction does best: not terrifying through monstrous revelation, but by revealing that the world—and the self—may be fundamentally unreadable. The city in O'Brien is a psychic trap, an ontological haze that does not lift at the end, but deepens.

In all three stories—Dickens's "The Drunkard's Death," Poe's "The Man of the Crowd," and O'Brien's "Broadway Bedeviled"— the city becomes more than setting. It is an enigma and a metaphor for the unstable self. Each story proposes a mystery, but none offers a resolution. Dickens provides a moral closure but leaves structural cruelty untouched. Poe stages a pursuit that ends not with discovery, but epistemic despair. O'Brien dramatizes madness as the only possible answer—and even that answer unravels under scrutiny. The city thus becomes a self-reflective paradox: it offers the illusion of visibility, yet resists interpretation. As each narrative collapses under the weight of its own ambiguity, we are left not with understanding, but with disorientation—a landscape where the only real horror is the impossibility of knowledge. This is the territory of weird fiction at its most profound, where what lies at the center of the story is not a monster, but a void.

Taken together, the works of Dickens, Poe, and O'Brien trace a descent into the psychological and narrative abysses of urban modernity, where the city is not merely observed but internalized. What begins in Dickens as a socially conscious gaze upon suffering becomes, in Poe, an obsessive fixation that dissolves the boundary between observer and observed, and in O'Brien, a full collapse of interior and exterior worlds. Each author stages the transformation of the flâneur from detached witness to haunted participant, a process that mirrors the philosophical arc implied in Nietzsche's warning: the one who observes darkness too long may absorb it. These stories do not merely depict the monstrous aspects of the city; they suggest that the city itself is a projection of the narrator's shadow self, an externalization of moral failure, alienation, and madness. As their narrators lose grip on stability, what emerges is a distinctly urban Gothic in which horror lies not in spectral figures or uncanny events alone, but in the unrelenting confrontation with the self. The uncanny city gazes back, and in doing so, exposes the shadow lurking within.

Works Cited

Amaral, Genevieve. "Edgar Allan Poe's Fear of Texts: 'The Man of the Crowd' as Literary Monster." *Comparatist* 35 (May 2011): 227–38.

Baumgarten, Murray. "Fictions of the City." In *The Cambridge Companion to Charles Dickens,* ed. John O. Jordan. Cambridge: Cambridge University Press, 2001. 106–19.

Botting, Fred. *Gothic.* London: Routledge, 2014.

Breslow, Julian W. "The Narrator in *Sketches by Boz.*" *English Literary History* 44 (Spring 1977): 127–49.

Cagle, Jeremey. "Reading Well: Transcendental Hermeneutics in Poe's 'The Man of the Crowd.'" *Edgar Allan Poe Review* 9, No. 2 (Fall 2008): 17–35.

Costigan, Edward. "Drama and Everyday Life in *Sketches by Boz.*" *Review of English Studies* 27 (November 1976): 403–21.

Crow, Charles L. *American Gothic.* Cardiff: University of Wales Press, 2009.

Dickens, Charles. *Sketches by Boz.* Ed. Dennis Walder. New York: Penguin, 1995.

Fink, Steven. "Who is Poe's 'Man of the Crowd'?" *Poe Studies* 44 (2011): 17–38.

Fisher, Benjamin F. *The Cambridge Introduction to Edgar Allan Poe.* Cambridge: Cambridge University Press, 2008.

Garcha, Amanpal. "Styles of Stillness and Motion: Market Culture and Narrative Form in 'Sketches by Boz.'" *Dickens Studies Annual* 30 (2001): 1–22.

Grech, Philip. "The Science of Psychopathy and Poe's 'The Man of the Crowd.'" *Edgar Allan Poe Review* 19 (Spring 2018): 53–75.

Grub, Gerald G. "The Personal and Literary Relationships of Dickens and Poe." *Nineteenth-Century Fiction* 5 (June 1950): 1–22.

Hayes, Kevin J. "Visual Culture and the Word in Edgar Allan Poe's 'The Man of the Crowd.'" *Nineteenth-Century Literature* 56 (March 2002): 445–65.

Hollington, Michael. "Boz's Gothic Gargoyles." *Dickens Quarterly* 16 (September 1999): 160–77.

———. *Dickens and the Grotesque.* New York: Barnes & Noble, 1984.

Howe, Daniel Walker. *What Hath God Wrought: The Transformation of America, 1815–1848.* New York: Oxford University Press, 2007.

Irish, John P. "Bohemian Horrors: The Life and Middle Speculative Writings of Fitz-James O'Brien." In Fitz-James O'Brien. *The Diamond Lens and Others (1855–1858).* Ed. John P. Irish. Dublin: Swan River Press, 2025. vii–xliii.

———. "Dreaming of Fantasy: The Life and Early Speculative Writings of Fitz-James O'Brien." In Fitz-James O'Brien. *An Arabian Night-mare and Others (1848–1854).* Ed. John P. Irish. Dublin: Swan River Press, 2025. vii–xxxviii.

———. "Premonitions of Death: The Life and Latter Speculative Writings of Fitz-James O'Brien." In Fitz-James O'Brien. *What Was It? and Others (1858–1864).* Ed. John P. Irish. Dublin: Swan River Press, 2025. vii–xxxvii.

Jen, Christina. "'Drop the Curtain': Astonishment and the Anxieties of Authorship in Charles Dickens's *Sketches by Boz.*" *Dickens Studies Annual* 49 (2018): 249–78.

Jung, C. G. *Aion: Researches into the Phenomenology of the Self.* Princeton, NJ: Princeton University Press, 1979.

Kopley, Richard. "Retracing Our Steps in Edgar Allan Poe's 'The Man of the Crowd.'" In Kopley's *The Formal Center in Literature: Explorations from Poe to the Present.* Rochester, NY: Camden House, 2018. 19–27.

Lloyd, Rosemary. *Baudelaire's World.* Ithaca, NY: Cornell University Press, 2002.

Mabbott, T. O. Editor's notes to "The Man of the Crowd." In *The Collected Works of Edgar Allan Poe, Volume II: Tales and Sketches (1831–1842).* Ed. T. O. Mabbott. Cambridge, MA: Harvard University Press, 1978. 505–18.

Mazurek, Ray. "Art, Ambiguity, and the Artist in Poe's 'The Man of the Crowd.'" *Poe Studies* 12, No. 2 (December 1979): 25-28.

Nietzsche, Friedrich. *Beyond Good and Evil/On the Genealogy of Morality.* Tr. Adrian Del Caro. Stanford: Stanford University Press, 2014.

Nord, Deborah Epstein. "*Sketches by Boz:* The Middle-Class City and the Quarantine of Urban Suffering." In Nord's *Walking the Victorian Streets: Women, Representation, and the City.* Ithaca, NY: Cornell University Press, 1995. 49–80.

O'Brien, Fitz-James. *The Lost Room and Other Speculative Fiction.* Ed. John P. Irish. New York: Hippocampus Press, 2026 (forthcoming).

———. *Thirteen Stories by Fitz-James O'Brien: The Realm of the Mind.* Ed. Wayne R. Kime. Newark: University of Delaware Press, 2012.

Poe, Edgar Allan. *Essays and Reviews.* Ed. G. R. Thompson. New York: Library of America, 1984.

———. *Poetry and Tales.* Ed. Patrick F. Quinn. New York: Library of America, 1984.

Polk, Noel. "Welty, Hawthorne, and Poe: Men of the Crowd and the Landscape of Alienation." *Mississippi Quarterly* 50 (Fall 1997): 553–65.

Rachman, Stephen. "'Es last sich nicht schreiben': Plagiarism and 'The Man of the Crowd.'" In *The American Face of Edgar Allan Poe*, ed. Shawn Rosenheim and Stephen Rachman. Baltimore: Johns Hopkins University Press, 1995. 49–87.

Schlicke, Paul. "'Risen Like a Rocket': The Impact of 'Sketches by Boz.'" *Dickens Quarterly* 22 (March 2005): 3–18.

Schwarzbach, F. S. *Dickens and the City*. London: Athlone Press, 1979.

Seed, David. "Touring the Metropolis: The Shifting Subjects of Dickens's London Sketches." *Yearbook of English Studies* 34 (2004): 155–70.

Slater, Michael. "Dickens's Life and Times—to 1839." In *Dickens' Journalism: Sketches by Boz and Other Early Papers, 1833–39*. Ed. Michael Slater. Columbus: Ohio State University Press, 1994. xi–xxii.

Sweeney, Susan Elizabeth. "The Magnifying Glass: Spectacular Distance in Poe's 'Man of the Crowd' and Beyond." *Poe Studies* 36 (2003): 3–17.

Weinstock, Jeffrey Andrew. "The Crowd Within: Poe's Impossible Aloneness." *Edgar Allan Poe Review* 7, No. 2 (Fall 2006): 50–64.

Wolle, Francis. *Fitz-James O'Brien: A Literary Bohemian of the Eighteen-Fifties*. Boulder: University of Colorado Press, 1944.

Dead Reckonings

"Infinity Round the Corner of Any Street"

ARTHUR MACHEN. *Autobiographical Writings.* Edited by S. T. Joshi. New York: Hippocampus Press, 2019. 481 pp. $30.00 tpb. ISBN: 978-1-61498-310-1.

Autobiographical Writings is a compilation of Arthur Machen's reflections on his life and on life in general. Collected within its pages, for the first time, are *Far Off Things* (an amalgamation of essays which originally were published individually in a column in the London *Evening News*), *Things Near and Far*, and *The London Adventure; or, The Art of Wandering*, along with supplementary essays and *Precious Balms* (selections of reviews—mostly bad—of Machen's books), and his early poem "Eleusinia."

In these works, Machen (1863–1947) presents his life not as a chronological sequence of events, but as a succession of meditations upon places, things, and phenomena he encounters in his rambling progress through life. He is possessed of a strong attachment to the Welsh borderland of Monmouthshire (which he always calls by its old Welsh name of Gwent), where he grew up, and whose lore and mystical outlook he has internalized deeply. At the end of his school years, Machen sets out for London to take the entry exam for medical school, but his humble ability in the nebulous regions of mathematics derails his career plan. Having glimpsed the magical metropolis, he returns home and resumes his life of rambling country lanes and reading high literature.

The problem is that his family is poor, and he must earn a living. Thus he spends the bulk of the 1880s living in a boarding house in London, earning barely more than his daily bread by working as clerk at a publishing house and as a tutor. At the end of the workday his real life begins: at night he explores the city streets and writes. Machen is increasingly disgusted by his work, and his initial, naïve fascination with the city wears thin when he runs out of the ready money that is necessary to enjoy its diversions. The dichotomy between not only city and country but the modern material world and his ancient mystical home becomes his focus.

Machen's writing takes on an attitude of wistfulness, dwelling on the passage of time, as well as the quality of timelessness, the ancient things of his homeland, nostalgia, and imagination. He writes *The Anatomy of Tobacco* (1884), *The Chronicle of Clemendy* (1888), *The Great God Pan* (1894), and *The Three Imposters* (1895)—a new literature, grounded in an old tradition of mellifluous sound and beauty. Machen has an eye for awe and a sense of the newness of everything, and it is the impression each experience makes upon him that is the vital matter under consideration. He is on a grail quest for truth and beauty, which are essentially the same to him. For Machen, "all literature can be but an approximation to the Truth," and what he writes about is the transcendent truth in his daily life in London, the essence behind the material forms recognized by the senses.

Machen is best known for his horror fiction, which blends ancient pagan pasts and dark ritual with modern life, and which reveals a cosmic reality of sublime beauty so terrible that many people are unable to survive a revelation of it. The first of these is *The Great God Pan*, a volume that includes the stories "The Great God Pan" and "The Inmost Light," in both of which tales women are the victims of hideous experiments by malevolent scientists who have no regard for human life. *The Three Imposters* is a celebrated frame tale that interweaves stories of pagan diablerie with ancient witchcraft. "The White People," a saga of loathsome mysteries and unspeakable atrocities, revolves around the discovery of a cryptical Green Book and the rearing of a girl as a witch.

Far Off Things, the collected essays Machen wrote for the *Evening News* over the course of several months in 1915 (in a column entitled "Confessions of a Literary Man"), is a group of unconnected essays—unconnected except in the sense that they are all various reminiscences of "the far gone times and suns of the 'seventies and early 'eighties when the scene of my life was being set." The wealth of Celtic and Arthurian relics that adorn Machen's rambles through country lanes informs his modern attitudes, and he credits the success of his "career in letters" to the "enchanted land" of ancient barrows. No matter the topic under discussion—the books of his childhood library in his father's rectory, which prepared him to know the Wonder in the world; country food; the relative merits of fantastic fiction and the realistic style; the decline of style and civility; poetry and beauty—Machen enriches his theme with a discourse on his closeness to the land and nature, storms, even the neighborliness of the people of Gwent, and houses with biographies: "The pride of race that belongs to the Morgans, Herberts, Meyricks that once lived in them has passed into their stones and still shines there." He discusses how he learned the art of writing (he began by imitating favorite authors) and the relativity of criticism—and he hurls some scathing denunciations of works of which he does not approve, such as Frazer's *The Golden Bough*.

All his fiction, Machen says, "has tried to realise my boyish impressions of that wonderful magic Gwent." He "wrote 'The Great God Pan' [as] an endeavor to pass on the vague, indefinite sense of awe and mystery and terror that [he] had received." For Machen, "the whole earth, down to the very pebbles, was but the veil of a quickening and adorable mystery" and the existence of God. He wants to create a story based on a description of an environment—not a plot—so that the reader, through reading it, could create his own internal story of the soul.

Things Near and Far (1923) is largely composed of Machen's thoughts on writing. It opens with a discussion of the pagan tumuli and Roman ruins of Gwent, which he often visits in his long walks in country lanes, and the poverty of his family, which occasions his exile to London in search of work. Interestingly, he obtains a position cataloguing for the publisher of his *The Anatomy of Tobacco*, and the manuscripts he catalogues deal primarily with occult subject matter. Machen heartily despises this work and uses his discussion of it to rant lengthily against Spiritualism.

In this book Machen evinces more self-pity than in *Far Off Things*, emphasizing the loneliness and poverty he experienced in London. His mother dies as he finishes the writing of *The Chronicle of Clemendy*, and his father soon after. He asks, "What is life?" And he concludes that we are all occupied with games, rather than with living. And yet, these games—whether mountain-climbing or book-writing—are vital for making "life tolerable, even entertaining, just as I add tomato sauce . . . to the cold mutton, to make that tolerable and even appetizing." He also asks, "Why do I write?" His meager arithmetical abilities notwithstanding, Machen computes that he has earned "fifteen pounds and a few shillings per annum" on average over a lifetime of writing—so that he can hardly be suspected of writing for gain—for it is poor remuneration for the author's laborious toil which entails frequent spirit-crushing failures and mounds of wadded-up and discarded sheets of paper. Why does he write? For the same reason he puts tomato sauce on cold mutton—to make life tolerable.

By 1890, he has lost his taste for London. But, having just finished a translation of Béroalde de Verville, and with some legacies in his bank account, he travels to Touraine to see the land of Verville. He returns to London with a renewed appreciation of it:

> And it is utterly true that he who cannot find wonder, mystery, awe, the sense of a new world and an undiscovered realm in the place by the Gray's Inn Road will never find those secrets elsewhere, not in the heart of Africa, not in the fabled hidden cities of Tibet.

Machen did not work from 1890 to 1900, except at literature. He translated *Le Moyen de Parvenir* and wrote *The Great God Pan*, "The

White People," *The Three Imposters, The Hill of Dreams, Ornaments in Jade,* and *Hieroglyphics.*

Things Near and Far is not a chronological account of these years, but a series of digressions from a nebulous center. He writes about the decline in the literary quality of the press (because, he says, it is catering to a new female readership) and the feminine infiltration into taverns (I can sympathize with his pangs at the loss of a comforting retreat). He writes of his struggles to write and then to get what he has written published; of his tenure as an actor in a traveling theatrical troupe, when his legacies had been exhausted; of the strange characters he meets in London—both in and out of the Hermetic Order of the Golden Dawn. What unites all these adventures is Machen's desire to read them as emblems of an ecstatic Greater-than-Thou.

Machen's flair for mysticism, consciousness-raising, the ecstatic, and transformational experiences is even more evident in *The London Adventure; or, The Art of Wandering.* For instance, he relates the story of a man in a tavern, who asks him how to spell "*exaltavit*," as in "*exaltavit humiles.*" The man becomes a friend, and Machen calls him a "messenger," for the phrase "*exaltavit humiles*" sustains him in his misery at being a poorly treated lackey in his penurious state. Another friend, meanwhile, keeps reminding him that it is time to begin writing the book he has promised to write about London in the spring. The friend repeats, "The leaves are beginning to come out," and Machen reflects, "One should hear and weigh all sorts of messages."

Machen continues his searches for mystery. He talks about his rambles when he lived in Soho in 1890, his London rambles of the 1880s, and his rambles east of the Gray's Inn Road from 1895 to 1900. He notes that he (and many of the rest of us) adore old things, but he finds "this love of antiquity for its own sake" puzzling. He ruminates that, outside of religion, all value is relative. And venerable institutions, such as Freemasonry, remain viable, while their original purposes and the meanings that underlie their rituals are forgotten: importantly, what survives is mystery. While the scenery east of the Gray's Inn Road is of recent date, neither venerable nor memoried, yet the stones of a doorstep in a new dwelling may have once been stood upon by "the Son Blessed of the Fire." Stone is a repository of mystery. He considers a séance he attended as a reporter sent to investigate a poltergeist incident: "I think something happened that the doors were opened; that the human spirit came into momentary contact with unconjectured worlds which it is not meant to visit."

Machen's thoughtful forays in this volume revolve around the concept that "wonder is everything," for we see only shadows, not essences: 'We, it appears, are to learn of high things, if at all, through little things, and thing of low estate." He considers "whether all the objects of nature are not purely symbolical: whether nature does not endeavor to talk to us and tell us amazing secrets by the signs and cyphers of trees and ferns and herbs and flowers and hills and streams."

He returns to the subject of writing, which he finds a terribly laborious process, frustrated by an inability to achieve an envisioned outcome: "The true tragedy lies in the juxtaposition of desire and impotence." Machen, who has been on both the giving and the receiving end of ridicule, asks why we laugh at the failed efforts of artists: "The jests of the good God are sometimes obscure."

Although he hates journalism, he appreciates the fact that he is sent to report on many strange places he might not otherwise have seen: "I found myself traversing unknown and unconjectured regions, happy as always in the faculty of find infinity round the corner of any street, within five minutes of anywhere." Strangeness is the essence of truth—examining an everyday thing as if it were a new discovery. He thinks of a familiar expression for this truth in words: "For ever and ever. Amen."

Writing—all art—is the quality that separates human beings from other animals, he says, and as far as the common equation of madness with genius—why, Keats is the saner person than one who cannot see the sublime in a girl or a bird.

The emotional tenor and abstraction of Machen's autobiographical writings rise over time, fraught with an increasingly taut and manic sort of desperation, traveling further and further from narrative into the gulfs and chasms of mystical meditations. Buffeted by financial hardships and literary setbacks, as well as the death of his first wife and his parents within a relatively short period of time, Machen's need for transcendence beyond the here and now becomes dire.

Precious Balms was published in 1924 when Machen was at the height of his fame. His works were being collected and reprinted and he was lionized in both England and America. He felt vindicated at last. He released this assembly of (mostly) bad reviews of his work, an ingenious response to old persecutors who might now eat their words. More than that, Machen's success was an indication that, through literature (and through his own efforts), the truth has won out. I conclude my discussion of *Autobiographical Writings* with one of the positive reviews in *Precious Balms*, written by Robert Hillyer in the *New York Times Book Review:*

> The triumph of mechanism, which is shown in its full glory by the late war and the wars that follow it, has, like all bad tyrannies, engendered a reaction. For years isolated voices were raised against it, but they spoke in syllables that were incomprehensible to the minds of men spellbound by the wonder of Things. In differing accents, protests came from writers as diverse in talent as Samuel Butler, Walter Pater and Arthur Machen. People took it for granted that such protests were the inevitable whine of the Old Order against Progress, an explanation at once so simple and inclusive that it could dispose of any objection calculated to disturb their satisfaction in the machinery of manufacture and the machinery of life. The world, indeed, was fast stampeding into a herd which would not tolerate the existence of unconverted individuals. Then suddenly the machine itself went wrong, and threatened, like the machine in the ballad, to transform its inventor into sausage meat. There was a wild flight of worshippers from the crumbling shrine of Moloch . . . the race was turning, had, in fact, turned, back toward an acknowledgment of the final mystery of life.

Katherine Kerestman

"The Oppressiveness of the Incomprehensible":
The William Hope Hodgson Mythos

WILLIAM HOPE HODGSON. *The Voice in the Night: Best Weird Stories of William Hope Hodgson.* Edited by S. T. Joshi. New York: Hippocampus Press, 2024. 302 pp. $20.00 tpb. ISBN: 978-1-61498-442-9.

JAMES CHAMBERS, ed. *Where the Silent Ones Watch.* New York: Hippocampus Press, 2024. 278 pp. $25.00 tpb. ISBN: 978-1-61498-443-6.

> "Rum things!–Of course there are rum things happen at sea–as rum as ever there were."
> —the opening line of "The Stone Ship"

The tide of H. P. Lovecraft fandom has lifted a lot of boats, bringing new attention to fellow writers such as Clark Ashton Smith and Manly Wade Wellman, and some who weren't even in his circle, but as fellow writers of pulpy weird fiction have been caught up in the whirlpool. This includes William Hope Hodgson (1877–1918), who died on the battlefield in the First World War, during the years Lovecraft was first beginning to publish short fiction.

Would William Hope Hodgson be as well remembered without the influence of Lovecraft, who wrote in "Supernatural Horror in Literature" of his "power in its suggestion of lurking worlds and beings behind the ordinary surface of life"? Even in that essay from the 1920s, Hodgson's work was described as "known today far less than it deserves to be." That is still the case in the larger world. Among readers of Hippocampus Press, which focuses on the work of Lovecraft and related weird writers, he is at least somewhat better known, so it is appropriate that the publisher recently brought out *The Voice in the Night*, a new collection of his work, in its Classics of Gothic Horror series.

The title story is often anthologized and was my initial entry point into reading Hodgson. It was the basis for the 1963 Japanese movie *Matango*, also known as *Attack of the Mushroom People*, a bizarre and even somber tale about a group of people shipwrecked on a deserted island who learn that eating the omnipresent fungi turns them into, well, mushroom people. Hodgson's original is much more stripped-down, told to the crew of another ship by a survivor who keeps his distance, but it is a disturbing tale of addiction and dehumanization, and it is no surprise it has been so influential.

Reading these stories all together can make them feel a little samey, with so many heavy fogs, putrid smells, and weed banks hiding giant sea creatures, and lots of nautical talk about fo'c'stles and jibbooms. It's like binge-watching all *The X-Files'* "monster of the week" episodes. I'd recommend taking your time with them, dipping into his weird world in smaller doses.

Hodgson's series of stories about the occult detective Carnacki, which is among his other best-known work despite their formulaic nature, is represented by "The Whistling Room." There is also a story about a statue of Kali that seems to come to life for revenge in a small English village, but the majority center around the sea, grounded in the author's personal experience and enlivened by the flourishes of his prose.

The horrors of *Jaws* have nothing on the sea monsters of "A Tropical Horror" and "From the Tideless Sea," and Hodgson excels at describing the ocean where "each felt the oppressiveness of the Incomprehensible about them," full of "the vastitude of the night and the *possibilities of the dark*." He gets extraordinary mileage from the stretches of seaweed in the Sargasso Sea: in "From the Tideless Sea" it is described as "a stupendous desolation of weed," "the Cemetery of the Ocean!" and "the vast Weed World."

Also published in 2024 was the anthology *Where the Silent Ones Watch*, edited by James Chambers. In it, several writers apply the Lovecraft Mythos model to Hodgson, spinning off his fiction into new stories and new directions.

I am neither a complete newcomer to Hodgson nor greatly knowledgeable about him; I have read a fair amount of his short fiction, but none of his novels. *The House on the Borderland* (1908) and *The Night Land* (1912) are particularly well regarded, and many of the stories here tie into those works. Even the collection's title was direct-ly inspired by *The Night Land*. I am guessing that in modern times the audience for seafaring horror stories probably isn't what it used to be. While I may have missed a little context here and there, that lack of familiarity wasn't any barrier to enjoying the tales. At worst, I was immersed in an alien environment and had to acclimate my way out, which could happen in any fantasy story, and that's not bad.

The thread of nautical horror appears in some stories, such as Nancy Holder's creepy "The Captain's Wife," but there would be a few more if it was catering to my taste. There was a noticeable shortage of giant monsters and other inexplicable sea phenomena, with the themes veering in a more cerebral direction. We always have Hodgson's own work, however, and I appreciated that the sto-ries weren't pastiches, but went in their own directions.

Among the twenty-six pieces, there is a Carnacki story (Adrian Ludens's "Resistance to Change"); a vlogger who explores "weird Americana, conspiracies, and things found on the dark web," who follows a story lead to an abandoned house and an otherworldly cult (Todd Keisling's "Little House on the Borderland"); and several po-ems.

A few stories are based on Hodgson's real life, from the circum-stances of his death in the Fourth Battle of Ypres to a controversial encounter with Harry Houdini. Curiously, one of the mysterious house stories, I assume drawn from *The House on the Borderland*, fea-tures a ghostly encounter with Philip K. Dick ("The House on the Scannerland," by David Agranoff). I spent the story trying to puzzle out its connection with Hodgson, apart from generally fusing Dick, with that nod to *A Scanner Darkly*, and the Borderland concept, but I didn't find it.

I recommend reading this collection, especially the more cosmi-cally oriented tales such as Michael Cisco's "Night Hearing" and Kyla Lee Ward's "The Battlements of Twilight," while listening to some spacy ambient music. I found that very effective.

Both these books have striking, and very different, cover art by Daniel V. Sauer: an almost Gustave Doré–like black and white drawing for the older work, and full color for the new one, emphasizing the cosmic horror elements.

As a set, these volumes provide a solid introduction to Hodgson's varied worlds, and the "possibilities of the dark" spun off from them.

Karen Joan Kohoutek

Nightmare Logic

LEIGH BLACKMORE. *Nightmare Logic: Tales of the Macabre, Fantastic and Cthulhuesque.* N.p.: IFWG Publishing International, 2024. $14.99 tpb. ISBN: 978-1-922856-73-9.

> He began to perform the Lesser Banishing Ritual in that habitually dolorous voice of his, vibrating the Divine Names with a nasal quality that always made me imagine his angels would appear clutching spray packs of Sinex to stop him.—"Uncharted"

Reading this collection of Leigh Blackmore's fiction feels very much, I imagine, as it would to peruse the notebooks scrawled by his urban mages and haphazard investigators of the occult. Fragments, hints, visions of tremendous clarity or deliberate obfuscation, paranoid observations of the neighbors; here and there, the complete record of some ghastly experiment. Runes, ciphers, the tantalizing suggestion of a world that can be manipulated by the right combination of words. The scribe might be written off as mad. And yet, these writings are so thoroughly embedded in the realities of urban Australia that a transference takes place: the mundane is refined and enchanted, while the numinous gains a concrete presence.

At its best, this is polished and mature work by an author who has earned his stripes. The vignette "The Wave" is perfection, conjuring a single moment in a single life that resonates with universal meaning. A story original to the collection, "The Squats," invokes horror within a row of inner-city terraces so convincingly that reading it felt like remembering something that happened to the friend of a friend when I was at university in the nineties. Offering a distinct change of pace, "The Roomer" leads the reader—in its rambling, ocker idiom—all but imperceptibly from a grim slice of life to—what, exactly? This isn't where we started, and yet it is surely the same world.

For the majority of stories, this world is Sydney's inner west or the south coast city of Wollongong. As invoked by Blackmore, it is full of begrudging beauty and rampant decay. His investigators are not a privileged elite, but struggling students and musicians, artists working dead-end jobs as they attempt to pursue higher goals, invalids and the suddenly single or unemployed contemplating the wreck of their ideals. But their world contains secrets, perhaps only available to those in such a liminal state. In "Uncharted" (quoted above), we are privy to a man's various attempts to recapture a childhood fantasy, which remains the only constant amid the upheavals of his life.

Blackmore displays considerable occult erudition in the likes of "Uncharted" and the darkly funny "Doctor Nadurnian's Golem," drawing on various Western traditions. He ventures further afield amid the erotic entanglements of the "The Hourglass." But even when he takes inspiration from the fictional Cthulhu Mythos, he treats its tenets with a seriousness and rigor that greatly enhances the effect of "The Horror in the Manuscript" and "The Return of Zoth-Ommog." Even the slightest stories demonstrate a thoroughly magical concern with transitions from one state to another: even the transit from Sydney to Wollongong, in the vignette "Imago," speaks to the desire to transform. But louder, much louder, speak the giant cicadas of "Beneath the Carapace." In this fantastical novelette, the protagonist travels from provincial Grynne to the decadent city of Beremythos in search of the fulfillment that has eluded him, only to discover his own transformation involves a higher price than a train ticket.

There is also considerable attention paid to the idea of sacrifice—its necessity in magic and, indeed, in daily life. Those chosen to feed Zoth-Ommog meet their deaths in a uniquely hideous way, in which memory is only part of the burden borne by those who survive. In other tales, the situation is more complex: the guilt of the protagonist in "Morsels" can only be expiated through a sacrifice he unconsciously enacts through his art. But the reader frequently feels the seekers are to some degree complicit in the horrors they experience. They may have created them wholesale, or at least be guilty of a latent hypocrisy.

> It dawned on him that nothing he could do would save him, for he believed neither in the possibility that these creatures could really exist, nor in the efficacy of any supernatural gimmick he might level at them.—"Cemetery Rose"

A personal favorite, "Cemetery Rose" is a story about why you should never, ever stay in Sydney's Rookwood cemetery after sunset.

Nightmare Logic covers a good thirty years of publication in a wide variety of venues, and the technical quality of the writing does vary, along with the completeness of the ideas expressed. As a chronicle of an author's developing voice, the early and experimental inclusions are not without interest, especially when combined with the author's biographical afterword, in which he speaks of his inspiration and intent. Amid the prose lurks a pair of short scripts—one an absurdist pastiche titled "Waiting for Cthulhu"—but no poetry. Blackmore is a notable dark poet and has two substantial collections available, *Spores from Sharnoth and Other Madnesses* (P'rea Press, 2008; variant text substituting some poems in *Sharnoth's Spores and Other Seeds*, Rainfall Books, 2010) and *Azathoth and Other Horrors: The Collected Nightmare Lyrics by Edward Pickman Derby* (IFWG, 2023). An introduction by Darrell Schweitzer rounds out this volume.

It is indisputable that Leigh Blackmore writes with intelligence and ingenuity, and at no stage of his career has quarter been asked or given. If you are seeking something provocative, beyond the staples of whatever genre you care to name, then you may well have found it. Just possibly, something may have found you.

Kyla Lee Ward

Long vs. Lovecraft

H. P. LOVECRAFT and FRANK BELKNAP LONG. *A Sense of Proportion: The Letters of H. P. Lovecraft and Frank Belknap Long.* Edited by David E. Schultz and S. T. Joshi. New York: Hippocampus Press. 2025. 850 pp. $75.00 hc. ISBN: 978-1-61498-174-9.

Toward the end of the editors' introduction to this hefty volume collecting the surviving correspondence between H. P. Lovecraft and Frank Belknap Long, David E. Schultz and S. T. Joshi lightly touch on the hardships of Long's last years. By then, to speak plainly, Long was barely surviving month to month on Social Security checks, coping with his mentally ill and often abusive wife, and all too aware that attention from the outside world was largely due to his long-ago friendship with Lovecraft, whose reputation in the field of fantastic fiction far exceeded his own. In short, his old age was grim.

Frank's youth was another matter. At the time the two met in person, during a trip Lovecraft made in April 1922 to New York City, the twenty-one-year-old Frank Belknap Long, Jr., was living with his parents in Manhattan, his birthplace. In the years ahead, particularly during the period of his New York exile, Lovecraft would be a regular guest at the Longs' Upper West Side apartment, where Frank's solicitous mother ensured he was always well fed. Thanks to the steady earnings of Dr. Long, a dental surgeon who treated patients in his home office, the family could afford the services of a live-in maid. Each summer the Longs motored in their Essex automobile to scenic vacation spots around New England and New York State. At least once, the three of them were accompanied by Frank's cat, Felis.

A letter to Lovecraft from late April 1926 shows that Long got off to a promising start as a freelance writer with the publication of his first book, *A Man from Genoa and Other Poems.* The New York Public Library ordered copies, as did Harvard and Columbia. Favorable reviews appeared in the *Boston Transcript* and the *Haldeman-Julius Monthly*, and copies sent to eminent authors prompted complimentary replies from George Sterling, Lord Alfred Douglas, and John Hall Wheelock. In a separate missive from the spring of 1926, FBL quotes an appreciative letter received from "the noblest of them all," George Santayana.

In addition, from bookseller and poet Samuel Loveman came news that the trade magazine *Publishers' Weekly* had mentioned *A Man from Genoa* "as one of the three outstanding books of verse of the year." In response, Lovecraft, recently returned to Providence from New York, congratulated him on his success: "Even the *Publishers' Weekly* praise is by no means to be despised." [Note: *PW* used an apostrophe in its name at this time.]

The first extant letter from Long to Lovecraft, dated 30 January 1924, demonstrates FBL's combative side. In it he takes issue with HPL's dismissal of Henry Fielding's bawdiness. After defending Fielding, Frank asserts: "I frankly enjoy pornography, for I hold it is pornography which gives a degree of charm to all really great writing, writing in the great tradition, which it would otherwise lack." A page later, he notes, "Most critics agree Poe was absolutely incapable of sexual desire," and adds: "a nature that lacks sex suffers in another way—the warmth and human sympathy which springs directly from sex." In a subsequent letter, HPL responds: "As for pornography— no, Child, I don't believe you enjoy it!" His playful rebuttal includes a moralizing poem in the manner of Dean Swift, "The Pathetick History of Sir Wilful Wildrake," originally composed for the benefit of Rheinhart Kleiner, another friend with a penchant for "wenching and bawdry."

Long also takes aim at Lovecraft's vaunting of the Nordic type: "the tall blond Nordic is overwhelmingly stupid, anyhow, and you ought to be thankful you haven't light hair and blue eyes." As FBL tells HPL in a September 1929 letter, "I . . . enjoy 'getting a rise out of you.'"

In a June 1926 letter, Frank makes a subtle effort to challenge Howard's racism. He quotes a passage from Anita Loos's bestselling novel, *Gentlemen Prefer Blondes*, in which the narrator expresses regret for almost giving her colored maid Joseph Conrad's *The Nigger of the Narcissus*, "which really would have hurt her feelings. I mean I don't know why authors cannot say 'Negro' instead of 'Nigger' as they have feelings just the same as we have." He cites another passage from the novel with a positive reference to Jews, but to no avail. In an August 1926 letter, Lovecraft, still smarting from his two years living among New York City's alien immigrant hordes, criticizes the boorish behavior of Samuel Loveman, whom he refers to as a "lowly Israelite." He goes on to expound on "the New York Mongoloid problem," which can be solved by conducting "a scientific wholesale deportation from which there will be neither flinching nor retreating."

Long shows good taste in recommending the works of Arthur Machen and M. R. James to Lovecraft, but his literary judgment isn't always sound. In a January 1927 letter, he hails "The Horror at Red Hook" as "a Brobdingnagian achievement," putting one of Lovecraft's most racist stories in a class with the best of Machen and James. A few months later, he is closer to the mark in his enthusiasm for "The Colour out of Space": "A gorgeously mephitic, effective and convincing tale! and I solemnly pronounce it the most magnificent thing of its kind you've yet done."

As for mainstream fiction, in the same letter in which he quotes Anita Loos, Frank extolls Herman Melville, "as great a genius as Poe or Hawthorne." *Moby-Dick* "is of course an epic, and I'm conscious it's a mighty book," though "vast portions of it are unspeakably dull." He prefers the "idyllic" *Typee*, "a dreamy but very realistic picture of life among the Marquesas." *Omoo*, *Typee*'s sequel, "is all that, and more." Unclear is whether Long was aware that Lovecraft had already read *Moby-Dick*, as revealed in a 1925 letter to his aunt Lillian Clark. Unfortunately, what if anything HPL might have said about Melville in response to FBL's comments is lost.

In a 1929 letter, Long calls Marcel Proust "the one really outstanding modern Gaul," and apologizes for having not yet read *Swann's Way*, the first volume of *Remembrance of Things Past*, which

Lovecraft gave him as a Christmas present months earlier, along with a poem "To a Sophisticated Young Gentleman." In a 1931 letter, Long thanks his friend for another volume in the sequence: "The Pr[o]ust was magnificent—you could not have selected a more welcome gift."

Toward the end of 1926, Frank writes: "It has occurred to me that we could make a great deal of money by coöperating in the production of magazine articles. The Sunday supplements usually pay from two to five cents a word for material, and the old women who read them are tremendously interested in Americana at the present moment." In particular, he has in mind subjects close to his friend's heart, including Colonial doorways, quaint Newburyport, New England churches, and curious Providence characters. In his next epistle, he writes, "Newport would be splendid!," suggesting Lovecraft was open to the idea. Long asks, "Couldn't you write me a two-thousand word article on South Main Street; and take five or six pictures with your pocket camera?" Alas, so far as is known, HPL failed to follow through on such a commercial project. A few months later, however, he penned what amounts to an exhaustive Newport travelogue, purely for the Longs' personal use on their summer driving tour of 1927.

In 1928, the pair launched a serious effort to make money. They ran an ad in *Weird Tales* announcing their "Critical and advisory service for writers of prose and verse; literary revision in all degrees of extensiveness." One client was Zealia Brown Reed, for whom Lovecraft in essence ghostwrote "The Curse of Yig," "The Mound," and "Medusa's Coil." Long, meanwhile, got stuck with revising a full-length novel of hers, a romantic melodrama. The letter from FBL to HPL complaining about this thankless task opens:

> Dear Theobaldus:
>   Have you gone suddenly quite mad? If you will look up the word "revision" in the Oxford English Dictionary you will discover that it is nowhere defined as *creation*—the creation of an original work of art. And do you imagine for a moment that I could

possibly produce 60,000 words of *original creative work* in five of six weeks—at ⅓ cent a word? Realism forsooth—it is I who am the realist. Certain statements in your letter *appall* me by their lack of orientation. . . .

Mrs. Reed's work doesn't approach literature at a single point—and you would have me, in five weeks, for a mere pittance, turn it into an original and vividly conceived novel, utterly accurate from a topographical, social, political, industrial, archaeological, architectural, and historical point of view. Help!

In this indignant rant, which includes a random sample of Reed's namby-pamby prose, Long hilariously blows up Lovecraft's unrealistic assumptions about the freelance revision business.

In a 1929 letter, Frank expresses "a dread of the future," adding, "I am destitute financially, without a prospect of making money in the months and years to come." His fifty-eight-year-old father "has not been well, and works much too hard." Left unsaid is that while his father remains alive, he doesn't have to worry about a roof over his head or enough food to eat. Dr. Long would die in 1940.

When, later in 1929, fellow poet and weird writer Donald Wandrei gives up his permanent position at the publisher E. P. Dutton, Long exclaims, "I would give two years of my already hideously consumed life for a position similar to the one he held." Another friend he envies for having a day job is August Derleth, whose last name he consistently mispronounces "Derluth." "For Gawd's sake remember the name is DERL*E*TH," an exasperated Lovecraft writes in a 1930 letter. "Don't mix it up with Duluth, Minnesota." In subsequent letters, he makes a point of spelling the name "Derl*E*th"; Frank pushes back with "Derl*U*th."

Lovecraft's last two letters to Long, dating from early 1931, occupy some ninety-five pages of text. Among a host of topics, he laments their mutual failures ("both you and I suffer from the handicap of having lived very circumscribed and eventless lives so far . . . We cannot hope to create realistic literature"), attacks the typewriter ("The typewriter is ruining prose style among the younger generation"), and bemoans the current troubles of New England ("the emigration of good old stock, the shifting of economic conditions, and the injudicious admittance of foreign scum"). One can't help wondering whether Long found Lovecraft's convoluted sentences running in page-long paragraphs, for all their Proustian flights, as tedious as he found parts of *Moby-Dick*.

Frank's remaining letters, from 1932 to 1936, fill about two dozen pages. Two of them take Lovecraft to task for his attitude toward sex. The first opens: "There are some statements in your last letter so HORRIBLY biased, so amazingly prejudicial and prudish and evasive that I honestly cannot believe that you really mean what you say"; "You're a puritan sex cripple, sir," he says in the second. Far from the gentle teasing of his 1924 letter on the subject, Long's tone is closer to that of his letter in which he harangues Lovecraft's illusions about revision work. As for Frank's claim of having slept with "women of various European nationalities over a period of five years," if true, one has to wonder about the circumstances. That he was paying for sex seems unlikely given his limited funds. Was he sneaking out of the family apartment at night? Did his parents know what he was up to? Did he ever have a girlfriend? He never mentions one. Perhaps in the end his claims of sexual experience are false, as Joshi suggests in a footnote in the introduction citing the opinion of Frank's wife, whom he married in 1960, on the question.

In his next to last letter, from 1935, Frank defends himself against the charge of neglecting "my best and oldest friend." HPL is apparently piqued that FBL has been delinquent in keeping up their correspondence. Long explains that he has been consumed with work: "I am merely seeking to avoid narrowing horizons ahead. To secure even a few of the good things in life, a wife, economic independence and freedom from the indignities of penny-pinching I am compelled temporarily to neglect all of the amenities. I haven't written a gracious, civilized letter to anyone in eight months." In his last letter, from 1936, he apologizes for not being more communicative, but he has been busy with "pulp hacking." "During the past three or four months The Man from Genoa has done very well from a putrid commercial point of view," he writes, "but then had a bad, uncreative period and used up reserves of capital and is at present not too solidly entrenched financially."

It would be Frank's tragedy that, along the way to outliving his oldest friend by decades, his fear of not securing even a few of the good things in life was only too justified.

Peter Cannon

Notes on Contributors

Dmitri Akers is a writer of the weird, living on Kaurna country. Apart from formal poetry, inspired by the Romantics, Dmitri mainly writes weird verse and weird fiction. His poetry and prose have appeared in *Penumbra, Spectral Realms, Skull & Laurel, Midnight Echo,* and *Spawn 2: More Weird Horror Tales about Pregnancy, Birth and Babies,* edited by Deborah Sheldon (IFWG Publishing).

Manuel Arenas is a writer of verse and prose in the Gothic Horror tradition. His work has appeared in various anthologies and journals including *Spectral Realms* and *Penumbra,* both from Hippocampus Press, and *Weird Fiction Quarterly.* He has two collections of prose and poetry, available at Jackanapes Press: *Book of Shadows* (2021) and *The Burning Ember Mission of Helldorado* (2024).

Ramsey Campbell is an English horror fiction writer, editor, and critic who has been writing for well over fifty years. He is frequently cited as one of the leading writers in the field. His website is www.ramseycampbell.com.

Lovecraft scholar **Peter Cannon's** latest book is *Long Memories and Other Writings* (Hippocampus Press, 2022). It contains further speculation on Frank's sex life.

Scott J. Couturier is a Rhysling Award–nominated poet and prose writer of the weird, liminal, and darkly fantastic. His work has appeared in numerous venues, including *The Audient Void, Spectral Realms, Tales from the Magician's Skull, Space and Time, Cosmic Horror Monthly,* and *Weirdbook.* His collection of weird fiction, *The Box,* is available from Hybrid Sequence Media, while his collection of autumnal and folk horror verse, *I Awaken in October,* is available from Jackanapes Press.

Aditya Dwarkesh hails from Mumbai, India. He now lives in the prairies of Canada as a Ph.D. student of mathematics. He is the author of "Who Killed Augustus Bourbaki?," which appeared in S. T. Joshi's anthology *Black Wings VII* (PS Publishing, 2023).

Adele Gardner is an active member of SFWA and HWA and a graduate of the Clarion West Writers Workshop with more than 500 stories, poems, illustrations, and articles published in *Analog, Clarkesworld, Strange Horizons, PodCastle,* and forthcoming in *Asimov's.* Adele's poetry collection, *Halloween Hearts,* is available from Jackanapes Press. Fifteen poems won or placed in the Poetry Society of Virginia Awards, Rhysling Award, and Balticon Poetry Contest.

Wade German's most recent full-length poetry collection is *Psalms and Sorceries* (Hippocampus Press, 2022). His first collection, *Dreams from a Black Nebula,* is also available from Hippocampus Press. Other titles include several slim volumes of his selected poems with Portuguese translation, most recently the chapbook *Noctivagations* (Raphus Press, 2024).

Joshua Green is an author of weird fiction, fantasy, and science fiction. His work has appeared or is forthcoming in *British Fantasy Society: Horizons, Strange Aeon, Spectral Realms,* and elsewhere. Currently he is working on the narrative-driven expansion for the critically acclaimed board game *Beast.*

Mario Sanchez Gumiel is a postdoctoral fellow at the University of Michigan, where he also received his Ph.D. in Romance Languages and Literatures (Spanish) in 2024. His research interests include nineteenth- to twenty-first-century world literatures and visual cultures in Spanish, posthumanism, utopia, science fiction, the weird, world cinemas, Spanish as a Second Language. He is also a certified teacher and examiner of Spanish by the Cervantes Institute.

John P. Irish is an educator and independent scholar specializing in nineteenth-century Gothic and speculative fiction. His research focuses on the intersections of urban modernity, the uncanny, and the weird in authors such as Fitz-James O'Brien, Edgar Allan Poe, and Charles Dickens. He holds a Ph.D. in Humanities from Southern Methodist University and has published widely on literature, philosophy, and popular culture. He teaches Humanities and History in North Texas.

Mark Howard Jones lives and writes in Cardiff, the capital city of Wales. He has edited both volumes of *Cthulhu Cymraeg: Lovecraftian Tales from Wales*. His latest collections of weird fiction are *Star-Spawned: Lovecraftian Horrors and Strange Stories* and *Tales from The Rain: Early Weird Fiction* (both Macabre Ink).

S. T. Joshi is the author of *The Weird Tale* (1990), *I Am Providence: The Life and Times of H. P. Lovecraft* (2010), *Unutterable Horror: A History of Supernatural Fiction* (2012), *Ramsey Campbell: Master of Weird Fiction* (2022), and other critical and biographical works. He recently assisted Ramsey Campbell in assembling a new edition of *Demons by Daylight* (forthcoming from PS Publishing).

Katherine Kerestman is the author of *Lethal* (PsychoToxin Press, 2023) and *Creepy Cat's Macabre Travels: Prowling around Haunted Towers, Crumbling Castles, and Ghoulish Graveyards* (WordCrafts Press, 2020), as well as the co-editor (with S. T. Joshi) of *The Weird Cat* and *Shunned Houses* (WordCrafts Press, 2023 and 2024). Her Lovecraftian and Gothic works have been featured in *Black Wings VII*, *Penumbra*, *Journ-E*, *Spectral Realms*, *Illumen*, *Retro-Fan*, *The Little Book of Cursed Dolls* (Media Macabre, 2023), as well as other discerning publications.

Karen Joan Kohoutek, an independent scholar and poet, has published about weird fiction in various journals and literary websites. Recent and upcoming publications have been on subjects including the Gamera films, the Robert E. Howard–H. P. Lovecraft correspondence, folk magic in the novels of Ishmael Reed, and the proto-Gothic writer Charles Brockden Brown. She lives in Fargo, North Dakota.

J. G. Maybrook writes poetry and fiction inspired by history, mythology, and folklore. A librarian by profession, he lives in upstate New York with his wife Hannah. Look for his work in *Lovecraftiania, Spectral Realms, Weirdbook Annual,* and other venues.

Maureen O'Leary lives in California. Her work appears in *Nightmare, Bourbon Penn, Chthonic Matter, Sacramento Noir, Black Glass Pages,* and Electric Literature's Recommended Reading, among other places.

Manuel Pérez-Campos of Bayamón, Puerto Rico is a long-time poet in the tradition of the weird, with work published in several venues.

Ann K. Schwader lives and writes in Colorado. Her newest collection, *Unquiet Stars,* is available from Weird House Press. Two of her earlier collections, *Wild Hunt of the Stars* (Sam's Dot, 2010) and *Dark Energies* (P'rea Press, 2015), were Bram Stoker Award finalists. In 2018, she received the Science Fiction and Fantasy Poetry Association's Grand Master award. She is also a two-time Rhysling Award winner.

John C. Tibbetts is Professor Emeritus at the University of Kansas in Film and Media Studies. His books include *The Furies of Marjorie Bowen* (McFarland, 2019), *The Gothic Worlds of Peter Straub* (McFarland, 2016), *Those Who Made It: Conversations with the Legends of Hollywood* (Palgrave Macmillan, 2015), *Peter Weir: Interviews* (University of Mississippi Press, 2014), and *The Gothic Imagination* (Palgrave Macmillan, 2012). He was awarded in 2008 the Kansas Governor's Arts in Education Award, presented by Governor Kathleen Sebelius.

DJ Tyrer is the person behind Atlantean Publishing and has been published in *The Rhysling Anthology*, issues of *Cyäegha*, the *Horror-zine*, *Scifaikuest*, *Sirens Call*, *Star*Line*, *Tigershark*, and the *Yellow Zine*. The e-chapbook *One Vision* is available from Tigershark Publishing. *SuperTrump* and *A Wuhan Whodunnit* are available for download from Atlantean Publishing.

Kyla Lee Ward is an award-winning author of horror and dark fantasy novels, short stories and poetry, as well as roleplaying games. She is also an actor and artist, a part-time medievalist and ghost host.

Lee Clark Zumpe, an entertainment editor with Tampa Bay Newspapers, earned his degree in English at the University of South Florida. His work has appeared in a variety of literary journals, genre magazines, and anthologies over the last two decades. Recent publication credits include *Dreams & Nightmares*, *Spectral Realms*, and *Star*Line*. In 2024, Hiraeth Publishing produced Lee's fourth poetry collection, *Wearing Winter Gray*. Lee lives in Florida with his wife and daughter.

www.ingramcontent.com/pod-product-compliance
Lightning Source LLC
Chambersburg PA
CBHW071258250626
47159CB00004B/1237